Trailer Park Mysteries

"Down the mean streets of Tullahoma, Mississippi, one waitress must go. Wanda Nell Culpepper, armed only with a deep sense of right and wrong and her own flaming temper, must protect her three children and her precarious financial situation against powerful enemies . . . A downhome treat."
—Charlaine Harris

"If you like rural Southern culture, or just need a break from the bustle of the big city, you should stop in at the Kountry Kitchen for some coffee. I'm sure we'll be stopping back next time we're passing through."
—Gumshoe Review

"Wanda Nell Culpepper is a steel magnolia to cherish. This heartwarming mystery will win legions of fans."
—Carolyn Hart

"A solid regional amateur-sleuth tale that uses the backdrop of the rural South to provide a fine who-done-it . . . Jimmie Ruth Evans provides a wonderful Mississippi mystery that stars a fabulous protagonist, a delightful eccentric support cast that brings Tullahoma—especially the diner and the trailer park—alive, and a surprising final peck."
—Midwest Book Review

"The Southern cozy at its best . . . delightfully constructed, care   nth."
          ce.com

Berkley Prime Crime titles by Jimmie Ruth Evans

FLAMINGO FATALE
MURDER OVER EASY
BEST SERVED COLD
BRING YOUR OWN POISON
LEFTOVER DEAD

Leftover Dead

Jimmie Ruth Evans

BERKLEY PRIME CRIME, NEW YORK

THE BERKLEY PUBLISHING GROUP
Published by the Penguin Group
Penguin Group (USA) Inc.
375 Hudson Street, New York, New York 10014, USA
Penguin Group (Canada), 90 Eglinton Avenue East, Suite 700, Toronto, Ontario M4P 2Y3, Canada
(a division of Pearson Penguin Canada Inc.)
Penguin Group Ltd., 80 Strand, London WC2R 0RL, England
Penguin Group Ireland, 25 St. Stephen's Green, Dublin 2, Ireland (a division of Penguin Books Ltd.)
Penguin Group (Australia), 250 Camberwell Road, Camberwell, Victoria 3124, Australia
(a division of Pearson Australia Group Pty. Ltd.)
Penguin Books India Pvt. Ltd., 11 Community Centre, Panchsheel Park, New Delhi—110 017, India
Penguin Group (NZ), 67 Apollo Drive, Rosedale, North Shore 0632, New Zealand
(a division of Pearson New Zealand Ltd.)
Penguin Books (South Africa) (Pty.) Ltd., 24 Sturdee Avenue, Rosebank, Johannesburg 2196,
South Africa

Penguin Books Ltd., Registered Offices: 80 Strand, London WC2R 0RL, England

LEFTOVER DEAD

A Berkley Prime Crime Book / published by arrangement with the author

PRINTING HISTORY
Berkley Prime Crime mass-market edition / January 2009

Copyright © 2009 by Dean James.
Cover illustration by Paul Slater.
Cover design by Judith Lagerman.
Interior text design by Kristin del Rosario.

ISBN: 978-0-425-22560-8

BERKLEY® PRIME CRIME
Berkley Prime Crime Books are published by The Berkley Publishing Group,
a division of Penguin Group (USA) Inc.,
375 Hudson Street, New York, New York 10014.
BERKLEY® PRIME CRIME and the PRIME CRIME logo are trademarks of Penguin Group (USA) Inc.

PRINTED IN THE UNITED STATES OF AMERICA

10   9   8   7   6   5   4   3   2   1

*Though she's half the world away in Bahrain,
Jan Spearman Giles nevertheless manages to offer
the kind of support and encouragement that keeps me
going when I think I can't go another step.
You're amazing, Jan, and every time I see your name
pop up in my e-mail in-box, I just start smiling.
Thank you for that.*

Acknowledgments

My editor, Michelle Vega, and my agent, Nancy Yost, helped make a very difficult year easier to get through, and I thank them for their support and understanding. It means more than you can ever know. Carolyn Haines is also there, whenever I need a shoulder to lean on. Tejas Englesmith, Julie Wray Herman, and Patricia Orr are always ready with encouragement and support when I need it. My amazing boss, Leah Krevit, has made the day job a joy, and I can't thank her enough for the opportunities she's given me.

One

Wanda Nell yawned and stretched, enjoying the luxury of a Saturday morning spent in bed. Now that she had only one job, working the lunch and dinner shifts Monday through Friday and every other Saturday at the Kountry Kitchen, she had more time to relax and pamper herself a bit. She turned on her side and reached for Jack, wanting to snuggle, but his side of the bed was empty.

Disappointed, Wanda Nell rolled over and peered at the clock on the nightstand. Nearly nine o'clock. Jack should be back soon. She sat up, pushing the covers aside. She stretched again before getting out of bed and padding bare-foot into the bathroom. She splashed some cold water on her face, and as she wiped the moisture away, she caught sight of the ring on her left hand.

"Good morning, Mrs. Pemberton," she said, her voice soft. She smiled at her reflection in the mirror. She and Jack had been married for six weeks now, and most mornings, she wanted to pinch herself to make sure it wasn't a dream.

A few minutes later, housecoat securely fastened and house shoes on, she went down the hall to the kitchen. The trailer was quiet around her. Jack had left over an hour ago, headed for the high school where he taught, to make use of the track. He had started running again, determined to shed some of the pounds he had gained over the past year or so from all the meals he had eaten at the Kountry Kitchen.

Juliet, almost sixteen now, had spent the night with one of her friends and wouldn't be home until sometime that afternoon. Ever since the wedding Juliet had been spending Friday nights away from home, with her best friend, with her grandmother, or with her sister, Miranda, and her new husband, Teddy. Wanda Nell appreciated Juliet's thoughtfulness, allowing her and Jack some time completely alone on the weekends.

Miranda and Teddy had been married two weeks before Wanda Nell and Jack, and ever since Miranda and her son, Lavon, had moved out, Wanda Nell had missed them. The good Lord only knew how aggravating Miranda often was, and how many battles Wanda Nell had waged trying to get her older daughter to do the simplest of household chores. Wanda Nell didn't miss that part, but she did miss seeing her grandson every morning and listening to his lively and imaginative conversations, usually directed at his stuffed rabbit.

Sighing, Wanda Nell grabbed the cereal box out of the cabinet, found a clean bowl and spoon, and set them all on the kitchen table before getting the milk from the fridge. She ate her breakfast slowly, thinking about the day ahead. School would be starting in a few weeks, and before Jack got snowed under with grading papers and dealing with his students, she wanted him to have some time to relax and have fun. He had been talking about writing another book, and Wanda Nell was proud of his accomplishments. He had published two moderately successful true crime books, and now he was itching to start another one.

Wanda Nell didn't want him pushing himself too hard,

between teaching high school English and researching and writing a new book, but she had begun to realize how important writing was to her new husband. Because it was so important, she would do whatever she needed to do in order to support him.

She was rinsing out her bowl in the sink when she heard the front door of the trailer open. "I'm up, honey. In the kitchen," she called out.

Before she finished drying the bowl, she felt strong arms slip around her waist and warm lips brush the side of her neck.

She leaned back against her husband for a moment, luxuriating in the feeling. "Mmm, you sure do smell good." She turned in his arms and looked up into his face.

Jack's eyes glowed behind the lenses of his rimless glasses. His brown hair was still slightly damp from the shower he had taken at school. "I didn't want to come back all hot and sweaty," he murmured. His lips sought hers, and they kissed for a while.

Wanda Nell finally pulled away, more than a little breathless. "Where did you learn to kiss like that? Just what kind of loose woman did you date before you met me?" She pretended to be annoyed.

"All it takes is the right inspiration," Jack said with a wicked grin. "I never even wanted to kiss a woman like that until I met you, love."

Laughing, Wanda Nell pushed against his chest. "It's lucky for you I like having you around, otherwise I wouldn't put up with that kind of talk."

"We don't *have* to talk." Jack pulled her closer. "If you know what I mean."

Wanda Nell agreed.

Sometime later, once again in the kitchen, Wanda Nell scrambled eggs while Jack made toast. They grinned at each other when they sat down at the table to eat. Neither spoke until they had finished, and Jack got up from the table to fetch two glasses and a pitcher of orange juice from the fridge.

After filling the glasses, he sat down and raised his glass. "To marriage."

Wanda Nell lifted her own glass and touched it to her husband's. "Amen to that. I never thought I'd see the day when I'd get married again."

"I'm glad you did. Otherwise, I might have had to kidnap you and run off with you somewhere till I could talk you into it."

Shaking her head at his nonsense, Wanda Nell tried to suppress a smile. At some point they would get over this giddiness and goofiness, but for now, they were both determined to enjoy every single second of being newlyweds.

"How was your run?"

"Good. My knees are holding up, and I'm up to three miles now. At this rate, I should be pretty comfortable with five miles a day by the time school starts next month."

"I probably ought to be out there with you," Wanda Nell said, thinking ruefully of her thighs. "I could stand to lose a few pounds, too."

"If you want to, you know you're welcome to come along. Chasing you around that track would give me even more incentive." He leered at her.

"Oh, behave." Wanda Nell tried not to laugh. She stood up and started gathering the remains of their late breakfast—or early lunch, she noted as she glanced at the clock. It was almost eleven.

Jack got up to help her. "I've got something interesting to tell you," he said, putting the juice away. "I think I've found what I want to work on for the new book. It just fell into my lap, so to speak."

"This morning? Because you sure didn't say anything about it last night." Wanda Nell turned on the hot water to rinse their plates and utensils before putting them in the dishwasher.

"I didn't know about it last night. There I was this morning, doing my stretches before I started my run, and old Gus showed up."

"The custodian? You mean he's still there?"

"Yeah, he is, but this coming school year is going to be his last. Can you believe it? He's been custodian at the high school for forty-seven years now."

"How old is he?" Wanda Nell asked. "Surely he's old enough to retire."

"He said he'd be sixty-six by the time he retires next spring, so he must have been about eighteen when he started the job."

"That's really something," Wanda Nell said, impressed. "I hope to goodness they do something real nice for him when he retires."

Jack shrugged. "With our school board, who knows?" He took the plates from Wanda Nell and put them in the dishwasher.

"So how did Gus give you an idea for a book?" Wanda Nell dried her hands, wrung out the dishrag, and draped it across the faucet before going back to the table to sit down.

"I guess he was just in one of those moods," Jack said, pulling her chair out for her. Once she was seated, he sat down, too. "Thinking about retirement, and thinking about the things that have happened at that school during the time he's worked there."

"What could have happened there that would be make a true crime book?"

"I was surprised, too," Jack admitted, "because I'd never heard the story until Gus told me. He said they found a girl dead on the football field thirty-one years ago, and the case was never solved."

Wanda Nell frowned. "I don't remember that at all. I

mean, I was only about eleven or twelve then, but I can't recall hearing about it."

"Gus said there was a big uproar for about a week, and then it just kind of faded away. Which is pretty strange, but Gus said he figured some big shot in town was probably involved, and it just got hushed up."

"Wouldn't surprise me a bit, not in this town." Wanda Nell paused for a moment. "Mayrene might know something about it. She almost always does, and she would have been in her twenties."

Mayrene Lancaster, who lived in the trailer next door, was Wanda Nell's best friend. Thanks to her job at Tullahoma's most popular beauty shop, Mayrene heard all the gossip in town that was worth hearing. She wasn't shy about sharing it with Wanda Nell, either.

"Was she in Tullahoma then?" Jack asked. "I thought she told me once she'd been here only about twenty years."

"Yeah, you're right. I'd forgotten that." Wanda Nell grinned. "She still might know something about it, though. The things she hears, you wouldn't believe sometimes."

"I definitely want to talk to her, then. Gus couldn't tell me many of the details, except that he did remember the girl was a complete stranger in Tullahoma. Nobody knew her or where she came from."

"At least not that they'd let on," Wanda Nell said. "She had to be in town for some reason, unless whoever killed her was just driving through and decided to dump her body here. But why on the football field, of all places? Seems to me, if I wanted to get rid of a dead body, I wouldn't be putting it somewhere like that, where it would be found right away."

"That's one of the things that really intrigues me," Jack said. "It does seem stupid on the killer's part, but it makes me wonder whether somehow it isn't important to why she was killed or who killed her."

"Maybe." Wanda Nell shrugged. "But there don't seem to be much to go on."

"Not at the moment, but surely there were police reports and articles in the paper, if nothing else."

"You could always ask Elmer Lee," Wanda Nell said. Elmer Lee Johnson, for a long time Wanda Nell's nemesis, was the sheriff of Tullahoma County. "He's only a year older than me, though, so he might not remember anything, either. But maybe he could look through the files at the Sheriff's Department."

"I'll keep that in mind, but he might be touchy about that. Since there's no statute of limitations on murder, the case is still technically open. He might not want someone like me having access to that kind of information. Plus I don't think he's all that fond of me."

Wanda Nell thought it wise not to respond to that last sentence. Elmer Lee had been a bit odd around Jack ever since he heard that Wanda Nell was getting married again. Even though he had come to the wedding, he hadn't stuck around for the reception. T.J., Wanda Nell's son, had told her more than once that Elmer Lee was carrying a torch for her, but Wanda Nell had never been sure. She had come to respect Elmer Lee, and sometimes she almost liked him, but she could never imagine being attracted to him.

One thing Jack said didn't register at first, but then the full implication of it hit her.

"If the case is still open," Wanda Nell said, frowning, "that means the killer could still be around here somewhere."

"Yes," Jack said, "although in thirty-one years, who knows what could have happened?"

"Even if the killer isn't around," Wanda Nell said, "somebody might still not be happy if you go poking around. Didn't Gus say the case got hushed up, more or less?"

"That's what he figured," Jack replied. "He didn't know that for sure."

"The point is"—Wanda Nell was growing more concerned the more she thought about it—"trying to find out who killed that girl could be dangerous. It's not like those other two cases you wrote about, where the killer was behind bars, or executed."

"I know," Jack said, "and it's certainly a risk. I thought about all that on the way home, but I just can't get the image of that girl, lying there dead and alone, out of my mind."

Wanda Nell sighed. "And you're the one always worried about *me* getting mixed up in murders." She sighed again. "But you're right, I don't like the thought of that poor girl just lying there, either. It's not right." For a moment she saw that girl lying on the football field, and her face looked like Juliet's. She suppressed a shudder.

Jack reached over and clasped one of her hands in his. "No, it's not right. Maybe me poking into this will do some good. Who knows?" He squeezed her hand. "Will you help me?"

"Of course, but we'd better be mighty careful. This whole thing could get pretty ugly."

Two

"Yoo-hoo! You two lovebirds up and out of bed? If you ain't decent, let me know, and I'll come back later."

Wanda Nell and Jack started at the sound of Mayrene's voice coming from the living room. They hadn't heard the trailer door open.

"We're in the kitchen," Wanda Nell called out. "Come on in." She and Jack exchanged amused glances. Mayrene had been carrying on like this ever since they got married.

The front door shut, and moments later Mayrene walked into the kitchen. She dropped a hand on Jack's shoulder and squeezed, grinning down at his upturned face. "What's up with you two?" She sat down. "As if I didn't know." She laughed.

Wanda Nell blushed. She couldn't help it.

Seeing her friend's face redden slightly, Mayrene laughed again. "Honey, I'm so happy for the two of you, I'm just about to bust. Every time I see the smiles on your faces, I say 'thank you, Lord' for getting you two together."

"I'm pretty thankful myself," Jack said. "Sometimes I still can't quite believe it."

"I'm just glad you two decided to stay here. I don't

know what I'd do if y'all had moved into Jack's house instead."

"We thought about it," Wanda Nell said. "It was closer to the high school, but since Jack was only renting, and the trailer is close to being paid for, it seemed like more sense for him to move in here."

"And it was a small house," Jack added. "There's actually more room here." He winked at Wanda Nell. They also had a bedroom with more privacy here, since it was at one end of the trailer and Juliet's bedroom was at the other. In the house he had been renting, there were two small bedrooms right next to each other.

Wanda Nell blushed again. Mayrene had never been in Jack's house, but she was shrewd enough to figure it out. To distract her friend, Wanda Nell asked, "Guess what? Jack's got an idea for a new book."

"Really?" Mayrene turned eagerly toward Jack. "You know I loved both your books. What are you going to write about now?"

"Something that happened right here in Tullahoma about thirty-one years ago." Jack paused, waiting to see if Mayrene would pick up on his cue.

Mayrene shook her head. "That long ago? I wasn't here back then, and I don't reckon I've heard tell of anything that you could make a book out of." She grinned. "I hear stuff you wouldn't believe down at the beauty shop, but most of it's about who's stepping out on a wife, or a husband who's too blind to see what's going on."

"Well, they found a girl's body on the football field," Wanda Nell said. "Gus, the custodian at the high school, told Jack about it this morning."

"I reckon Gus would know," Mayrene said. "He knows about everything going on at that school, let me tell you." She waggled her eyebrows. "His wife comes to the shop, and I do her hair. She's told me some pretty juicy stuff."

"Have you ever heard about this dead girl?" Jack asked.

Mayrene shook her head. "It's news to me. How old was she?"

"Gus didn't really say, but she couldn't have been that old, or he would have said 'woman' instead." Jack frowned. "That's something I'll have to check out."

"Gus also said there was a fuss over it for about a week, and then it all just died down," Wanda Nell added. "He reckoned some big shot in town got it hushed up."

"So they never found out who killed her?" Mayrene shook her head knowingly. "If that's the case, then somebody got paid off somewhere. You can bet on that."

"You're probably right," Jack said. "And if I could find out who did *that*, then I'd probably be a lot closer to knowing who killed her, and why."

"Yeah, and you may be stirring up a hornets' nest if you start digging into this," Mayrene said.

"He knows that," Wanda Nell replied. "And so do I. But I don't like the thought of that poor girl being killed, and nobody having to answer for it. She had to have some family somewhere, surely, and they at least deserve to know what happened."

"Yeah, I see your point," Mayrene said, "and I don't think some bastard should get away with killing a girl, even if it was thirty-something years ago. I don't know what I can do to help, but you know you both can count on me."

"Thanks," Jack said. "I'm going to be looking for leads anywhere I can find them."

"I know what I can do." Mayrene's face took on a sly look.

"Start talking about it down at the beauty shop," Wanda Nell said.

"Of course," Mayrene responded. "I told you, all kinds of stuff gets talked about there. Ain't no reason I can't prod it in the direction I want, instead of just waiting to hear what somebody else wants to talk about."

"I appreciate that," Jack said. "But I want you to be careful. If word of this gets around too quickly, it might make things more difficult for me."

"You don't want to tip your hand too soon," Mayrene agreed.

"Exactly." Jack nodded, the light glinting off his glasses as his head moved.

"Good point." Mayrene glanced back and forth between Jack and Wanda Nell. "How about, then, if I hold off poking around for a bit until you've had time to do some digging on your own?"

"Thanks," Wanda Nell said. "I think that's a good idea."

"That's settled, then." Jack stood up. "I think, if you two will excuse me, I'll go start making some notes about this." He grinned. "I know you have other things you want to talk about that don't necessarily include me."

He blew Wanda Nell a kiss before he left the kitchen.

"You two are just so dang cute." Wanda Nell tried hard not to blush again at Mayrene's description.

"That's enough of that," Wanda Nell said. "Now let's talk about you."

"What about me? Ain't much to tell that I know of."

"Don't give me that. We haven't seen much of you this week, so I figured you had a hot date every night."

Mayrene snorted. "Don't I wish."

"So what's going on? I thought you and Dixon were doing real well." Wanda Nell watched her friend in concern. Mayrene had been dating Dixon Vance, a policeman in Tullahoma, for several months now, and Wanda Nell had thought everything was fine with them.

Mayrene shrugged. "I don't know."

"Come on now, you know you can tell me. Have y'all had a fight?"

Mayrene looked away, and when she finally turned to

face Wanda Nell again, her face was red. "Yeah, we did. And it wasn't the kind you can have fun making up afterwards."

This was sounding pretty bad. "So what was it about?"

"He thinks I should go on a diet," Mayrene said, her voice so low Wanda Nell could barely hear her.

"He *what*?" Wanda Nell wasn't sure she had heard correctly.

"A diet," Mayrene repeated, her voice louder. "He thinks I need to lose weight."

Wanda Nell knew she had to choose her words carefully. As long as she had known Mayrene, her friend had been more than a bit plump. She could probably stand to lose about twenty pounds, but Mayrene had always seemed perfectly comfortable with her weight. It certainly hadn't kept her from finding plenty of men to date.

"Why does he think that?" Wanda Nell asked. That was the safest response she could manage right then.

Mayrene started to tear up. She wiped her eyes with the back of her right hand. When she spoke, she was clearly indignant. "Dixon told me the other cops were kidding him about him going out with the Pillsbury Doughboy."

"And he told you that?"

Mayrene nodded.

"You don't look anything like that silly thing."

"You're just saying that because you're my best friend." Mayrene dashed back more tears.

"Of course I'm not. You may be a little plump, but you're not obese like that stupid doll, or whatever it is."

"Thank you, honey." Mayrene's voice was gruff with tears still unshed. "I needed to hear that."

"I still can't believe he would say something like that to you. What kind of jackass is he?"

Mayrene managed a brief smile. "I thought he was *my* jackass until a few days ago."

"Does this mean you told him he could put it where the sun don't shine?"

"Sort of." Mayrene didn't meet Wanda Nell's gaze.

"You didn't tell him off?"

"Not exactly." Mayrene sighed after a brief pause. "I let him know he hurt me pretty bad, and that I wasn't real happy with him right then. But I didn't kick him out and tell him not to come back."

"Well, frankly, I'm surprised at you," Wanda Nell said. "I don't think I've ever known you to put up with that kind of crap from anybody, let alone a man."

"I know. But I really did think I had found somebody good, and I guess I hate to let him go completely."

"What did he do when you told him how much he hurt your feelings?"

"He said he was sorry, but then he went on about how it would be good for my health, and all kinds of stuff like that."

"They never learn when to just keep their mouths shut, do they?"

"Nope. I told him I didn't much appreciate him criticizing me that way, even if he was concerned about my health. Which, frankly, I don't think he was. He was more concerned about his pride."

"I'm sorry to say it, but you're probably right." Wanda Nell shook her head. "So what's happening right now?"

"Nothing. I told him I wasn't sure if I could go on seeing him, knowing he felt like that. Then he stomped off, and I haven't talked to him since."

"He hasn't called you?"

"Nope, and I sure ain't called him, I can tell you that."

"Good for you. It's up to him to apologize."

"It sure is." Mayrene frowned. "The only thing is, it's been four days now, and I still haven't heard from him."

That wasn't good, but Wanda Nell didn't want to make

Mayrene more unhappy by pointing it out. "You know how men are, it takes them a little longer to get over these things and think about how it really was their fault. He'll call you."

"We'll see. But I'm not sure what I'm going to say to him."

"Listen to what he has to say first," Wanda Nell advised. "Then you'll know what to say back to him."

"I guess you're right. It's not like I got much choice at the moment."

Wanda Nell reached forward and patted her friend's hand. "You hang in there. If he's too stupid to realize how wonderful you are, then you don't need him."

Mayrene smiled her thanks. She got up from her chair and pulled a paper towel from the roll near the sink. After blowing her nose a couple of times, she wadded the paper towel up and threw it in the bin under the sink.

"Okay if I come in?" Jack said from the doorway of the kitchen.

"Sure, honey," Wanda Nell said. Mayrene resumed her seat.

Jack advanced into the room. "How would you like to go visit your buddy Elmer Lee this afternoon?"

Wanda Nell grimaced. "How would I like to go to the dentist's office and have a root canal instead?"

Jack and Mayrene laughed.

"He's not that bad," Mayrene said. "I mean, I know he don't like it much if he thinks you're stirring up trouble, but he can't blame you if Jack wants to write a book."

"He'll think I put Jack up to it just to drive him crazy," Wanda Nell said. "You just wait and see."

Three

"I'm ready, Jack." Wanda Nell paused in the doorway of what had been her bedroom until a couple of months ago. When Miranda and Lavon moved out, Wanda Nell had taken over their bedroom and started turning her old room into a study for Jack.

Jack looked up from his computer for a moment to smile at her. "Just let me shut this down, and I'll be ready to go, too."

Wanda Nell watched as he tapped at the keyboard, then punched the button on the monitor before pushing back his chair to stand. Jack had been saying he was going to teach her to use the computer, and Juliet had been after her to learn, too. She reckoned it was something she ought to know about, but for now she couldn't figure out what she'd need to use the thing for.

Jack bent over his desk to retrieve something from one of the drawers, and Wanda Nell couldn't help admiring the view. He was wearing jeans, and they were molded to his body in all the right places. He was wearing the cowboy boots her son T.J. and his partner, Tuck, had given him for his birthday. Wanda Nell had always liked the look of a man in boots, and she was glad Jack enjoyed wearing his so much.

He turned to face her and grinned. He knew what she had been thinking. She was amazed at the way he seemed to be able to read her mind so often. It had never been like this with her first husband, Bobby Ray. But then Bobby Ray never cared much about what anyone else thought or felt. He had been concerned only with himself most of the time.

"Okay, let's go." Jack stepped forward and hit the light switch.

"Yes, sir." Wanda Nell led the way down the hall to the front door. She scooped up her purse while Jack opened the door.

Stepping out into the hot July afternoon, Wanda Nell blinked. She paused to pull her sunglasses out of her purse, and once they were in place, she could see better. Jack followed her down the two steps to the ground and then moved around her to get to his car first.

"Let me open all the doors and get the air conditioner going, honey. We'll get fried if we don't let it cool off a little first."

"Thanks," Wanda Nell said. She stepped under the shade provided by her one-car carport. They planned to have it extended to make room for Jack's car, but they hadn't gotten around to it yet.

Jack climbed out of his car and joined Wanda Nell in the shade. "The air will cool off enough in a minute, so we'll be able to stand getting in."

They waited about a minute before going to the car. The worst of the hot air had blown out when Jack had opened all the doors. Now they were all shut, the car was blasting cold air, and Wanda Nell didn't feel like she was having some kind of hot flash.

As Jack carefully backed the car out of the driveway

and pointed it toward the road that would lead them out of the trailer park and into town, Wanda Nell said, "How much did you tell Elmer Lee when you talked to him?"

"Not a lot. I told him I wanted to talk to him about an old case, and that I was thinking about writing a new book. I guess things must be pretty quiet around the Sheriff's Department this afternoon. He didn't really ask me any questions, just said to come on in and talk."

"Does he know I'm coming with you?"

"No. I didn't think to mention it to him." Jack glanced sideways at her. "Do you think it'll make a difference?"

"Who knows with Elmer Lee?" Wanda Nell shrugged. "He might not want to talk much with me around. But maybe I can goad him into it if we need to."

Jack laughed. "If anybody can do it, you can." He patted her knee. "But Elmer Lee's basically a good guy. He believes in doing the right thing, and I'm sure he'll feel that way about this case."

"You're right," Wanda Nell said. "I guess I don't always give him enough credit, but he sure as heck don't make it too easy sometimes."

"What time is Juliet coming home?" Jack asked. "I forgot all about her supposed to be coming back this afternoon, and it's already half-past one."

"It's okay. I called her and told her we had an appointment and wouldn't be home till later. She's going to get Miz Hankins to drop her off at Miz Culpepper's house, and we're going to pick her up there when we're done with Elmer Lee."

"We could have picked her up from the Hankins's house." Jack paused. "But you wanted a reason to go by Miz Culpepper's house, didn't you?"

Wanda Nell laughed. "Yeah, I thought as long as we were going to talk to Elmer Lee about this case, we might as well talk to Miz Culpepper, too. She's lived in Tullahoma for over fifty years now, and I reckon she'll know something about it. Old Judge Culpepper was always in the middle of everything."

"If he was, what if he was involved in this particular case? What if he was part of the cover-up, if there was one?"

They had reached one of the main intersections in town now, and Jack signaled a right turn. They were only about five minutes from the town square, where the Sheriff's Department and county jail were located.

"I thought about that," Wanda Nell said. "She can be a bit touchy where her husband is concerned, but he's been dead a long time now. I can't see where it'll hurt to ask her about it."

"You know her better than I do," Jack said. "So I think I'll turn that interview over to you." He laughed. "After all, I'm not sure she really likes me that much."

"Gee, thanks. Of course she likes you, otherwise she wouldn't have insisted we have the wedding at her house. I think it was her way of finally making peace with me, and with Bobby Ray's death."

"I guess you're right," Jack said, "but I do feel a little uneasy whenever I'm around her."

"You'll get used to her. It's taken me a long time, but I finally realized that her bark really is a lot worse than her bite. She's been lonely for a long time, and the good Lord knows Bobby Ray wasn't much of a son to her. But now she's getting attention all the time from T.J. and Tuck and the girls."

"Not to mention Belle."

Belle Meriwether was Mrs. Culpepper's cousin, and she had recently come to live with the older woman as a companion. Belle had never married and had no brothers or sisters, and she seemed to enjoy living with her cousin and looking after her. Mrs. Culpepper often said Belle had never met a silence she couldn't fill, and she snapped at Belle pretty often. Everyone figured she must enjoy it, though, because she had perked up quite a bit since Belle had moved in.

"Thank the Lord for Belle," Wanda Nell said. "I don't know what we'd do without her."

By now they had reached the town square, and Jack drove around to the side near the Sheriff's Department building and parked at the courthouse.

Wanda Nell waited until Jack opened the car door for her. She wasn't used to such treatment and would have been more than happy to open the door for herself, but Jack got so much pleasure out of such courtesies, she didn't have the heart to disappoint him. Besides, it was a nice change to have someone taking care of her.

As they crossed the street, Wanda Nell glanced at the building where Tuck's law office was located. He and T.J. sometimes worked in the office on Saturdays, especially when Tuck had a case that needed overtime. The windows were dark this afternoon, and Wanda Nell hoped they were enjoying some time off. They were supposed to come to dinner with her and Jack and Juliet tomorrow night, and she looked forward to seeing them.

Jack held open the door to the Sheriff's Department, and Wanda Nell stepped inside. The air here was very cold, and she shivered as she removed her sunglasses and stowed them in her purse.

"Brrr . . . it's like an icebox in here," Jack said. "I should have worn my jacket. Are you warm enough, honey?"

"I'll be okay," Wanda Nell said. "I'm sure it'll be warm enough in Elmer Lee's office before too long."

Jack laughed as they moved forward to the desk. He informed the officer on duty they had an appointment with the sheriff, and the officer picked up his phone and punched a button.

After a brief conversation, the officer waved them toward a door. Wanda Nell knew the way all too well. She had been here more times than she cared to recall.

She and Jack walked down the hall to Elmer Lee's office, and she was thankful to note it actually was warmer there, thanks to the sun streaming through one window.

"Afternoon," Elmer Lee Johnson said, standing up from behind his desk. "Howdy, Wanda Nell. Or I guess I should say, Miz Pemberton. I didn't know you were coming."

"Didn't I mention that?" Jack said. "Sorry."

"No problem. Y'all have a seat, and tell me what I can do for you."

"Thanks for talking to us, Elmer Lee," Wanda Nell said. "I know you're usually pretty busy around here."

Elmer Lee shot her a sharp glance, but evidently decided that she wasn't being sarcastic. "It's a slow day for once. And I'm always happy to talk to the good people of Tullahoma County." The corners of his mouth twitched.

"And we appreciate that," Jack said, shifting in his chair.

Elmer Lee sat down again. "So what case did you want to talk about? You didn't say much on the phone."

"I guess I didn't." Jack's tone was light. "Well, it's about an old case from thirty-one years ago. Back when we were all still in junior high, I guess."

Elmer Lee frowned. "Yeah, I would have been about thirteen then. But I don't remember anything from back then. It's something that happened here in Tullahoma? Or somewhere in the county?"

"Right here in Tullahoma," Wanda Nell said. "I didn't remember it either, but I guess we were too young to pay much attention to something like that."

"Maybe so," Elmer Lee replied, "but I used to watch all those detective shows. I thought I was pretty sharp, and I wanted to be Jim Rockford when I grew up."

Wanda Nell was surprised. She had never heard Elmer Lee say anything that personal before.

"I know what you mean," Jack said. "I loved that show, too. But to get back to the case I'm talking about. Thirty-one years ago, or so I'm told, they found the body of a dead girl one morning on the football field at the high school. As far as we know, the case was never solved."

Elmer Lee frowned at them, his eyes narrowing for a moment. "I do remember that, sorta," he said after a moment. "I remember my mama telling me she didn't want me out after dark for a week or two, and when I cut up about it, she told me she didn't want some maniac killing me like he did that poor girl on the football field."

Wanda Nell shifted in her chair. Hearing what Elmer Lee had said stirred a memory in her. "I didn't remember anything until you said that just now, but I remember Mama telling me and Rusty we had to come straight home from school for a couple of weeks and to be sure we didn't miss the bus for anything."

"And then what?" Jack looked at Elmer Lee.

"Nothing. After a couple of weeks or so, my mama didn't seem as uptight about it as she had been, and I guess we all just forgot about it." He frowned. "I wonder what did happen about that case. Something must have happened, or else everybody would have still been all worked up over it."

"The person who told me about it," Jack said, "well, he told me he thought it got hushed up for some reason. According to him, it was never solved, just got swept under the carpet, so to speak."

Elmer Lee evidently didn't like the sound of that, Wanda Nell decided, judging by the scowl on his face. He was pretty touchy about the reputation of the Sheriff's Department.

"I don't know about that," Elmer Lee said. "I can't remember who was sheriff back then, but I suppose it's possible."

"Is there any way you could check your files to find out what happened?" Jack tensed slightly as he waited for an answer. Wanda Nell didn't move or say anything. She didn't want to aggravate Elmer Lee in any way.

"You got me curious, too," Elmer Lee said. "Y'all sit here for a few minutes, and I'm gonna go have a look at our old files. Most of them are here, so I should be able to find it pretty quick. Can you narrow it down any more than thirty-one years ago?"

Jack frowned for a moment. "I think the person who told me said it was late in the spring, not long before school was out. He seemed pretty certain it was thirty-one years, though."

"That means April or May, then," Elmer Lee said. "I'll start there first." He got up from his desk and walked to the door of the office. "Y'all wait, and I'll be back."

When he had gone, Wanda Nell and Jack looked at each other. "He's taking this better than I thought he would," Wanda Nell said.

"He's a fair man," Jack responded, "and he doesn't like the thought of an unsolved murder any more than we do. I was pretty sure he'd come through."

"Let's just hope he finds something," Wanda Nell said.

They fell silent, waiting. Wanda Nell glanced at the clock on the wall nearby, and she watched as three minutes, then five, then ten ticked by. She was getting restless, and she knew Jack was, too.

"What's taking him so long?" Wanda Nell asked.

"There may be a lot of files to go through, especially since we don't know exactly when."

"We know close enough," Wanda Nell said. "Unless Elmer Lee can't subtract too well."

"I heard that, Wanda Nell." Elmer Lee went to his desk

and sat down. In his hands was a file folder, but to Wanda Nell it looked very, very thin.

"Is that it?" Jack asked, sounding disappointed.

Elmer Lee glanced down at the folder in his hands. "What's left of it, yeah."

Four

"What do you mean, what's left of it?" Wanda Nell asked, her voice sharper than she meant it to be.

"What do you think I mean, Wanda Nell?" Elmer Lee's face darkened.

"Sorry," Wanda Nell muttered.

Elmer Lee glared at her for a moment before he spoke again. He tapped the folder lying on his desk. "There's only two sheets of paper in this file, and that ain't right."

"So somebody took the rest of the file," Jack said, the disappointment obvious in his voice.

"Yeah." Elmer Lee almost bit off the word. It was obvious to Wanda Nell that he was very angry, and she was glad that, for once, she was not the cause of his anger.

"So what's left in the file?" Jack asked, his tone mild.

Elmer Lee opened it and scanned the two pages before saying anything. "Not much. Just some brief details about the victim. Young woman, about eighteen to twenty, blunt trauma to the back of the head. She was completely naked, no kind of I.D. on the body, and no clothes anywhere nearby. No mention whether they ever identified her."

"Does it say anything about who found the body?" Wanda Nell asked.

Elmer Lee shook his head. "Not even that. Hell, it doesn't even say who the investigating officer was. There's a note on the second page that just says the case was basically closed because of lack of evidence."

"It does look like somebody hushed it up," Wanda Nell said.

"Yeah," Elmer Lee agreed, "and I wonder who the hell it was. This reeks to high heaven, and I don't like it. I don't like it one damn bit."

"Then is it okay with you if we dig into it, try to find some leads?" Jack leaned forward, his eyes fixed on Elmer Lee.

The sheriff stared off into space for a moment. Then he faced Jack. "I'm kinda of two minds about it. I hate like hell that something like this got covered up, because it ain't right. Nobody should get away with killing a girl like that." He paused. "But if somebody went to this much trouble to cover it up and put a halt to the investigation, that means somebody with some power around this town was involved. And if you go digging it up now, well, the you-know-what could really hit the fan."

"We're prepared for that," Jack said, after glancing at Wanda Nell for her approval. She nodded. "That girl deserves to have a name, and to have justice done for her sake."

Elmer Lee grinned. "Damn right she does."

Wanda Nell thought that grin of Elmer Lee's didn't bode too well for someone. He was like an old hound dog. Once he got the scent, he'd follow it as far as he could, and then some.

"You'll back us up if we need it?" Wanda Nell asked. She wanted to be absolutely clear with Elmer Lee.

"I will," Elmer Lee responded, his voice firm. "I'm going to be doing some digging into this myself. And

I'm gonna trust you to share anything you find out with me. This case ain't closed, as far as I'm concerned, and if we can find out who did it, that person's going to pay for it."

"We'll be glad to cooperate," Jack said, "but you're going to have to do the same with us. Share information, I mean." His tone was as firm as Elmer Lee's.

"Sure," Elmer Lee said. "I understand that."

"Then is it okay if I have a copy of what's in that file?"

"Yeah." Elmer Lee stood, the folder in his hands. "Y'all hang on a minute."

As soon as he was out of the room, Wanda Nell turned to her husband. "Well, that went a lot better than I thought it would."

Jack smiled. "It did. But I'm not really surprised. I knew Elmer Lee would want to get to the bottom of this as much as we do."

"Yeah, I guess so," Wanda Nell admitted. "I sure do wish there had been more to go on in that file, though."

"I do, too," Jack said, "but I guess I'm not all that surprised it's been tampered with. Seems like Gus was right about the whole thing being covered up."

"Since there's not much to go on in that file, what are we going to do next?" Wanda Nell asked.

"First, I guess we'll go and talk to Miz Culpepper," Jack said. "We might as well find out what she remembers about it. She might have some kind of lead for us."

"And if she doesn't?"

Jack grinned. "Then we go to the library, of course. I want to look at back issues of the local paper. There's bound to be something from back then."

"You don't think somebody got at the newspaper, too, do you? Maybe anything that was in the paper got taken out, too."

"It's possible, I guess," Jack said, "but I'm betting there'll be a little information, at least a couple days' worth, before the investigation got shut down."

Elmer Lee came back in the room, and Jack and Wanda Nell stood. Jack accepted the two sheets of paper Elmer Lee held out. "Thanks again, Sheriff. We both really appreciate this."

"Just be careful, Pemberton." Elmer Lee's face was stern. He nodded toward Wanda Nell. "And keep an eye on that wife of yours. Don't let her go off chasing some wild hare and get us all in trouble before we make any progress."

Jack coughed, and Wanda Nell cast her husband a suspicious glance. He'd better not be laughing. She looked hard at Elmer Lee. He wasn't smiling, but she was pretty sure she could detect a glint of humor in his eyes.

"I'll be sure and let you know if I find any wild hares that need chasing, Elmer Lee," Wanda Nell said sweetly. "Or maybe I should just start calling you Elmer *Fudd*." She walked out of the office without waiting to see how the sheriff responded to that.

Jack was close on her heels. He was trying hard not to laugh as he put an arm around her. "Honey, what am I going to do with you? I swear, you and the sheriff sound like siblings who are always squabbling."

"Just what I need," Wanda Nell said. "Elmer Fudd for a brother." She laughed. "I bet he'd love that."

Jack grinned at her. They didn't speak again until they were outside the Sheriff's Department. They made their way to the car. Jack had parked in one of the few patches of shade, and the car wasn't as hot inside as it could have been.

They sat for a moment, letting the car cool down. The ride to Mrs. Culpepper's house would take about three minutes. She lived on Main Street, just about three blocks from the town square. Since the library was farther down Main Street, it made sense for them to stop at Mrs. Culpepper's first.

"If we're lucky, Belle will have some cold lemonade or iced tea," Wanda Nell said as Jack backed the car out of the parking space.

"I could go for that. This heat is something." Jack pulled a handkerchief from his pocket to mop sweat from his forehead.

A couple of minutes later Jack pulled the car into the driveway at the Culpepper house. Every time she saw it, Wanda Nell still felt a bit overwhelmed. She had grown up with two hardworking parents, living in either a trailer or a very modest house, and the Culpepper house was a stark reminder of the difference between her and Bobby Ray's growing up. A beautiful antebellum mansion, the Culpepper house had been in the family for generations, and the antiques it contained were worth a fortune. All the time she was married to Bobby Ray, Mrs. Culpepper had never let her forget all that.

The old woman had mellowed in the last couple of years, and Wanda Nell was grateful for that, mostly for the sake of her children. Mrs. Culpepper was their grandmother, after all, and they should be part of her life, especially since Wanda Nell's parents were gone. Wanda Nell had finally realized, too, just how lonely Mrs. Culpepper had been, and the attention from her grandchildren had worked wonders on her personality.

Belle answered the door, and her plump face split into a wide grin the moment she saw them. "Howdy, you two. My, aren't you both a sight for sore eyes." She stepped aside to let them enter. "I tell you, Wanda Nell, I think you're looking younger and even more beautiful since the wedding. Lucretia and I were looking at the pictures just the other day, and Lucretia was saying to me, 'Look at that girl and how pretty she is. I don't know when I've seen a more beautiful bride.'"

Neither Wanda Nell nor Jack attempted to stem the flow.

They had both known Belle long enough to realize that nothing short of the Last Trump—or her cousin Lucretia— could stop Belle from talking once she got going.

Wanda Nell was still blushing and Belle still talking when they entered what Mrs. Culpepper had always called the drawing room. The old lady was sitting in her favorite chair, and she smiled at them as they entered. The smile dimmed slightly as she glanced at her companion.

"Good Lord, Belle," Mrs. Culpepper said, her tone milder than usual, "Wanda Nell and Jack will be deaf soon if you don't stop all that yammering in their ears. Take some pity on their poor eardrums, and hush." She motioned toward the sofa on her right. "Y'all come on in and sit down, and try to ignore the Tower of Babble, if you can."

Belle laughed. "Now, Lucretia, I swear I don't talk half as much as you say I do. I was just telling Jack and Wanda Nell about you and me looking at their wedding photos the other day, and how you were saying what a beautiful bride Wanda Nell was."

"And so what if I was?" Mrs. Culpepper demanded. "I've got a right to my opinion, though the good Lord knows I have to take a shovel to the side of your head to get a word in most of the time."

Wanda Nell and Jack exchanged amused, but slightly exasperated, glances. This was what any visitor experienced, the constant verbal battle between the two women. Wanda Nell noted, however, the sparkle in Mrs. Culpepper's eyes and the bloom of health in her cheeks. Having Belle around actually made her appear younger than her seventy-odd years.

"I bet you two could use something nice and cool to drink," Belle said, standing in front of Jack and Wanda Nell. "I do declare, I think this July is about as hot a one as I can ever remember. You probably could fry an egg out there on that sidewalk. Would you believe I tried that once when I was little bitty girl? I heard my mama talking to somebody about how hot it was and that she could fry an egg on the sidewalk, so I sneaked one and took it outside. I cracked it, and you know what? It actually did cook. I just about blistered the skin off my feet, it was so hot."

Mrs. Culpepper seized her chance the moment Belle paused for a breath. "Why don't you go on in the kitchen and get us all some of that lemonade you made, Belle? Do something productive for once, and don't just stand there talking till somebody's ears fall off."

Belle smiled. "I surely could use some lemonade myself. I'll be back in a minute with some for everybody." With that she turned and headed for the kitchen.

"I swear, that woman will be the death of me yet," Mrs. Culpepper said. "If I don't kill myself just to get away from the sound of her voice, she'll drive me insane and I'll be running out into traffic and get hit by a car."

"You'd be bored to death without Belle," Wanda Nell said, trying not to smile. "And you know it."

"I reckon you're right," Mrs. Culpepper replied. "It's actually kind of fascinating, listening to her talk, sort of like being in one of those mazes. You never know when you're going to get to the center of it all, because there are so many detours and blind alleys."

Wanda Nell and Jack exchanged glances again. Mrs. Culpepper probably hadn't realized it, but when she did get a word in edgewise, she sounded more and more like Belle all the time.

"Now what brings you two by here?" Mrs. Culpepper asked. She flapped a hand at Belle, who had come back with a tray bearing a pitcher and four glasses. "You go on and pour that up for us, and then sit down over there and be quiet. I want to hear what Wanda Nell and Jack have to say, not you."

"Of course," Belle said. "I want to hear what they have

to say myself." With that, she set the tray on a table and began filling the glasses. Wanda Nell waited until Belle finished and took a seat before she spoke.

"We just happened to be downtown, and we thought we'd stop by. Juliet spent the night with one of her friends last night, and the girl's mama is going to drop Juliet off here for us to pick her up. We were sure you wouldn't mind."

"Of course not. She's such a sweet girl, I like having her here. She can spend the night here anytime she wants, you just remember that."

"Thank you," Wanda Nell said. "We appreciate that. And I know Juliet enjoys spending time with you and Belle."

"She's a good girl," Belle said.

"So what have you two been up to?" Mrs. Culpepper asked. "Are you settling in okay in that trailer?"

Jack nodded. "Yes, ma'am. We're doing just fine. Wanda Nell's trailer is actually bigger than the house I was renting, and it's nice to have more room."

"Good. I used to worry about my grandchildren growing up in that trailer park, but then I finally realized what really mattered was *how* they were raised, not where."

That was as close to an apology as she would ever get, Wanda Nell realized. She smiled at Mrs. Culpepper, knowing that a spoken "thank you" would simply embarrass the old lady.

"Jack is starting to work on a new book," Wanda Nell announced, "and I'm going to help."

"That's exciting," Belle said. "You know, Lucretia and I have read both your other books, Jack, and I can't tell you how thrilling they are. I swear I stayed up all night reading them."

"What's the new book about?" Mrs. Culpepper asked after glaring at Belle for a moment. Belle sat back and sipped at her lemonade.

"This one's going to be about a murder that occurred

right here in Tullahoma." Jack paused at Mrs. Culpepper's sudden intake of breath.

Realizing what she must have thought, Jack hastened to reassure her. "This is about an old murder, nothing recent."

Mrs. Culpepper relaxed, and Jack continued. "Thirty-one years ago, someone found the body of a girl on the football field at the high school. The case was never solved."

"Oh, how terrible," Belle said. "That poor child. And her poor parents. What an awful thing, to lose a child, and to lose one like that. Who was she?"

"Nobody knows," Wanda Nell said. "She wasn't ever identified, from what we know so far." She glanced at Mrs. Culpepper and was shocked to see how pale the old woman had become.

Belle had noticed it, too. She set down her glass and got up from her chair. "Lucretia, what on earth is the matter with you? Do you need one of your pills?"

"You'll have to excuse me," Mrs. Culpepper announced, her voice thin. "Belle, help me upstairs. I need to lie down."

Belle shot a worried glance at Wanda Nell and Jack. "I think we should call your doctor," Wanda Nell said.

"No, I don't need a doctor," Mrs. Culpepper snapped, her voice stronger. "I just want to lie down."

Jack had jumped up from the sofa. "Let me help you," he offered.

Mrs. Culpepper waved him away. "Belle will look after me, won't you, Belle?"

"Of course, Lucretia." Belle assisted her cousin from her chair. "I'll get you upstairs, and you can lie down and rest. I'm sure you're just tired."

Jack and Wanda Nell watched as Belle escorted Mrs. Culpepper toward the grand staircase in the front hall. Mrs. Culpepper had recently installed a chair lift on the stairs, and Belle put her in it.

Wanda Nell and Jack heard the whir of the machinery as Mrs. Culpepper slowly ascended the stairs, Belle treading up them behind her.

Jack sat back down on the couch and looked at Wanda Nell. "That wasn't good."

"No, it wasn't. She knows something, and I bet it involves the old judge. He must have been involved somehow."

Five

"Do you think she's going to be okay?" Jack asked, the concern obvious on his face. "The last thing I wanted to do was give her a stroke or a heart attack."

Wanda Nell squeezed his hand. "We didn't do that, honey, I'm sure. She was upset, but Belle will give her something to calm her, and she'll be okay. Let's just wait till Belle comes back downstairs."

Jack squeezed back. "Thanks, love."

Though she had done her best to reassure Jack, Wanda Nell was worried. Mrs. Culpepper did have heart problems, partly the result of years of drinking way more than she should have, but she had been doing pretty well for the past year. Wanda Nell prayed that they hadn't caused her to have a setback.

Jack and Wanda Nell waited in silence until Belle came padding down the stairs about ten minutes later. They both rose from the sofa when Belle entered the drawing room.

"How is she?" Jack asked.

"She had a little shock," Belle said, "but she's going to be just fine. I gave her one of those little tranquilizers the doctor prescribed, and she's already dropping off to sleep.

When she wakes up, she'll be just as ornery as ever. Don't you two worry about her."

"Did she say anything?" Wanda Nell asked as she and Jack sat back down on the sofa.

"Not much," Belle replied, after a sip of her lemonade. "She did say, 'Tell them I'm sorry,' but I don't really know what she meant by that. She did seem to get a shock when you told her about that poor dead girl." She eyed Jack and Wanda Nell over the rim of her glass.

Wanda Nell glanced at Jack, and he nodded. She took a breath before she spoke. "The thing is, there was probably some kind of cover-up over the murder. Because somebody important here in Tullahoma was involved."

"And you're thinking it could be Thaddeus," Belle said. She carefully set her glass on the table beside her chair. She leaned forward slightly. "It sure wouldn't surprise me. Thaddeus James Culpepper was about as crooked as a mountain road, let me tell you. And poor Lucretia didn't have much choice but to put up with him."

"Thaddeus James?" Jack asked. "I reckon that's the first time I've ever heard him called anything besides the old judge."

"T.J. is named for him," Wanda Nell said, making a wry face. "Now you know why he prefers being called T.J."

"I'm sorry we upset Miz Culpepper," Jack said. "The last thing we wanted to do was make her ill."

"It's not your fault, Jack, dear." Belle shook her head. "It's the fault of that awful man she was married to for so long. Thank the Lord he went off to his reward years ago, and I reckon I know right where he is this moment, roasting away. Him *and* all those floozies he used to carry on with. It was disgusting."

"Still, dragging up the past can't be anything but hurtful to her," Wanda Nell said.

"Lucretia's a lot stronger than you think she is," Belle

replied. "Don't you think she isn't. She had a little shock, but once she's had some time to think about it, she'll understand. I know she'll feel sorry for that poor girl, and she'll tell you that child ought to have justice. You'll see. I know her better than anybody."

"I hope you're right," Jack said. "We knew this was going to be tough, but I didn't want it to be tough on Miz Culpepper."

The doorbell rang, and they all started. Belle made a move to get out of her chair, but Wanda Nell forestalled her. "I'm sure it's Juliet," she said. "I'll go."

Belle subsided in her chair and smiled. "Thank you, dear."

Wanda Nell walked to the front door and opened it. Her younger daughter stood there, small overnight bag in hand and a purse slung over her shoulder.

"Hi, Mama." Juliet smiled.

"Hi, sweetie," Wanda Nell said, stepping aside to let her pass into the hall. "Did you have a good time?"

"I did. We went to a movie last night, and then we stayed up talking till about two in the morning. Miz Hankins let us sleep late, too."

"Good," Wanda Nell said, giving Juliet a hug. "But you don't need to be staying up late too often, okay? Even if it is a weekend."

"Okay, Mama." Juliet rolled her eyes. Wanda Nell pretended not to notice.

Juliet followed her mother into the drawing room. "Hello, Belle," she said, stooping to give the older woman a quick hug and a peck on the cheek. "How are you?"

"I'm just fine, honey." Belle beamed at her.

"Where's Grandmama?" Juliet asked, waving at Jack. She perched on the arm of Belle's chair.

"She's upstairs having a little rest," Wanda Nell said. "We were talking, and she was a bit tired." She stared at

Belle, willing her not to say anything to Juliet. Belle winked at her.

Juliet looked down at Belle. "She hasn't been out working in the flower beds in this heat, has she?" Juliet frowned. "I told her I'd do the weeding for her, but I guess I forgot."

"No, honey," Belle said, patting Juliet's hand. "She hasn't been out in the heat. She was just a little tired, like your mama said. Don't you worry about her."

Juliet didn't appear wholly convinced. She was still frowning. "Mama, would you mind if I spent the night with Grandmama and Belle tonight? I can work on the flower beds this evening, when it's cooler out, and then Grandmama won't have to worry about them. And I can go to church with her and Belle in the morning." She glanced down at Belle again. "Is it okay with you, Belle?"

"Of course it is, honey," Belle said, beaming. "You know how much Lucretia and I love having you here. That'll be just the thing to perk her up." She turned to look at Wanda Nell. "You don't mind, do you, Wanda Nell? Juliet's no trouble at all, none at all."

"Of course I don't mind." Wanda Nell smiled at her daughter. "I'm real proud of her for wanting to help her grandmama like this. Do you have something to wear to church tomorrow, though?"

"Yes'm. I have a dress here that I can wear. It's in the closet in my room upstairs."

"That's settled, then," Jack said. "We can pick you up after church tomorrow, if you like." He stood up and held out his hand to Wanda Nell. She grasped it and stood beside him.

"I can just come with T.J. and Tuck. They won't mind coming by here to get me when they head out there for dinner." She paused. "Unless you need me to help with dinner or help clean the house, Mama."

"That'll be fine," Wanda Nell said. "I don't think there's

anything you really need to do about cleaning tomorrow, honey. So we'll see you tomorrow evening."

Juliet came to her mother for a goodbye kiss, then gave Jack a quick hug. He smiled fondly at her.

Belle went with them to the front door while Juliet scampered up the stairs, heading for her room on the second floor. "Don't y'all worry about a thing," Belle said. "Lucretia's going to be just fine."

"Thanks, Belle." Wanda Nell gave the older woman a kiss on the cheek. Jack did the same, and Belle blushed a little.

"Call us if you need anything," Jack said on his way out the door.

"I sure will," Belle answered.

Wanda Nell waved goodbye before she got in the car, and Belle waved back. The front door shut as Jack started the car and turned on the air conditioning. Mrs. Culpepper's driveway was heavily shaded, and Wanda Nell was thankful. The car cooled quickly, and Jack backed down the driveway into the street.

"You mind if we go to the library?" Jack asked as he drove down Main Street.

"Of course not. I'm as curious as you are to see if we'll find anything. There's got to be *something*."

"I sure hope so," Jack said, "or this book isn't going anywhere very fast."

"Elmer Lee might turn up something, too," Wanda Nell reminded him.

"True." Jack turned the car into the parking lot at the library. He glanced at his watch. "It's three-thirty, and I think they close at five on Saturdays. So we should have time to find something, if there is anything, in the back issues of the paper."

There were only a couple of other cars in the parking lot, and the library was very quiet when they walked inside. A teenager was looking through the shelves in one section, and a mother with two young children in tow was browsing the shelves in another area. Wanda Nell and Jack walked up to the front desk.

"Afternoon, Miz Lockett," Wanda Nell said to the librarian. Mrs. Lockett had worked at the library since Wanda Nell was in grade school, and Wanda Nell suddenly realized just how young Mrs. Lockett had been in those days. She was only in her mid-fifties now, so she probably hadn't been long out of college when Wanda Nell went to the library for the first time.

"Why, hello, Wanda Nell." Mrs. Lockett smiled. "How are you doing? And Jack. What a pleasure to see you both. Congratulations, by the way. I read about your wedding in the paper."

"Thank you," Wanda Nell said, and Jack echoed her.

"Now what can I do for you?" Mrs. Lockett asked.

"We need to look at back issues of the newspaper," Jack said. "From thirty years ago or so."

Mrs. Lockett nodded. "They're all on microfilm, I'm afraid. I keep hoping somehow we'll get the money to digitize them and get them online, but probably not in my lifetime." She gave a quiet chuckle. "So we're left with outdated technology."

Jack laughed. "That's fine. I think I remember how to use a microfilm reader."

"Good," Mrs. Lockett replied. "The local paper is in cabinets in that second room down the hall, and there are a couple of readers on the tables in there. If you need help with anything, you just come and let me know."

"Thank you, we will," Wanda Nell said. She followed Jack down the hall to the room the librarian had indicated. Jack flipped the light switch on, and he and Wanda Nell stared for a moment at the wall of cabinets.

Stepping closer, they began examining the labels on the

drawers, looking for the local paper. "I guess I never realized just how much they have in here," Wanda Nell said. "They've got the *Commercial Appeal* from Memphis, and the *Clarion-Ledger* from Jackson, too."

"That reminds me, we should probably check those papers, too, just in case," Jack said. "It might have made one of them before the cover-up started."

"How about I start with the Memphis paper, while you look at the Tullahoma one?" Wanda Nell asked. She started hunting for the drawer with the right dates on it.

"Good idea," Jack said. He wandered away from her. "Here's the Tullahoma paper." He bent to peer more closely at the labels.

Wanda Nell found the drawer she needed and pulled it open. Inside were several rows of boxes containing microfilms. Using one finger, she skimmed over the labels, looking for the correct month. "Got it," she said, extracting the box from the drawer.

"I'm not having any luck yet," Jack said.

Wanda Nell was only half-listening. She took her box to one of the readers and sat down at the table. There was a diagram that explained how to load the film on the machine, and she examined it closely. "That looks easy enough," she muttered. She extracted the roll of microfilm from the box and began to load it. Behind her she could hear Jack opening and closing drawers.

Once the microfilm was properly loaded, Wanda Nell started going through it, looking for the right date to start. "Honey," she called, "did Elmer Lee say anything about a date on that file?"

"No, he didn't, but I've got the copy right here."

Wanda Nell turned to watch as he pulled the folded papers from his jeans pocket. He unfolded them and scanned them quickly. "Looks like the body was found on April twenty-third."

"Thanks." Wanda Nell got to that date on her roll of film and began carefully going forward. She was dimly aware of Jack's continuing to open and shut drawers while she worked.

She had made her way through April twenty-fifth without finding any reference to a murder in Tullahoma, when the increasingly loud sounds of frustration coming from behind her broke through her concentration.

Wanda Nell turned in her chair, staring at her husband in concern. "Honey, what's going on?"

"It's missing," Jack said, frowning. "I've looked through most of the drawers now, thinking it might simply be misfiled. But it's just not here. The box we need just isn't here."

Six

Jack cursed, and Wanda Nell shook a finger at him. "Honey, don't forget you're in the library. Don't be talking like that."

"Sorry," Jack muttered. "I guess I should have expected this."

Wanda Nell got up and went over to him, slipping a consoling arm around his waist. "Well, if we had any doubts about somebody trying to cover the whole thing up, I guess we don't anymore."

"We sure don't."

"But it does tell us something," Wanda Nell added in a more encouraging tone. "There must be something in the paper that would help us, if someone went to all the trouble of stealing the microfilm from the library."

"Good point." Jack's face brightened for a moment. "But where are we going to find other copies of the paper?"

"First, let's make sure there's not something in the Memphis or Jackson papers," Wanda Nell said. She nodded in the direction of the microfilm reader she had been using. "I've been through the twenty-fifth in the *Commercial Appeal*, and I haven't found anything so far."

"I'll check out the *Clarion-Ledger*." Jack moved toward the drawers containing the Jackson paper. "I'm willing to bet, though, we're not going to find anything in either one."

"Maybe not," Wanda Nell said. "But somewhere, I bet you, we'll be able to find a copy of the missing Tullahoma paper. You just wait and see."

Jack grinned at her. "That's just one of the many reasons I love you, darling. The Unsinkable Wanda Nell."

Wanda Nell shook her head at him. "Get to work," she said, trying to sound stern.

"Yes, ma'am."

Wanda Nell turned her back on him and resumed her examination of the Memphis paper. She went carefully through the whole week after April twenty-third, but she never found a mention of the murder, or any mention at all of Tullahoma. She stopped looking, rewound the reel, took it off the machine, and put it back in its box.

Jack was now sitting at the table next to her, using the other reader. "Any luck so far?" she asked.

"No. I'm up to the twenty-sixth, and nothing so far. How far did you look?"

"Through May first."

"That was probably enough," Jack said. "If there wasn't some kind of mention by that point, there probably never was. Let me just go that far here, and then we'll try to figure out what to do next."

Wanda Nell waited in silence while Jack finished examining his reel of film. After about seven or eight minutes, he leaned back, pulled off his glasses, and rubbed at his eyes. "Now I'm getting a headache from staring at that screen."

"Didn't find anything?"

"No, not a blessed thing. No mention of Tullahoma at all." He rewound the roll, extracted it, and stuck it in its box.

"Let's go talk to Miz Lockett," Wanda Nell said. "She needs to know there's a box missing, and maybe she'll know of another way we can find what we're looking for."

"Let's not make a big deal out of it, though," Jack said. "I don't want to stir up anything at this point."

"Okay." Wanda Nell followed him out of the room, flipping off the light switch as she went.

At the front desk Mrs. Lockett was checking out a stack of books for the mother and the two children. Jack and Wanda Nell waited, increasingly impatient, as the mother kept interrupting the proceedings to admonish her children. Finally, the woman started herding them toward the door.

With a tired smile, Mrs. Lockett turned her attention to Wanda Nell and Jack. "Did you find what you needed?"

"Well, no, we didn't," Jack said, sounding slightly apologetic. "The one reel of film we needed seems to be missing."

"Oh, dear. Where could it have got to? Maybe someone just misfiled it, and it's in another drawer somewhere." She came from behind the counter and started for the microfilm room.

"We checked for that," Jack said, and Mrs. Lockett halted.

"You looked through *all* the drawers?" Mrs. Lockett asked, her head cocked to one side.

"Well, no, not through all of them," Jack admitted. "But I checked all the drawers for the Tullahoma paper. I didn't check anywhere else."

"Then the box you need is probably somewhere in one of the other drawers," Mrs. Lockett said. She came back to the desk. "If you don't mind waiting a couple of days, I'll have one of the high school students who works here during the week go through all the drawers on Monday to see if he can find it." She smiled at them. "I'm sure it's there somewhere." She pulled a slip of scrap paper from a slot behind the desk and handed it to Jack. "Just put your name and phone number on this for me, and I'll call you on Monday."

"Thank you, I'd appreciate that very much." Jack glanced sideways at Wanda Nell before he picked up a pen from the counter and wrote down the information Mrs. Lockett had requested.

Neither Wanda Nell nor Jack thought the student would ever find the missing box, but they weren't going to tell Mrs. Lockett that. That wouldn't serve much purpose at this point.

"What happened to the paper copies of the newspaper?" Wanda Nell asked. "I don't imagine you still have them somewhere around, do you?"

"Heavens, no." Mrs. Lockett laughed. "We got rid of them once we were able to have them microfilmed. They took up so much space—and the dust!" She wrinkled her nose. "Ordinarily I hate getting rid of something like that, but we were certainly able to make better use of the space once they were gone."

"So they just got thrown away?" Jack asked.

"Well, no," Mrs. Lockett said, surprising him and Wanda Nell. "We gave them to the Tullahoma County Historical Society. And as far as I know, they still have them all."

"Oh, I didn't know that." Wanda Nell was trying to maintain a casual tone. "Does the Historical Society let people look at them?"

"I don't see why not," Mrs. Lockett said. "Though they're open only a couple of days a week. They have to depend on volunteers to do everything, and I think that's about all they can manage these days."

"If we wanted to have a look at their collection," Jack asked, "whom should we call?"

"The president of the society, probably," Mrs. Lockett

said. "I'm sure you both know her—she taught at the high school for about forty years, until she retired a few years ago. Miss Ernestine Carpenter. She even taught me. It was her second year teaching at the high school."

Wanda Nell turned to Jack with a smile. "We sure do know her," Wanda Nell said. "In fact, she came to our wedding."

"Well, then"—Mrs. Lockett beamed at them—"there you are. I know Miss Ernestine will be more than happy to help you. Y'all just give her a call, and I know she'll fix you right up."

"Thank you, we will," Jack said. "We really appreciate all your help."

"You're more than welcome," Mrs. Lockett replied. "And I'll have our student worker look for that missing box. I'll call you when he finds it."

"Thank you, Miz Lockett," Wanda Nell said. "We'll be seeing you."

"Bye now," Mrs. Lockett called after them.

In the car again, the air conditioner blasting once more, Wanda Nell adjusted her sunglasses. "It's only about four-fifteen. What say we give Ernie a call right now?"

"Fine by me," Jack said. "Curiosity's really getting to me, I have to say."

Wanda Nell pulled her cell phone out of her purse and started punching buttons. She had put Ernie's number in her phone address book back when her brother Rusty had been involved in a nasty local murder. Ernie had been a big help to her during that awful time. Since then she had chatted with Ernie a few times, and Ernie had been there, beaming, when Wanda Nell and Jack were married.

There was no answer, so Wanda Nell ended the call and checked her book for Ernie's cell number and punched it in. The phone rang three times before Ernie answered.

"Hello, there, Wanda Nell. How are you and Jack doing?" Ernie asked, her voice cheerful and loud.

"We're doing just fine. How about you?"

They exchanged pleasantries while Ernie inquired about the health of everyone in Wanda Nell's family. After about three minutes, Ernie finally wound down long enough for Wanda Nell to broach the subject of her call.

"Jack and I were just at the library talking to Miz Lockett, and she told us you're the president of the Historical Society."

"I am, for all my sins," Ernie said with another laugh. "Are you and Jack interested in volunteering? We're always looking for help, let me tell you."

"Not exactly," Wanda Nell said. "We were hoping you could help us with something. Miz Lockett told us that the library gave the Historical Society its copies of all the old Tullahoma newspaper when they got the microfilms of them."

"Yes, they did," Ernie said. "Do you need to look at them?"

"We sure do, if that's possible. The ones we needed to see, well, the library didn't have them. There was a box of microfilm missing."

"How strange," Ernie said. "Is this something urgent?"

"Well, I wouldn't say *urgent*," Wanda Nell replied. "But we'd sure like to get a look as soon as we can. It's kind of important."

"Can you tell me what it is?" Ernie asked. "You know how nosy I am, and right now I'm about to pop from curiosity."

Wanda Nell laughed. "Of course we can tell you. We'll probably have some questions to ask you anyway, besides just looking at the newspapers."

"Good," Ernie said. "I'm actually in Tullahoma at the

moment, doing some shopping. Where are you and Jack right now?"

"Sitting in the parking lot at the library." Wanda Nell gave Jack a thumbs-up with her free hand, and he grinned. He had heard most of what Ernie had said, her voice was so strong and clear.

"Then meet me at the Historical Society," Ernie said. "I can be there in about seven or eight minutes."

"Where is it?" Wanda Nell asked. "You know, I don't think I've ever even seen the building. At least not that I can recall."

"It's nothing remarkable, sad to say," Ernie responded with a laugh. "It's just a couple of blocks from the library, in one of the old houses off Main Street. Go back down Main Street, take a right on Elm, and it's the second house on your right."

"Thanks, Ernie. We sure do appreciate this."

"See you in a few minutes," Ernie said, and she broke the connection.

Wanda Nell put away her phone and repeated the directions to Jack. He squeezed her hand quickly before he put the car in gear and drove out of the library parking lot.

In less than two minutes they were parked at the curb in front of the house that was home to the Tullahoma County Historical Society. Like Mrs. Culpepper's larger and grander house, this building was also antebellum, but on a more modest scale.

"This is what they call Greek Revival, isn't it?" Wanda Nell asked. "Like Miz. Culpepper's house."

"Yes," Jack replied. "The Culpepper house is a lot bigger, but this one looks like a little jewel box on the outside. I don't think I've ever noticed it before."

"Me neither," Wanda Nell said. "I've never had much call to drive down this street, but it sure is a nice one. All these old homes, and most of them look like they've been really taken care of."

"How would you like to live in one of them?" Jack asked, and something in his tone made Wanda Nell look at him.

"You're not kidding, are you?"

Jack shrugged. "Well, you never know. If one of my books took off and sold really well, who knows? I could quit teaching and actually write full-time. And maybe we could afford a house like this. Would you like that?"

"I don't know. I've never even really thought about something like that. I've never been able to look all that far ahead, past the next payment on the trailer."

"I know, honey, but there are two of us now, and we can dream as big as we want, together."

Wanda Nell smiled at him. "I'll have to think about it. But to be honest, the first thing that occurs to me is, how the heck would I keep a house that size clean?"

Jack laughed. "We'd hire a maid, honey."

"Me, with a maid? Are you serious?"

A bright red, late-model Jeep pulled up beside them, and the driver honked. Startled, Jack and Wanda Nell peered at the driver as the vehicle pulled into the driveway. It was Ernie.

Jack and Wanda Nell got out of the car and walked up the sidewalk to the front door. Ernie, dressed in a comfortable cotton dress and sensible, low-heeled shoes, met them at the door. At six feet, Ernie was only a bit shorter than Jack, and she had the bearing of a woman who never doubted that she was in command of any situation.

After a quick hug, Ernie pulled a key from her purse and unlocked the door. "Come on in. It probably smells a little musty in here, but there's not much we can do about that. Too many old things."

Wanda Nell's nose wrinkled as she and Jack stepped

into the front hall. Ernie was right, it did smell a bit funny. Ernie flipped a couple of light switches, and the shadowy hallway came into sharper focus.

"Looks like we've stepped right back into the Civil War era," Jack said.

"As much as we've been able to, we've kept the house looking like it did back then," Ernie said. "The elderly lady who left the house to the Historical Society fifty years ago was the daughter of a Confederate officer, and when she inherited the house, she kept it as much as possible in the state it had been in during her father's time."

"Remarkable," Jack said. "Truly remarkable, and a little bit macabre."

"You don't know the half of it," Ernie said. "You ought to be here alone in the evening, working. I've seen some interesting things, let me tell you."

Wanda Nell peered around her. One thing she didn't like was ghost stories.

Seeing Wanda Nell's reaction, Ernie chuckled. "Don't worry. Miss Ina never comes out during the daytime."

"About those newspapers?" Jack asked.

"Right," Ernie replied. "I'll show you where they are, and you can tell me what you're looking for. Follow me." She turned and headed down the hall to a room near the rear of the house.

"This is the library," Ernie said, once they were all inside, "but of course you can see that, with all the bookshelves." She waved a hand around. "The newspapers are in these cabinets, and I believe there are markers on the shelves to indicate the years, and so on." She moved toward a series of metal file cabinets in one corner of the room. They were the only jarring, modern note in the room, as far as Wanda Nell could see.

Jack walked over to the cabinets and started peering at the labels. "Here's the drawer," he said, turning to Wanda

Nell for a moment. She held up crossed fingers, and he grinned.

Jack pulled open the drawer and began examining the contents. Wanda Nell held her breath while Ernie watched, her eyes burning with curiosity.

Seven

Wanda Nell couldn't stand it any longer. She moved beside Jack and peered into the drawer as he continued to examine its contents. As she watched, he pulled a handful of newspapers from the drawer.

"Here they are." Jack's shoulders relaxed.

"Thank goodness. I was afraid they'd be missing from here, too." Wanda Nell heaved a sigh of relief.

"Okay, you two, You had better fill me in now." Ernie said. "Why did you think the papers you wanted might be missing?"

"I guess we'd better start at the beginning." Jack clutched the papers to his chest as he shut the file drawer with his other hand.

"Good idea," Ernie replied. "Y'all come on over here, and let's sit down and talk about it." She motioned them toward a desk with some chairs in front of it. She pointed at the chair behind the desk for Jack, and she and Wanda Nell sat down across from him.

Stacking the newspapers neatly in front of him as he sat, Jack said, "It all started this morning when I was at the high school having my morning run. I saw old Gus, the custodian, and he got to telling me about how, thirty-one years ago, they found a dead girl on the football field one morning."

"Oh, my goodness," Ernie said. "I'd forgotten all about that."

"I'd been thinking about working on a new book, and as soon as Gus told me about this case, I was hooked. He said the case was never solved, and he thought it was hushed up."

"From what I remember, there weren't all that many details to go on," Ernie said. "Or so everyone was led to believe. But that doesn't mean somebody wasn't pulling strings to make sure the investigation didn't progress very far."

"Somebody was obviously pulling strings," Jack said. "We've already talked to Elmer Lee, and he checked their files. He found a file, all right, but there were only two sheets of paper in it. Very few details."

"And when you went to the library to look for information in the newspaper, you found that the issues you wanted were missing," Ernie said, her brow furrowing. "Somebody tried to remove as many traces of the case as they could." She shook her head. "I suppose I shouldn't really be that surprised. It wouldn't be the first time something like that happened around here."

"Probably not," Jack said. "But it does tell me there's bound to be at least *some* useful information in the newspaper."

"You go on ahead and look." Ernie rose from her chair. "I think one of the bits of information you'll find is the name of a suspect who quickly disappeared, as I recall. His name escapes me just now. I'm going to check something in our records, and I'll be back in a minute."

Jack nodded before he began examining the small stack of newspapers in front of him. Wanda Nell got up from her chair and went to stand beside him at the desk.

There was an item about the body in the April twenty-fourth issue. It didn't say much—just that the body of a young woman had been found on the football field at the high school. There was no mention of the person who found the body. The Sheriff's Department was investigating, and that was about it.

Jack laid that issue aside and began looking through the one for April twenty-fifth. The case earned a little more coverage on this date. The Sheriff's Department had thus far not been able to identify the young woman, estimated to be eighteen to twenty years old. No one in town had come forward with any information by press time, and anyone who might know something was asked to call the Sheriff's Department.

The twenty-sixth and twenty-seventh were weekend days that year, and the local paper didn't publish on the weekends. On the twenty-eighth, the paper stated that the Sheriff's Department was questioning someone in connection with the case, but that was it.

Jack turned and looked up at Wanda Nell. "So far I sure don't see anything worth stealing the microfilm over, do you?"

"No. It sure is strange."

With a sigh, Jack picked up the next issue. The headline leaped out at them: "Tullahoma man questioned in murder." Jack and Wanda Nell quickly scanned the item. According to the paper, the Sheriff's Department had questioned one Roscoe Lee Bates extensively in the case, but no charges were pending against Mr. Bates, age nineteen.

"At least we have a name now," Wanda Nell said, relieved. "That's who Ernie was talking about. Didn't she say he disappeared?"

Nodding, Jack laid the issue aside and unfolded the next one, April thirtieth. There was nothing about the murder on the front page, nor was there anything on the other pages.

The May first issue was also devoid of any mention of the murder. Jack pushed the remaining few issues aside. There seemed little point in looking any further.

"I guess we know when the cover-up set in," Wanda Nell said. She walked around the desk and sat back down in her chair.

"Find anything?" Ernie asked as she came back into the room. She was holding a file folder, her face alight with curiosity.

"We found one thing," Jack said. "The name of a young man the Sheriff's Department questioned in connection with the case. Then coverage of the murder stopped abruptly April twenty-ninth. We looked at April thirtieth and May first, and there was nothing."

Ernie resumed her seat, brandishing the folder. "That fits with the information I have here." She glanced from Jack to Wanda Nell. "This is a file of some of the records we keep on the provenance of donations to the Historical Society. I wanted to check the records for the copies of the paper we've received. I thought I remembered something odd."

"Like what?" Wanda Nell asked.

"I was pretty sure I remembered that when we received the papers from the library, there were some gaps in what they had." Ernie held up her file folder again. "And, sure enough, I remembered correctly. The issues you just looked at were missing, along with a few others here and there over the years."

"So where did these come from then?" Jack asked.

"From the father of one of the Historical Society members," Ernie said with a brief smile. "A real pack rat. He had every issue of the paper going back to when it was founded, in 1903."

"Thank the Lord someone had kept them," Wanda Nell said.

"Exactly. The fact that those issues"—Ernie pointed toward the stack of newspapers on the desk in front of Jack—"were missing from the library's set makes it pretty obvious someone really wanted to try to erase as many traces of the murder as possible."

"Thanks to an elderly pack rat, they didn't quite succeed," Jack said.

Ernie smiled. "Even pack rats have their uses." She waved a hand around. "Otherwise this house would hold a lot less local history than it does."

Wanda Nell grinned. "Then the next time I clean out my house, I'll know where to send the stuff I want to get rid of."

"You never know what we might want," Ernie said. "Now, what was the name of the young man the Sheriff's Department was questioning? I still can't quite dredge it up."

Jack glanced down at the issue of the newspaper with the information. "Roscoe Lee Bates, age nineteen." He looked up again. "Did you know him? You said something about a suspect disappearing."

Ernie leaned back in her chair. "Roscoe Lee Bates. So that's who it was." She shook her head. "I don't know why I couldn't remember his name. Yes, I knew him. At least briefly, I should say. He was in one of my classes at the high school for about three months, and then he dropped out of school."

"When was that?" Wanda Nell asked. "Was it when the murder happened?"

"No, I'm pretty sure it wasn't. I think it was probably the year before that. The boy was average, but he never applied himself all that much. He could have graduated if he'd put a little effort into it, but he just gave up partway through his senior year."

"Can you think of any reason the police might consider him a suspect?" Jack asked. "I mean, was he known to be a troublemaker, or anything?"

"Not really. Now that we're talking about him, I'm remembering more and more. No, he was basically a good boy, just lazy. He also had difficulty making good decisions, so he occasionally got in trouble—nothing really serious, though." She cocked her head to one side and stared into space. "He was a very handsome boy, and so he always had plenty of girls buzzing around him even though he was pretty quiet most of the time. He certainly liked girls, so I can easily imagine his chatting up a stranger in town, especially if she was pretty."

"There must have been some kind of connection, then, between him and the dead girl," Wanda Nell said. "You don't think the Sheriff's Department would have picked somebody at random, do you?"

"I'd sure hate to think they'd stoop that low," Ernie said. "But if somebody in town with a lot of money and influence was willing to pay, the sheriff at that time might have been bought off."

"Who was the sheriff back then?" Wanda Nell asked. "I was only about ten or eleven, and I sure don't remember."

Ernie's mouth twisted in distaste. "I hate to say it, but he was a distant cousin of mine. Claude Carpenter. He had the morals of an alley cat, and was as venal as they come. It was a shameful day for this county when he was elected sheriff, let me tell you."

"Was he in office very long?" Jack asked.

"A couple of terms," Ernie replied. "Then he had a heart attack and died, just when he was about to run for a third time."

"So we can't question him," Jack said, sighing.

"No, but one of his deputies might still be around. I'm sure Elmer Lee can check on that. One of them might be able to tell you something. If they weren't paid off, too, that is."

"Let's get back to Roscoe Lee Bates," Wanda Nell said. "About his disappearing. What do you think happened?"

"Do you think he could have been murdered, too?" Jack asked.

"I suppose it's possible. But I think it's just as likely that he ran off because he was afraid of what might happen if he didn't. He came from a poor family, and I seem to recall that his father wasn't around, just his mother and a younger sister."

"He would have made a pretty convenient scapegoat then," Jack said.

"Exactly. Too young, too inexperienced, not bright enough, and certainly with no influence—he would have been a prime target if someone wanted to frame him for the murder."

"He also could have done it, you know," Wanda Nell said. "Although if he had, it seems kind of silly for anyone to go to the extremes of covering it up when they had the killer all along."

"Maybe, honey," Jack said. "Maybe he *was* the killer. But maybe someone in town was more afraid of something else."

"Like what?" Ernie asked.

"Who the girl really was. To me, that's the simplest explanation. If there's any way to find out *why* she came to Tullahoma, I think we'd find the key to the whole situation."

"Maybe she wanted something from somebody here"— Ernie continued Jack's train of thought—"and that someone wasn't willing to give it. That person killed her, and Roscoe Lee Bates looked like an easy scapegoat."

"But if he disappeared, it would be a lot easier for the whole thing to just fade away," Wanda Nell said.

She, Jack, and Ernie looked at each other. "It's certainly plausible," Ernie said.

"But in order to find out what the dead girl wanted here in Tullahoma," Jack said, "we're going to have to find out who she was."

"Yes," Wanda Nell said. "And how are we going to do that?"

Jack turned to Ernie. "You mentioned that this Bates boy had a mother and a sister. Are they still in Tullahoma?"

Ernie thought for a moment. "I'm pretty sure Mrs. Bates died many years ago. I don't know about the sister. I seem to recall she married someone local before her mother died, but at the moment I can't think of his name. I certainly haven't run across her in a long time, and I have a pretty good memory for former students." She smiled at Wanda Nell.

"You sure do." Wanda Nell smiled. "So you taught this girl?"

"Yes, and I think she was three or four years younger than her brother. Her name was Sandra." She paused. "Sandra June Bates. Her mother's name was June, I believe."

Wanda Nell exchanged glances with her husband. "Now I guess we have to track down Sandra June Bates. She's our only link to her brother, and if we can find her, she might know something about what happened to him." Jack crossed his arms and leaned back in the chair. "But how are we going to find Sandra Bates?"

"First off," Ernie said, "I'll do my best to remember who it was she married. Once you have that name, it should be easier. Of course, she could have been married and divorced seven times since then, but hopefully she won't be that hard to trace."

Wanda Nell stood up. "Once again, Ernie, you've been tremendous help."

Ernie smiled at her former student. "It's my pleasure, of course, Wanda Nell." Her smile faded. "I hate to think of that poor girl lying somewhere nameless, unavenged. If I can do anything to correct that, I'll be proud to do it." She stood.

"That's how we feel," Jack said.

"Hang on a second." Wanda Nell was struck by a sudden thought. She stared into space for a moment. "What happened to the girl's body? Would they have buried her somewhere?"

"Good point, honey," Jack said. "In big cities, they often keep unclaimed bodies in the morgue for years. But here, well, I don't know." He looked at Ernie. "What do you think?"

Ernie frowned. "They might have turned her body over to the state, but I'm thinking that if someone went to such great lengths to cover this all up, she was probably buried in town or somewhere nearby. And probably in an unmarked grave."

"That's awful," Wanda Nell said around a sudden lump in her throat. The thought of such a careless burial struck her as particularly sad. Jack slipped an arm around her, and she laid her head on his shoulder.

"It is." Ernie's voice huskier than usual. "She deserves better than that."

"We have to find her, Jack." Wanda Nell lifted her head and looked into Jack's eyes. "And give her back her name."

"We will, honey. One way or another, the good Lord willing, we'll do that for her."

Eight

On the drive home from the Historical Society, neither Jack nor Wanda Nell found much to say. Wanda Nell was still gripped by the image of an unmarked grave, and that grieved her.

"Surely somebody, somewhere knew her," she said, startling Jack.

"Yes. She had a life somewhere else."

"I wonder why someone didn't come looking for her," Wanda Nell said. "Don't you think it's strange that nobody did?"

"As far as we know, honey, nobody came looking for her. But the sad fact is, young women—and young men, too, for that matter—go missing all the time, and a lot of them are never found. Some people disappear because they want to, and this girl could have been one of them. Why, I don't know. But it happens all the time."

"I guess you're right," Wanda Nell said, feeling even sadder. "This sure is a depressing case."

"Yes. It's pretty damn awful, all the way around. And I guess that's one reason I'm even more committed to try and figure it out. For the sake of some nameless, faceless girl."

"That's the best reason there is," Wanda Nell said with a sad smile at her husband.

Jack nodded. "This morning, when Gus told me about it, all I could think about at first was what an interesting subject for a book it would make. But now it's much more than that. Even though we have no idea who she is at this point, I feel like I have a duty to do what I can to make things right for her." He shook his head. "At least as right as you can, after all this time."

Jack pulled his car in behind Wanda Nell's in their driveway, and for a moment they sat, the motor still running. With a sigh Jack switched off the air conditioner and then the ignition.

Wanda Nell didn't wait for him to open her door. She got out and followed him up the stairs to the door of the trailer. Jack unlocked it, and Wanda Nell preceded him inside.

"What are you going to do now?" Wanda Nell asked as she set her purse down on the table near the door.

"If you don't mind, I'm going to do some work on this, but if you need me to help with something, it can wait."

Wanda Nell smiled. "No, you go ahead. I've just got some laundry to finish, and I don't mind doing it by myself."

Jack gave her a quick kiss before disappearing down the hall to his study. Wanda Nell knew she probably wouldn't see him for a couple of hours. When he was working, he got so focused he lost all track of time.

Wanda Nell headed for the small utility room close to their bedroom. She switched on the light and began loading the washing machine. Once that was done, she pulled a load of whites from the dryer and began folding them.

As her hands performed a task they knew all too well, Wanda Nell let her mind wander over the events of the day. It seemed like longer, but it had been only this morning when Jack first told her about the case. They had certainly made some progress today, despite the best efforts of someone to cover it all up.

There were still big obstacles in the way, though. Who was the dead girl? And why had she come to Tullahoma? Wanda Nell sighed and stacked a newly folded towel on top of the others she had done.

If they could find Sandra June Bates, and if she knew what had happened to her brother, they might have a good chance of figuring this thing out. If he knew something, that is, and hadn't been picked at random to be the scapegoat.

If, if, if. Wanda Nell frowned. Too many of them at this point, but she knew that wasn't going to stop Jack, and it certainly wouldn't stop her, either. With Ernie Carpenter on their side, she reflected, they surely couldn't fail. Ernie had the determination and drive to help them see it through.

Before they had left the Historical Society, Ernie had promised to do whatever she could to help. Wanda Nell, struck by a sudden inspiration, suggested looking through the newspapers to find an announcement of Sandra June Bates's wedding. Ernie said she would look, but she doubted she'd find anything. The Bates family wasn't the kind to pay for a wedding announcement in the paper, and she didn't think Sandra June Bates had married a man whose family would have done it, cither.

"But I promise I'll look," Ernie said, "and who knows? We might get lucky. Or else I'll finally dredge up the boy's name from my memory."

Wanda Nell smiled fondly. Ernie did have an amazing memory, especially for her former students. If she couldn't remember this one person, he probably hadn't been a student.

Jack had already mentioned going through the records

at the county courthouse, because if Sandra June had been married in Tullahoma County, the marriage license would be on file. He was planning to do it on Monday.

There was no need for Jack to do that, Wanda Nell realized. Her son, T.J., could easily do it for him. In his work with his partner, Tuck, T.J. often did research of this kind at the courthouse. They knew him there, and no one would pay much attention to him. Jack, however, had rarely done this, and if he wanted to keep a low profile for as long as possible on this case, then it would be better to have T.J. do the job.

Wanda Nell laid aside a hand towel and went to the kitchen. She picked up the phone and punched in the number of T.J.'s cell phone.

After three rings, T.J.'s voice came on the line. "Hey, Mama, how are you?"

"I'm fine, honey, how about you?" T.J. sounded more and more like his father all the time. She pushed that thought away.

"Pretty good. We're just relaxing a bit before deciding what to do for dinner."

"He means deciding which one of us is going to cook it," Tuck said, his voice surprising Wanda Nell.

"You'd better do it," Wanda Nell said. "I'm not sure T.J.'s learned enough yet."

Tuck laughed, a rich, warm sound, and Wanda Nell could easily picture his handsome face as he gazed lovingly at her son. "I don't know, he's a pretty fast learner. He's at least picked up on how to boil water."

Wanda Nell heard the sounds of a brief scuffle as T.J. recaptured the phone. "Don't pay any attention to him, Mama," he said, laughing. "And just for that, he's going to have to cook dinner *and* clean up afterward."

"You two are something else," Wanda Nell said, trying not to laugh. "You be good, and help."

"Yes, Mama," T.J. said, in his best good-boy voice. "Now, did you have some reason for calling other than to tell me to behave?"

"I did. I was hoping you'd do a little work for Jack on Monday, if you have time."

"Sure, Mama, what is it?"

"Well, we'll give you all the details tomorrow night when you come over for dinner. We need you to look through the county marriage records for us. We need to find out if someone got married here, and who she married."

"That's easy enough. They've got a lot of the records computerized now. How long ago was it, do you know?"

"We're not sure." Wanda Nell thought for a moment. Ernie had said Sandra June was several years younger than her brother, who was nineteen at the time. If the girl had married right out of high school, that would put it at twenty-six or twenty-seven years ago. "Twenty-five years ago, give or take a couple of years, most likely. But we really aren't sure."

"They haven't gotten that far back with the computerized records," T.J. said, "but it's still not that hard. I'll be happy to do it for Jack, Mama. Is he working on a new book?

"He is, and we'll tell you all about it at dinner."

"Sure," T.J. said. "Hang on a minute, Tuck wants to talk to you."

"Wanda Nell," Tuck said, "about dinner tomorrow. Why don't y'all come over here instead? It's our turn. You've cooked for us the past three Sundays, and we ought to be doing it for you. I promise I won't let T.J. burn anything."

Wanda Nell heard her son's voice raised in mock protest. "I guess that would be okay. I do love cooking for y'all, though."

"We know," Tuck said, "but it means a lot to both of us to have y'all here."

"Of course. We'll be happy to come."

"About six-thirty?"

"We'll be there," Wanda Nell said, and hung up the phone.

"Was that T.J. you were talking to?" Jack startled her. She hadn't heard him come into the kitchen.

"Yes, it was. Tuck wants us to come over there for dinner tomorrow, instead of them coming here."

"That's fine. I thought I'd call T.J. and ask him if he would mind looking at the courthouse for records of the marriage. I don't think he'd mind, do you?

"He already said he wouldn't," Wanda Nell said with a grin.

Jack laughed. "Well, I guess it's like my mama always said. Great minds are like catfish."

"They swim in the same channels." Wanda Nell had heard this one before.

"Exactly," Jack said, and his slow, sexy smile made Wanda Nell shiver just a little bit.

After a long, gentle kiss, Wanda Nell pushed him away. "You'd better get back to work, and I'll start thinking about something for supper."

"Yes, ma'am. Whatever you say—for now, at least." His smile told her that later it would be different.

Wanda Nell stared after him as he left the kitchen. She was having a hard time thinking about food. She shook her head, trying to clear it.

With a sigh she went over to the refrigerator. Maybe actually looking at the food inside it would help her focus on something else.

She stared at the contents of the fridge. There was some hamburger meat and about half a chicken from a previous meal, as well as some broccoli in the vegetable drawer and a pot of leftover peas.

The ringing of the phone brought her out of her reverie.

She shut the door of the fridge and walked over to the phone.

"Hello."

"Mama, it's me," Miranda said.

"Hi, sweetie." Wanda Nell braced herself. She could tell from the tone in those three words that something was wrong. "What's going on?"

"Oh, Mama, what am I going to do?" Miranda was obviously upset.

"What about? Tell me what the problem is." Talking to Miranda when she was like this always tried her patience.

"Oh, it's Teddy. I just want to slap his hard head sometimes."

"What is it this time?" Wanda Nell suppressed a sigh. Miranda wasn't adapting as well to marriage as she had hoped. About once a week she called her mother because of some sort of problem she was having with her new husband. Usually it was because Teddy had put his foot down about something, and Miranda didn't like that, not one little bit.

Wanda Nell's sympathies lay with her son-in-law most of the time, because she knew all too well just how exasperating Miranda could be. The girl didn't want to lift her hand to do much of anything, even looking after her son. Now another baby was on the way. What would Miranda do with two children to look after?

"He's just so mean. Why does he have to be that way?"

"What did he do that was so mean, sweetie?" He probably asked her to clean the house. He worked long hours as a mechanic at a garage in town, and Miranda was at home all day, not doing much of anything. "Did he fuss at you about cleaning the house?"

"No, it's not that," Miranda said, her tone sullen. "I done all that today, and I'm about worn to a frazzle. I wish we had a maid."

Like you did when you lived with me, Wanda Nell thought, but she didn't say it. There was no point.

"So what is it, then?" She couldn't quite keep the sharpness out of her voice.

"I'm trying to tell you, Mama," Miranda snapped back. "Nobody ever listens to me."

Wanda Nell gripped the phone hard and willed herself not to respond to that.

After a moment of silence, Miranda went on. "It's about T.J. He called and invited us to come over for dinner tomorrow night at his house with y'all."

Wanda Nell's heart sank. Teddy Bolton was a very nice young man in most respects, despite all those tattoos on his arms. But he was always kind of skittish with T.J. and Tuck. He wasn't ever rude, but he just never looked too comfortable around them.

"Does he not want to go?"

"Not really. And I swear I could just bang him upside the head with a baseball bat. Not that it would do any good, probably. I told him T.J.'s my brother, and I love him. It don't matter who he lives with. and Teddy better just get over it."

"It's going to take a little time," Wanda Nell said. "Most of the time he's okay. You know he was raised in that church, and how conservative they are." She had gone to church one morning with Miranda and Teddy, and she had been shocked at some of what she had heard there. To her mind, true Christians ought to have more compassion than those people seemed to have.

"I done told him I'm not going back to that church no more," Miranda said. "I don't care what he says."

Wanda Nell couldn't blame her for that, and she was glad Miranda was standing up for her brother.

"So is he going to come to dinner?"

"I told him he better, but he's acting real stubborn. I

don't know whether he'll really go or not, but I'm going to be real upset if he don't. Will you come get me and Lavon if Teddy won't come?"

"Of course, sweetie." Wanda Nell hoped this wouldn't drive Miranda and Teddy so far apart that it broke up the marriage. Surely Teddy would come around eventually. "But I'm hoping Teddy will change his mind. The more he can see how much T.J. and Tuck care about each other, I think maybe he'll understand."

"I sure hope so, Mama. I'm getting awful tired of talking to him about it."

"Sometimes talking doesn't do much good," Wanda Nell said. "It's what people do that counts. I know Teddy thinks a lot of both me and Jack, and if he sees how we feel about the situation, well, I'm hoping he'll begin to understand."

"Maybe," Miranda said, not sounding too hopeful. "But you'll come and get me and Lavon, right?"

"We will. Now try not to fret too much, and let up on Teddy. Let him come around on his own. I'm sure he will." She made that last statement with more confidence than she really felt, but at heart she did believe in Teddy's fundamental decency.

After a few questions about Lavon and about how Miranda was feeling during her pregnancy, Wanda Nell said goodbye to her older daughter.

She had barely put the phone down when it rang again. She managed to push the Talk button and say hello.

"Wanda Nell, I found out who Sandra June married," Ernie said. "The game's afoot."

Nine

"What?" Wanda Nell said, startled.

"Sorry," Ernie said. "I'm quoting Sherlock Holmes, couldn't help myself."

"It's okay. I thought I'd heard that somewhere before." Wanda Nell gave a little laugh. "But how did you find out?"

"I was right about there not being a wedding announcement, though I certainly looked. But it finally dawned on me that there probably *would* be an obituary for Mrs. Bates in the paper."

"And the obituary would mention any survivors."

"Exactly."

"So did it mention Sandra June?"

"It sure did. Her husband's name was Pete Havens, and at the time they were living in Water Valley."

"How long ago was this?"

"Twenty-four years."

"That's quite a while ago," Wanda Nell said. "I wonder if she's still in Water Valley."

"I don't know. I called you right after I found this. I haven't even looked in the phone book yet. I figured you and Jack would want to take it from here."

"Thank you so much, Ernie. I can't wait to tell Jack."

"You go on ahead and do that. Y'all just call me and let me know what you find out."

"We sure will. Talk to you soon."

Wanda Nell hung up the phone, ready to run down the hall to share the news with her husband. But she decided to look in the phone book first. She pulled it out of a drawer and began flipping through the pages. The book covered all of Tullahoma County, plus some of the small towns in a couple of neighboring counties. Even so, it wasn't a very thick book.

Wanda Nell found the section for Water Valley and began scanning the names. Her finger trailed down the appropriate page, and she frowned. There was only one Havens listed, but the initials were T.M. That sure didn't sound like a Pete Havens or a Sandra June Havens, unless Pete was only a nickname. That didn't seem too likely, however.

In twenty-four years, the couple could have moved away from Water Valley. "I knew it wouldn't be that easy," Wanda Nell muttered. As quickly as she could, she started going through each section of the book. She found three more listings for Havens, but not one of them for a P or an S.J.

Frowning, she stuck the phone book back in the drawer. She'd better go tell Jack.

Down the hall, she paused in the doorway to watch her husband at the computer for a moment. He was sitting and staring at the screen. He didn't look like he was reading anything, so he was probably lost in thought.

"Honey, Ernie called." For the moment Wanda Nell wasn't going to bring up the subject of Miranda and Teddy. That could wait.

"I thought I heard the phone ring a couple of times," Jack said, turning to her. "What did Ernie have to say?"

Wanda Nell shared Ernie's information with her husband. "That's great. Now at least we have something to go on. Did you look in the phone book already?"

"I did." Wanda Nell shook her head. "No luck. I found only one Havens in Water Valley, and the initials didn't match. I went through the rest of the book, and no luck there, either."

Jack grinned. "It's okay, honey. We'll let the Internet do its magic, and we'll see if we can find them another way."

"How?" Wanda Nell asked.

"Pull up that chair over there, and come sit beside me. I'll show you," Jack said. He was already tapping at the keyboard, and Wanda Nell dragged the chair over next to him. As she sat, she watched the computer screen change.

"This is a Web site called Anywho.com. You can look up people all over the country here, as long as they have a listed phone number."

"Goodness. So someone could use that and find us?" Wanda Nell wasn't sure she liked that idea.

"They could, but let's not worry about that for the moment. I want to see if we can track down Mr. and Mrs. Pete Havens."

Wanda Nell watched as he typed. He put the name Havens in one box and Pete in another. Then he chose Mississippi for the state and clicked a button labeled Search.

The screen changed, and Wanda Nell squinted to read it.

"No Pete Havens in Mississippi," Jack said, disappointed. "Let's try it again with just the last name."

This time when the screen changed, they had results, eighty-four of them. Wanda Nell watched as Jack scrolled through the pages.

On about the seventh screen, they saw a couple of P. Havenses with different middle initials listed, and Jack paused to note their names and addresses on a pad of paper beside the computer. There was no Sandra or S. Havens.

"There's the only one I found in Water Valley." Wanda Nell pointed to the screen.

Jack made a note of that one, too. "Probably related in some way, so if these other two don't pan out, we can try calling this T.M. Havens." He thought a moment. "Or just show up on his or her doorstep, since it's not that far away. Sometimes that works better."

"If you say so."

Jack reached for his cell phone. "I tell you what, let's go ahead and call these two P. Havenses, and see what happens."

"Okay." Wanda Nell was curious to hear how he was going to handle this. She pushed her chair back slightly and watched while Jack punched in the first number.

Someone answered after a moment, and Jack spoke. "Hi, there. I'm sorry to bother you, ma'am, but I'm trying to track down a high school classmate of mine, Pete Havens. We're going to have our twenty-fifth reunion this summer, and we've all kinda lost track of ol' Pete. But we sure would like to see him, if he can come. Is this his house, by any chance?"

If she hadn't been looking right at him, Wanda Nell would have sworn it was somebody besides Jack on the phone. His voice was different. He had made it a little deeper and rougher-sounding, and his drawl was much more pronounced. She shook her head. This was a side of her husband she hadn't seen before.

Jack listened for a moment. "Well, thank you kindly, ma'am. I knew it was kind of a long shot, but ol' Pete was such a great guy, we really do want to find him." He listened for a moment, said "thank you" one more time, and ended the call.

"I've never heard you talk like that before. Where did that come from?"

Jack grinned at her. "Did I ever tell you about the plays I did when I was in college?"

Smiling, Wanda Nell shook her head. "No, you didn't."

"Does it bother you, honey?"

"Well, it surprised me a bit. It seems a little dishonest."

"I suppose it is. But it's basically harmless. I'm not trying to scam somebody into buying something, or anything like that. Just looking for a little information."

"Okay, but if I get any calls like that from now on, I can tell you I'm gonna be real careful about what I say."

"That's a very good idea. If you don't want me to make another call like that, I won't."

"No, it's okay, honey. We're doing this for an important reason, and I don't reckon it's gonna hurt anybody. At least anybody that doesn't deserve it."

Jack smiled his thanks. Consulting his notes, he punched in the number for the second P. Havens. When someone answered, Jack went through the same routine. He received the same answer, and after a couple more remarks, he thanked the person and ended the call.

"Well, no luck with either of them," he said, his shoulders drooping a bit. "So I guess we'd better try talking to this Havens in Water Valley. If we're lucky, he or she'll be related to Pete and know where he is now."

"So do you want to go over to Water Valley and try to talk to them in person? Or call them instead?"

"I think we should go to Water Valley," Jack said. "We know that Havens lived there, at least twenty-four years ago. So maybe if we ask around, someone will know him and maybe where he went—and Sandra June, too. That is, if T.M. Havens can't help."

"Or won't," Wanda Nell said.

"That's a possibility. Not everybody wants to talk, but we'll just have to try."

"When do you want to go?"

"Tomorrow, after lunch. People will be home from church, probably relaxing, and that's a good time. And if we don't have any luck tomorrow, I can always go back on Monday."

"But without me," Wanda Nell said. "I have to go back to work on Monday."

"I know, honey, and I'd sure rather you were with me," Jack replied. "We need to keep moving forward, though, and I doubt Melvin would be all that happy about you asking for more time off." Melvin Arbuckle owned the Kountry Kitchen, where Wanda Nell worked.

"Especially since he gave me two weeks off with pay for our honeymoon. That was real sweet of him, and I don't want to impose on him if I don't have to."

"We'll just have to see how it goes tomorrow," Jack said. "But I have a feeling that solving this whole thing will probably mean a bit of traveling. Especially if we're lucky enough to find Roscoe Bates somewhere. I just hope it's not at the other end of the country."

Wanda Nell and Jack spent a quiet evening without any family around. They listened to music while they read, Jack absorbed in a historical mystery and Wanda Nell in a new book by a Southern writer, Mary Saums. She loved the two older women in the book and their relationship. It made her think of Mayrene, and she wondered how Mayrene was doing. She wasn't home this evening, and Wanda Nell hoped her best friend had been able to patch things up with Dixon Vance. Mainly, she hoped Dixon had had the sense to apologize to Mayrene for what he had said. Men could be so dumb sometimes.

Sunday morning dawned quiet and hot. Wanda Nell slipped out of bed without waking Jack and padded into the kitchen to put on some coffee. Once the coffeemaker was going, she stood at the sink, gazing out the window. This was the time of day she had always liked best, especially when her grandson would come into the kitchen, his stuffed bunny dragging behind him. She missed his bright chatter, but it was good that Miranda had her own home now. Wanda Nell just prayed that everything would work out between Teddy and Miranda.

By the time Jack wandered into the kitchen in search of caffeine, Wanda Nell was on her second cup of coffee.

"Good morning, sleepyhead. Sit down, and I'll get you some coffee."

Jack yawned. "No, I'll get it. Stay where you are."

Wanda Nell sipped her coffee while she watched her husband. His coffee poured, Jack turned back to her with a smile. He dropped a kiss on her forehead before he sat down at the table with her.

"How about some breakfast?" Wanda Nell asked.

"In a little while. Let's just sit and enjoy being alone together for a bit." He stretched out a hand to her, and she clasped it.

They spent a leisurely morning, lingering over breakfast. While they were clearing away after the meal, Wanda Nell asked Jack what time he wanted to leave for Water Valley.

"It takes, what? About thirty minutes to get there?"

"At the most. And on a Sunday there won't be much traffic out that way."

"Then let's leave about one. By the time we get there, people will be home from church and done with lunch. That ought to be a good time to talk to anybody. Depending on how long it takes, we can find somewhere to eat lunch while we're there."

They walked out the front door of the trailer a few minutes past one, both of them dressed less casually than they usually did on a Sunday. Wanda Nell had insisted. "If I'm going into someone's home on a Sunday, I want to look nice."

Jack loosened his tie before they set off in the car. "Are you sure I have to wear this?" He grimaced. "I don't even wear them to school half the time anymore."

"Yes, you do," Wanda Nell said. "If I'm wearing panty-hose and heels, you have to wear a tie." She grinned at him.

Jack stared into the mirror and sighed. "Henpecked already." He turned and winked at Wanda Nell. "I love it."

"Pay attention to your driving." Wanda Nell pretended to be stern. "I don't want to end up in a ditch before we get even a mile from home."

"Yes, ma'am."

During the drive they discussed how they would approach this T.M. Havens. Jack thought they should be as honest as possible about why they were looking for Sandra June Havens, and Wanda Nell agreed. They would be discreet, but they both felt directness was probably the best approach.

Jack had double-checked the address on the Internet, getting directions, and when they reached Water Valley, he had no trouble finding the street.

"Nice neighborhood," Jack said, gazing with appreciation at the old trees that lined the street. "These houses are pretty old, from at least around World War I, I'd say." He pulled the car to a stop in front of a two-story frame house with a wide verandah around the front and one side of it. "This is it," he said after consulting his notes.

Wanda Nell sat looking at the house for a moment before Jack shut the car off. "I wonder what we'll find out."

"Only one way to know that. Come on, honey, let's go knock on the door." They got out of the car.

"Your tie," Wanda Nell said. She straightened it, and Jack's hands closed over hers for a moment. Smiling, he finished the job. He took her arm as they walked up the sidewalk and the five steps to the verandah.

Jack opened the screen door, holding it with his shoulder. There was no doorbell, only an ornate brass knocker. Jack lifted it and rapped it three times. He and Wanda Nell waited for almost a minute, and Jack was about to use the knocker again when the door opened.

"Yeah, whadda ya want?"

Wanda Nell and Jack stared at the girl who had opened the door. Her hair was an improbable shade of red, straight out of a bottle of henna, Wanda Nell figured. She had a ring in her nose and multiple rings in her ears. Her eyes were sullen as she slouched in front of them, her tight jeans riding low on her hips.

"We'd like to speak to Mister or Miz Havens," Jack said, his voice firm. "We're not selling anything, but we do have an important matter to discuss."

"Ain't no Mister," the girl said. "Just Granny." She stared at them, her eyes hostile.

"Then could we speak to Miz Havens?" Wanda Nell asked.

"Who is it, Lucinda?" A strong voice came from somewhere behind the girl.

Lucinda turned. "I done tole you not to call me that. My name is Britney now." Her body was stiff with annoyance, and Wanda Nell had to suppress a smile. The girl was only about fourteen, though the hair and rings and makeup aged her by six or seven years.

"You were christened Lucinda, and that's what I'm going to call you, missy." The woman's voice came clearly to them, and as Jack and Wanda Nell watched, the woman herself appeared from the gloom of the hallway.

She was short, erect, and neatly dressed in a faded house dress. Wanda Nell judged her to be in her midseventies. Her hands were gnarled from arthritis, and her expression was severe as she regarded her granddaughter. Lucinda stomped off, leaving her grandmother at the door.

"What do you folks want? I've got no use for salespeople

or Jehovah's Witnesses. You can just go on about your business if that's what you're after."

"We're not," Jack said. "My name is Jack Pemberton, and this is my wife, Wanda Nell. Are you Miz Havens?"

The woman's eyes narrowed a moment. "I am," she said in a grudging tone. "What is it you want?"

"We're from Tullahoma," Jack said. "And we're trying to find a Sandra June Bates, who was married to a Pete Havens about twenty-four years ago."

An expression of outrage settled on Mrs. Havens's face. "If that tramp owes you money, you're not getting one red cent from me." She stepped back and slammed the door in their faces.

Ten

Wanda Nell and Jack stared at each other in dismay. "What now?" Wanda Nell asked.

Jack took a deep breath. "Please, Miz Havens," he called out, his voice strong. "She doesn't owe us any money. We don't even know her, but we need to find her. Please talk to us."

They waited, and for a moment there was nothing but silence. The heat of the day was beginning to get to both of them, and Wanda Nell could feel herself wilting. She didn't wear pantyhose all that often, nor heels, and her feet were starting to ache. Jack looked as hot as she felt, and she knew he was itching to loosen that tie.

Jack had lifted a hand to rap on the door again, and it opened. Mrs. Havens stood there, her face clouded with suspicion. "Are you sure she doesn't owe you any money?"

"No, ma'am," Jack said. "As I said, we don't even know her."

"Then what business do you have with her?" The elderly woman now seemed more curious than hostile.

"It's a long story," Jack said. "And I don't think it really has anything to do with you. It's about her family, really.

Not her husband's family," he hastened to add when Mrs. Havens's expression turned doubtful. "Her own family."

"Well, I guess you can come in." Mrs. Havens stood aside and motioned for them to enter.

"Thank you, ma'am," Wanda Nell said and gave her a friendly smile. "We sure do appreciate it. It's getting awful hot out there."

"It's July," Mrs. Havens said.

"Yes, ma'am," Wanda Nell replied meekly.

"Come on in here," Mrs. Havens said after she had shut the door behind Jack.

The house was cool and dim, and Wanda Nell felt better, just being off the hot verandah. Even with the shade it provided from the afternoon sun, it wasn't any good against the oppressiveness of the humid day.

She and Jack followed Mrs. Havens into a room that reminded Wanda Nell a lot of Mrs. Culpepper's front room. Many of the pieces of furniture looked even older than the house, but it was all gleaming with polish and dust-free. Mrs. Havens obviously kept a spotless home.

"Sit there," Mrs. Havens said. She sat in an elderly armchair upholstered in deep red material, indicating they should take their seats on a sofa covered in the same fabric. Wanda Nell found it surprisingly comfortable, and she ran her hand appreciatively over the bit of vacant seat between her and Jack.

"Thank you," Jack said. "We appreciate you taking the time to talk to us, and I apologize for intruding on your privacy."

Mrs. Havens's face softened a fraction at Jack's obvious courtesy. "I reckon it's okay. But get on with it."

"Yes, ma'am." After a quick glance at Wanda Nell, Jack went on. "I'm a teacher at the high school in Tullahoma, and I'm also a writer. I'm doing some research for a book right now, and my wife is helping me."

Wanda Nell smiled demurely at their hostess while the old lady assessed her thoroughly. "You both look respectable."

"If you'd like," Wanda Nell said, "you can call the sheriff of Tullahoma County, and he'll vouch for us. His name is Elmer Lee Johnson."

Mrs. Havens gave a sudden bark of laughter. "You don't mean old Ezekiel Johnson's boy, by any chance?"

Amazed, Wanda Nell nodded. "Why, yes, ma'am. That was Elmer Lee's daddy. Did you know him?"

Mrs. Havens laughed again. "Know him? I almost married him." She shook her head. "I haven't heard that name in years. So Zeke's son is a sheriff? That's one for the record books, I have to say." She shook her head, smiling and obviously enjoying some private joke.

"Elmer Lee's a good man," Jack said. "He's a fine sheriff."

"The sins of the father," Mrs. Havens said. "My, my, I bet Zeke is spinning in his grave. His son a sheriff. My, my."

Wanda Nell and Jack exchanged looks. Wanda Nell didn't remember anything about Elmer Lee's daddy besides his name, and Jack was just as stumped.

Taking pity on their confusion, Mrs. Havens explained. "Zeke Johnson was about the biggest bootlegger in Tullahoma. That's why my daddy wouldn't let me marry him. Zeke took over after his daddy died, and my daddy knew all about it. So I married somebody a lot more respectable."

Wanda Nell shook her head. "Well, I am truly amazed, Miz Havens. I never knew that about Elmer Lee's family." It did explain a lot, though, about Elmer Lee. He sure hadn't followed in his daddy's footsteps.

"I reckon it's neither here nor there," Mrs. Havens said, "but it sure is funny."

"Yes, ma'am," Jack said. "But about Sandra June Bates. We know she married a Pete Havens. Was that your son?"

Mrs. Havens scowled. "To my everlasting sorrow, she did. I had a real sweet girl picked out for him, she lived just down the street from us. But once he met that painted whore, he was bewitched, I swear." Her twisted fingers gripped the arms of her chair, and Wanda Nell could see the pain it caused her.

"We had no idea," Wanda Nell said. "Like my husband told you, we didn't know her, not even very much about her."

"Her family was bad. Her daddy ran off and left her slut of a mother and that brother of hers." Her eyes widened in shock. "That's why you want to talk to her, isn't it? Her brother."

"Yes, ma'am," Jack said. "I guess you know about him disappearing."

"I sure do. That's one of the reasons I didn't want my Pete getting mixed up with that family. Her brother killed a girl and ran off, and her just as wild as she could be. No telling how many men she'd been with before she trapped my son into marrying her."

Neither Jack nor Wanda Nell was sure just what to say next. After a moment, Wanda Nell spoke, her voice soft. "Miz Havens, what happened to your son? Did he divorce Sandra June?"

Mrs. Havens looked away from them for a moment, her body tense. Finally, with a deep sigh, she faced them. Wanda Nell could see the glint of tears in her eyes, but the old lady was determined not to cry in front of them. It showed in the way she sat, her back a ramrod in the chair.

"Pete died sixteen years ago. He was killed in a car wreck. He was going after that tramp, because she'd run off with some man. He was desperate to get her back. I told him he ought to let her go, but he wouldn't listen to me." Her voice broke, and the tears streamed down her face.

For a moment Wanda Nell sat, Jack stiff with distress beside her. Acting on instinct, Wanda Nell got up and went over to her. Kneeling in front of the elderly woman, she took those gnarled hands in her own and held them. "I'm so sorry," she said, trying to hold back her own tears. "I'm so sorry we caused you pain. We surely didn't want to do that."

Mrs. Havens stared down at Wanda Nell. "It's not your fault," she said, her voice little more than a hoarse whisper. "You had no way of knowing."

"Is there anything I can get for you?" Wanda Nell asked, still clasping her hands.

Shaking her head, Mrs. Havens said, "No, I'll be all right in a moment. I'm sorry you had to see me this way." Gently she pulled her hands away, and with her right, fumbled in a pocket of her dress. She pulled out a heavy cotton handkerchief and dabbed at her eyes.

Wanda Nell gave her one last consoling pat on the arm before she stood. Resuming her seat beside Jack, she reached for his hand. He squeezed it, and his eyes thanked her. He was still distressed by Mrs. Havens's reaction. Wanda Nell offered an encouraging smile, and his shoulders relaxed. He mouthed the words "thank you."

Wanda Nell glanced back at their hostess. Mrs. Havens had regained control of her emotions, and she was gazing at them with a resigned look in her eyes.

"What happened after that?" Jack asked.

"She had the nerve to come back here and try to apologize to me. My husband was still alive at the time, and he almost had to throw her out the door. I just thank the Lord she and my son never had a child." A slight smile passed over her face. "Lucinda's my only grandchild, my daughter Elizabeth's child. Elizabeth and her husband are in New York on business. Her husband is a doctor in Oxford."

"I'm sure you're very proud of them," Wanda Nell said.

"I am. But nothing ever makes up for losing a child. Do you have any children?"

"Three," Wanda Nell said, "and one grandson with another one on the way. I can't imagine what it would be like to lose one of them."

"I pray you never do," Mrs. Havens said. "But you want to find that woman. Why, though? Are you writing a book about that poor girl her brother killed?"

"Yes, ma'am," Jack said. "They've never tried anybody for the murder, and I'd like to see whoever killed her brought to justice. She deserves that much. We still don't even know who she was."

"Good luck to you," Mrs. Havens said. "I get a letter from that woman every few years." She sniffed. "She's probably as drunk as Cooter Brown when she writes them. They're so full of maudlin self-pity, you wouldn't believe."

"Do you still have any of those letters?" Jack tried not to sound too hopeful.

"I don't. I can't even believe I read them, but I do. And once I do, they go straight into the trash."

"Do you have any idea where she is these days?" Wanda Nell asked.

"There's always a return address. Like she thinks I'm going to write back to her and forgive her. I know it's my Christian duty to forgive her, but the Lord strike me dead, I can't." Mrs. Havens sighed and shook her head. "The last one I got was about two years ago, maybe less. I seem to recall she was living in Tullahoma again."

"Do you know what name she was using?" Jack asked.

"She married again at some point. The name on the return address was Baker. Other than that, I don't know. I couldn't tell you the address."

"You've given us something to go on," Jack said. "We sure do appreciate that. I'm very sorry that we caused you so much distress with all this. It's not what we intended." He and Wanda Nell stood.

"You couldn't know," Mrs. Havens said, looking up at

them. "I know I should just let all this hatred go, but I can't. I just hope the Lord will forgive me, come Judgment Day."

"No one can blame you," Wanda Nell said. "I know I'd have a hard time forgiving somebody for something like that."

"You find that brother of hers, if he's still alive." Mrs. Havens's tone was suddenly fierce. "Make him pay for taking some other mother's child away from her. He should pay for what he's done."

"We're going to do our best," Jack said. "I promise you that. Thank you again for talking to us."

Mrs. Havens rose from her chair, and Wanda Nell touched her arm. "We can see ourselves out. Thank you."

Mrs. Havens's gaze softened. "Bless you for your loving heart." She took Wanda Nell's right hand in her two misshapen ones and held it for a moment.

Wanda Nell had to hold back tears until she and Jack were out on the verandah again, the door shut behind them. Without a word, Jack pulled a handkerchief from his pants pocket and handed it to her. He wrapped his arm around her as she wiped her eyes and blew her nose. She tucked the handkerchief in the small purse she was carrying and extracted her sunglasses.

"This is tougher than I figured it would be," Jack said, donning his own sunglasses against the fierce afternoon sun. He led his wife down the sidewalk and back to the car. Waves of heat from the pavement struck them as Jack opened first her door, then his. They stood, letting the hot air inside the car dissipate a moment. Jack got in and started the car, turning up the air conditioning.

Wanda Nell got in and shut her door. They sat there for a moment. "Feeling better, honey?" Jack asked.

"Yes. I just feel so sorry for her. How awful to lose a child that way."

"Yeah." Jack put the car in gear and drove down the

street until he reached the next intersection. "It just breaks my heart to see someone living like that, after all these years."

"Some things you just never get over." Wanda Nell stared out her window, but all she could see was Mrs. Havens in her grief.

"Do you feel like getting something to eat before we drive back? I'm sure we can find a decent restaurant somewhere in town."

"I'm not really hungry right now," Wanda Nell said. "But I could use something to drink."

"Okay, love." A couple of blocks after they turned, Jack pulled into the parking lot of a convenience store and parked, leaving the car running. "I'll be right back. What would you rather have, a bottle of water or a Diet Coke?"

"How about both?" Wanda Nell managed a brief smile.

"Sure thing." Jack closed the door, and Wanda Nell sat, the cool air making her shiver suddenly.

Jack returned in a couple of minutes, carrying a plastic bag. Back behind the wheel, he opened the bag and extracted a bottle of water and then a Diet Coke. Wanda Nell took them both, tucking the soda in the pocket on the door. She twisted the cap off the water and drank deeply while Jack did the same.

"That's better. I was pretty parched."

"Me, too," Jack said. "This heat really takes it out of you, and fast." He set his bottle in one of the two cupholders between his seat and Wanda Nell's. He backed the car out of the parking lot and headed toward the highway that would take them home.

"I wonder how many Bakers there are in Tullahoma," Wanda Nell mused after they had been out of Water Valley and on the highway for several minutes.

"It's a pretty common name," Jack said, "but there shouldn't be too many in a town the size of Tullahoma."

"If she's even still in town."

"Yeah." Jack sighed. "Tracking her down could take a while, unless we get a break and actually find her in town."

"I bet we will," Wanda Nell said with a confidence she didn't entirely feel. "I tell you what, why don't we stop for a bite to eat when we get back to town? Maybe some pizza, or a hamburger. One of those fast-food places on the highway. Then we can hunt up a phone book and just see how many Bakers there are."

"Sounds fine to me," Jack said. "Thanks again, love, for being with me on this."

Wanda Nell smiled at him. They were silent for a few miles before she spoke again. "You know, seeing that house reminded me of Miz Culpepper. We're going to have to talk to her again at some point. From the way she reacted yesterday, she must know something." She shook her head. "But I'm wondering if it'll be too much for her."

"We do need to talk to her," Jack said. "But I don't want to upset her too much. I'm a little worried about her heart condition. I'd hate to be the cause of her having a stroke."

"Yeah, me, too. Maybe we should talk to Belle first, see what she thinks."

"Good plan," Jack said.

They drove the rest of the way to Tullahoma in silence. Jack turned off the highway, into the parking lot of the pizza place. By this time the after-church lunch crowd was gone, and only a few of the tables and booths had occupants. Jack guided Wanda Nell to an empty booth.

Moments later a young waitress took their drink orders while they looked over the menu. By the time the waitress was back with their iced tea, they were ready to order.

"You think they might have a phone book we could look at?" Jack asked.

"Most places do," Wanda Nell said, "even if they're not out somewhere. Do they still have a pay phone here?"

"I'll look." Jack slid out of the booth. "I'm going to the restroom, and I'll check it out."

"Good idea. I'll go, too." Wanda Nell slid out, taking her purse with her.

When Wanda Nell came back to their booth, she found her husband poring over the phone book. "Where did you find it?" she asked as she sat down. "There wasn't one by the pay phone."

"I asked the waitress, and she brought it to me. There are eleven Bakers here in Tullahoma. I haven't looked in the other sections yet."

"Might as well start there," Wanda Nell said.

"Do you mind if I start calling now?" Jack asked. "There aren't many people around. And as long as we're waiting for our food . . ." His voice trailed off.

Wanda Nell nodded. "Go ahead. I'm as curious as you are."

Jack withdrew his cell phone from his jacket pocket. Consulting the phone book, he punched in the first number. When someone answered, Jack gave a spiel similar to the one he had used when looking for Pete Havens. Only this time he was looking for Sandra June Bates to invite to the reunion.

He had called the first four Bakers in the book, with no success, by the time the waitress brought their mini-pizzas. Wanda Nell loved pepperoni on a thick crust, and Jack loved Italian sausage on a thin crust.

After eating one of the four slices of his pizza, Jack picked up his phone again. He glanced at Wanda Nell.

"Go ahead," she said. "Just don't let your pizza get too cold."

"I like cold pizza." Jack smiled before he looked for the next number.

While Wanda Nell slowly ate the rest of her pizza, Jack alternated between phone calls and bites of pizza. He had called four more Bakers, two of them with no answer, when, on the next call, his body stiffened. Wanda Nell put down her last bite of pizza to watch.

"So you're Sandra June Bates?" Jack said. "You won't remember me, but I'd like to talk to you about the reunion and a few other things. Would you have time to talk to me and my wife today?" He listened for a moment. "Why, sure, we can come on by right now, if it's convenient for you. Let me just double-check your address." He read out of the phone book. "Right. Good, I know where that is. We'll be there in less than ten minutes." He ended the call and stuck his phone back in his pocket.

"We've found her," Jack said, his eyes alight with excitement. "Let's go."

Eleven

Jack paid the bill, his fingers drumming impatiently on the counter while he waited for their waitress to count out his change. "Thank you," he said, pushing a couple of dollars back to her for a tip. She smiled.

"Where does she live?" Wanda Nell asked when they were in the car. Jack had been in such a hurry to get out of the restaurant, she hadn't asked him before.

"In that new development, just off the highway, on the east side of town." Jack pulled out of the parking lot and headed toward town. After a few blocks he took a cutoff that would save them a few minutes and take them to the east–west highway that cut through the middle of Tullahoma.

Traffic was light, and they made it to the entrance to the subdivision in about ten minutes. On the way, Wanda Nell had asked what the woman sounded like.

"Very quiet voice, not much intonation. Almost like she was drugged."

"Or drunk?" Wanda Nell asked, remembering what Mrs. Havens had told them.

Jack shrugged. "Maybe, but she wasn't slurring her words. Her voice just sounded flat."

"Was she very curious?"

"Not really," Jack admitted. "I thought it was a bit strange, but I wasn't going to turn down the opportunity."

The house where Sandra June Baker lived stood at the end of a cul-de-sac on one of the side streets a few blocks from the subdivision entrance. The houses here were modest, Wanda Nell noticed, and most of them looked pretty much alike. The yards were clean, and there were some trees. A few children were playing outside, but most of them were probably inside, where it was much cooler.

Jack stopped the car in front of the Baker house, checking the number he'd written down. A bungalow surrounded on three sides by young trees, it appeared well-maintained, with a neatly manicured lawn and white walls. There were a few flower beds, their contents drooping in the heat.

Wanda Nell stepped out of the car before Jack could open her door. She shut the door and followed him to the front of the house.

Jack punched the doorbell and held it for two seconds. Moments later the door opened, and a thin woman who appeared to be in her sixties gazed blankly at them. "Pardon me, ma'am," Jack said, "we're here to see Miz Sandra Baker." He exchanged a quick glance with Wanda Nell. This woman appeared too old to be the woman they were trying to find.

Maybe she's Sandra June's mother-in-law, Wanda Nell thought.

"Come on in," she said, her voice dull. She turned and walked away from the door, leaving them to enter and then shut the door behind them.

The front door opened directly into what appeared to be the living room. The woman had gone from the door to flop down in worn armchair whose threadbare fabric spoke for the condition of every stick of furniture in the room. Wanda Nell found it depressing. The outside of the house looked so nice, but inside, it was pitiful.

At least it appeared to be clean, she was glad to note. She followed Jack to a sofa near the woman's chair, and they both sat down. Wanda Nell shifted slightly, because she had sat on a spring. Her new position wasn't much better, so she resigned herself to being uncomfortable.

The woman still hadn't spoken again. She regarded them with blank, incurious eyes.

Jack introduced himself. "And this is my wife, Wanda Nell. I believe it was you I spoke to on the phone. Like I told you, we're looking for Sandra June Bates."

The woman stirred, a small, listless movement. "I'm Sandra June Bates. Baker now, that is."

Wanda Nell had figured that Sandra June must be in her late forties by now, from what they knew about her, but this woman looked at least twenty years older. The skin around her eyes was puffy, and her complexion was sallow. Her hair had been bleached too many times, and it looked dry enough for kindling, as Wanda Nell's mama would have said. The shapeless dress she wore appeared clean enough, though it had faded from many washings.

"Miz Baker," Jack said. He hid his surprise pretty well, Wanda Nell noted. "When we spoke on the phone just a little while ago, I told you I wanted to talk to you about a high school reunion. I'm afraid I misled you a little."

No expression of outrage appeared on Sandra June Baker's face. Her expression didn't change at all. She just stared at Jack.

"Do you remember, thirty-one years ago, a girl being found dead on the football field at the high school?" Jack spoke gently.

For the first time · spark of interest appeared in the

woman's face, but it quickly faded. "I guess so." Her tone hadn't changed.

"I'm writing a book about it," Jack said, "and my wife is helping me. We're trying to find out what really happened."

Still the woman didn't react. Wanda Nell watched her, puzzled. She wasn't drunk; Wanda Nell had seen enough drunks to know the signs. She was probably taking some kind of pill that made her this way. Maybe some kind of antidepressant or a tranquilizer.

Jack persevered, despite the lack of response. "We know your brother was questioned by the Sheriff's Department, but he disappeared before he could be charged with anything."

"Roscoe's gone," Mrs. Baker said. She stirred for a moment in the chair, then went still again.

Wanda Nell glanced at Jack. He raised his eyebrows. Wanda Nell decided to step in for a moment.

"When you say he's gone," she said, her voice gentle but firm, "do you mean just gone away? Or has he died?"

Mrs. Baker regarded her for a moment. "Just gone."

"Do you have any idea where he is now?" Wanda Nell asked.

"Why do you want to know?" The woman's voice grew stronger for a moment.

"We want to talk to him, find out whether he knew anything about the girl," Jack said. "Nobody even knows her name, or where she came from."

"We don't think your brother killed her," Wanda Nell added. "We think it's possible somebody else killed her and tried to blame your brother."

"He didn't kill her, I don't care what anybody said."

"Do you know where he is?" Jack asked. "We'd sure like to talk to him, and I promise you we wouldn't tell anybody where he is now."

"If we can prove somebody else did it, he could come

home again," Wanda Nell said. For some reason, she really believed that Roscoe Bates was innocent, despite what Mrs. Havens had said. Mrs. Bates heard the sincerity in her voice, and for the first time, she smiled.

The smile fled, however, when she heard the sound of a car pulling into the driveway.

"You'll have to go," she said, becoming agitated. "My husband." Alarm shone in her eyes. "I can't talk to you anymore."

Wanda Nell and Jack stood. Mrs. Baker was obviously distressed. She flinched when she heard a door open and close, and heavy footsteps approaching. Jack pulled his notebook and a pen out of his pocket and scribbled something. He tore the paper out and pressed it into Mrs. Baker's hand.

"Sandra June," a deep voice called out. "Have you got company in the house?"

Mrs. Baker clutched the paper for a moment, staring at them almost wildly. She stuffed the paper into the bosom of her dress. When her husband came into the room, she was calm again. She turned to him, her head down. "These folks stopped by. I didn't invite anybody." Her voice had gone flat again, and Wanda Nell could feel the fear emanating from her.

Mr. Baker was a tall man, several inches over six feet, and massively built. He wore a dark suit and tie, and his face had a grim, mean look to it that made Wanda Nell want to grab Mrs. Baker and carry her out of the house. "What do you folks want? Can't you see my wife is ill? She don't need strangers here pestering her."

"We're sorry," Jack said, standing his ground. "We didn't mean to impose on your wife."

Wanda Nell stared the man right in the face. "We're just visiting people in the neighborhood around here on behalf of our church and our pastor." She hoped the Lord would forgive her such a lie, but she would have said anything it took right then to protect the poor woman trembling in front of her.

Mr. Baker regarded her, his hostility undiminished. "We already belong to a church, and we got no mind to change to another one. I think y'all had best go on about your business and do the Lord's work somewhere else."

"We surely will," Wanda Nell said, not flinching.

Mr. Baker's face darkened, but before he could say anything else, Jack took Wanda Nell's arm. "We'll be going now. Goodbye, Mrs. Baker. We're sorry for bothering you."

Mrs. Baker didn't appear to have heard him. She hadn't moved since her husband came into the room. Wanda Nell hated to leave her in that house, but she didn't see any other option.

She and Jack walked to the front door. Jack opened it, and once they were both outside, he closed it firmly.

Neither of them said a word until they were in the car and on their way out of the subdivision.

"What a horrible man," Wanda Nell said. "Do you think he'll beat her because she let us in the house?"

"The Lord only knows." Jack's voice was as grim as the look on his face. "Men like that ought to be horsewhipped. Even if he's not abusing her physically, he's sure doing it mentally. I bet he makes her take whatever pills have got her like she is."

Wanda Nell shivered. "What can we do for her?"

"I don't know. I guess we could tell Elmer Lee about the situation. We need to tell him we found her, anyway. Maybe he can do something."

"I sure hope so," Wanda Nell said. After a moment, she reached in her purse for her cell phone.

"Are you going to call him right now?" Jack asked. By

now they were passing through the center of town, and they'd soon be taking the turn toward the reservoir and the trailer park.

"No. I'm calling T.J. and Tuck. I want to see if they'll invite Elmer Lee to have dinner with us tonight."

"You really think he'll come?"

"He gets along just fine with Tuck and T.J. now." Wanda Nell held up her free hand.

"Hey, sweetie, it's your mama. Yes, we're still planning to be there for dinner. Have you heard back from Miranda yet?"

She slumped against the seat. "I was afraid of that. I hope Teddy will stop some of this foolishness before too long." She listened for a moment. "I know, sweetie, I know. Look, since they aren't coming, would you mind inviting someone else instead?" She mentioned Elmer Lee.

"Thanks, honey. Will one of y'all call him? It's because of this case, the one Jack wants to write about. We'll explain it all when we see you tonight." After a brief pause she said, "Love you, too," and ended the call.

"So they're going to invite Elmer Lee?" Jack asked.

"Yes. T.J. said he thought it would be pretty interesting to have Elmer Lee sit down at their table with all of us. According to T.J., he's practically a part of the family anyway."

"Kind of like an annoying big brother, huh?" Jack teased.

"Annoying is right," Wanda Nell said. "But he has his uses, thank goodness."

"That he does," Jack said. "And I hope he can do something about Miz Baker."

"Do you think she knows where her brother is?"

"I think she does. And I think she might have told us if her husband hadn't turned up when he did. I'm afraid we may not get another chance to talk to her now."

"Well, if we can't, maybe Elmer Lee can," Wanda Nell said.

"Yes, but I promised her we wouldn't tell anybody else where her brother is." Jack turned the car off the highway onto the reservoir road. They would be home in less than five minutes.

"We may not have a choice," Wanda Nell said. "I'm worried about her. You know, I don't think I'm going to wait until tonight to talk to Elmer Lee. The minute we get home, I'm going to call him."

"Okay, honey," Jack said. "I think you're right. That's one of the reasons I love you so much. You have the biggest heart of anybody I know." He turned his head to give her a brief smile.

Wanda Nell couldn't speak for a moment because of the big lump in her throat. She pulled off her sunglasses and let her eyes speak for her.

As they came down the drive into the trailer park, Wanda Nell looked ahead to their trailer, the first one on the right. The next one belonged to Mayrene, and Wanda Nell spotted a pickup in front of it. "Looks like Dixon is here," she said. "I hope he's apologizing to Mayrene."

All of a sudden, they heard loud noises and one very loud voice coming from Mayrene's trailer. Then came the sound of something big crashing inside the trailer. Wanda Nell and Jack stared at each other, appalled. Wanda Nell ran toward Mayrene's door, with Jack right behind her.

She leaped up the steps, almost slipping in the unaccustomed heels. With a deep breath, she wrenched open the door, praying her best friend wasn't hurt.

Twelve

Wanda Nell stood in the doorway of Mayrene's trailer and gawked at the sight in front of her. Jack, peering over her shoulder, gave a snort of laughter.

Instead of finding her friend lying dead or dying on the floor, Wanda Nell saw Dixon Vance sitting amidst the remains of Mayrene's once-elegant coffee table in front of the couch. Small, foil-wrapped articles lay scattered about him, along with the shards of at least two vases and numerous artificial flowers of various kinds. Mayrene stood unharmed, hands on hips, a few feet away.

She stopped glowering at Dixon long enough to turn to Wanda Nell. "Do you know what this jackass had the unmitigated gall to bring me, thinking he was gonna cozy back up to me?"

"From the looks of it, a box of chocolates." Jack's voice was mild, with a hint of suppressed humor.

Wanda Nell looked at Dixon with pity. The man didn't have a clue when it came to Mayrene. He just sat there, still a bit dazed from what had happened. He shrank back as Mayrene took a couple of steps toward him.

"I'm not gonna throw anything else at you," Mayrene

said in tones of deep disgust as she stared down at him. "I'm getting over my mad now. Get up from there, why don't you?"

"Hell, Mayrene honey." Vance got up off the floor, brushing away candy and artificial flowers. "All I was trying to do was make it up to you for the other day. I didn't mean to hurt your feelings again."

"Well, telling me I needed to go on a diet and then bringing me a box of chocolates didn't make a whole lot of sense, did it?" Mayrene's tone had not softened. "If I'm too much woman for you, mister, then you better pack up your little red wagon and drag it somewhere else."

Wanda Nell was feeling distinctly unnecessary at this point, and Jack had already backed down the steps. "We'll leave you two to work this out," Wanda Nell said. "But don't throw anything else, okay?" She was trying hard not to laugh. The sight of the big policeman cowering in front of Mayrene had been a funny sight.

Mayrene flapped a hand in her direction. "I'm just fine, Wanda Nell. Y'all go on home, and if I need help burying the body, I'll give you a holler."

"Mayrene, don't talk like that, sweetie," Dixon said in protest.

Wanda Nell didn't wait to hear any more. She stepped away from the door, shut it firmly, and turned to stare at her husband. Jack had a huge grin on his face, and Wanda Nell shook her head at him.

"Come on, let's get inside before there's any more fireworks," she said, coming down the steps and grabbing his arm. "Mayrene's going to be just fine."

"Yeah, I don't think Dixon will lift a hand against her." Jack allowed himself to be tugged along. "Not if he values his life, that is."

Wanda Nell giggled. "Can you believe him giving her candy after telling her she need to go on a diet?"

"Not the brightest thing in the world to do," Jack said, following her up the steps to their door. He reached past her with his key and unlocked it.

Stepping inside, Wanda Nell laughed again. "No, it sure wasn't, but if she lets him hang around long enough, he'll figure it out, I guess."

"He must care about her if he hasn't already run out." Jack pushed the door shut and leaned against it.

"He does," Wanda Nell said, "and Mayrene knows it. Once she blows up like that, she gets over it real fast. They'll be okay. But I bet you he'll buy her something pretty nice now. And it won't be something to eat." She laughed.

"Do you throw things when you get mad?" Jack asked, a slight grin on his face.

"No, and I don't hit, either. But you might get some frost on certain parts of your anatomy before I'm over my mad."

Jack laughed. "Then I'm going to do my best not to make you mad at me."

"Making up afterward sure can be fun," Wanda Nell said.

"True." Jack followed Wanda Nell into the kitchen. "But we can have fun without anybody getting mad at anybody else."

"I know." Wanda Nell smiled for a moment. Then her expression sobered. "I better call Elmer Lee. I forgot about it for a few minutes, thanks to Mayrene."

"Okay, honey," Jack said. "If you need me for something, I'll be in the study, writing up some notes." He gave her a kiss on the cheek.

Wanda Nell picked up the phone as Jack walked out of the kitchen. She punched in the number for the Sheriff's Department. When someone answered, she asked to speak to the sheriff and gave her name. For a moment she was convinced she heard the man on the other end sigh, but she decided to ignore it.

After nearly a minute, Elmer Lee came on the line. "What is it now, Wanda Nell?" He sounded tired.

"Don't you ever go home?" Wanda Nell asked, trying to sound sympathetic.

"No, because I might miss one of your phone calls." Elmer Lee sighed heavily. "Sorry, Wanda Nell, I don't mean to take it out on you. We had a long night last night. A coupla bubbas got into it at one of their homes last night, and there was more trouble this afternoon with their wives. I swear, sometimes I really wonder about people."

"I know," Wanda Nell said. "But it's a good thing y'all are there to get things sorted out."

"I guess so," Elmer Lee said. "Now, what was it you called about? I'll be seeing you in a little while anyways."

"Well, I'm kinda worried," Wanda Nell said. She launched into an explanation of their visit to Sandra June Baker, promising that Jack would give him the full details of how they had found her. "I swear her husband's keeping her drugged up, and she looks like he's abusing her somehow."

"Did you see any physical signs, other than her acting drugged?"

"Well, no," Wanda Nell said, after having thought about it for a moment. "No heavy makeup, or long sleeves, or anything like that. And she didn't move around like she was hurt. Just sluggish."

"I'll check with the police and see if there've been any complaints about that address. But I don't think there's much anybody can do, until she makes a complaint herself."

"I figured that, but I still felt like I had to tell someone."

"I'll talk it over with the police, and they'll be alert in case any calls come from over there," Elmer Lee said. "And now that y'all have found her, I'll need to talk to her about her brother. That'll give me a chance to assess the situation."

"Good. Jack's hoping maybe she'll call him at some point, if she can ever get away from that husband of hers long enough. We think she knows where her brother is."

"Then we sure need to talk to her."

"You're not going over there right now, are you?"

"No, now don't get all upset," Elmer Lee said. "Going over now wouldn't do a whole lot of good, probably. I'll give her a day or so, to see if she gets in touch with Jack. If she doesn't, then I'll for sure go and see her when her husband ain't around."

"Good," Wanda Nell said, much relieved. "Thanks."

"I'll see y'all in a little while for dinner," Elmer Lee said.

Wanda Nell said goodbye and put the phone back on its cradle. She was still concerned for Sandra June Baker, but at least now Elmer Lee knew about the situation. If there was anything to be done, he would see that it got done.

Wanda Nell walked down the hall to the door of the study and peeked in. Jack was engrossed in working on his computer, listening to music, and she decided not to interrupt him. She tiptoed away, deciding she would read for a while. Soon she was engrossed in her book, and when she finally glanced at the clock, she saw that they would need to leave in a few minutes for dinner with Tuck and T.J.

Setting the book aside, Wanda Nell went back to Jack's study. He was dozing in the recliner in the corner. She sat down on the arm of the chair and brushed his hair back from his forehead. "Time to wake up, honey."

Jack blinked at her. He yawned. "I guess I did nod off there for a while. What time is it?"

"Almost time to leave for dinner, if we're going to get there on time."

"Good thing we don't have to change, then," Jack said. "All I need to do is hit the bathroom and put my boots back on, and I'm ready to go."

"Go right ahead. We might need to go by Miz Culpepper's and pick up Juliet on the way. T.J. may have picked her up already, so I'll check with him first."

Jack pulled his boots back on while Wanda Nell went back to the kitchen to use the phone. She punched in the number, and after three rings, Tuck answered the phone.

"Hey, Wanda Nell. Y'all heading this way soon?"

"We are. I was just calling to see if T.J. had picked up Juliet, or if we need to do it."

"She's here already," Tuck said. "So y'all just come on. T.J. probably already told you it's just going to be us and Elmer Lee, I'm afraid. Miranda called. They can't come."

Wanda Nell heard the slight note of hurt in his voice, and she wanted to jerk a knot in Teddy's tail. "Don't pay any attention to that. It's just something he's gonna have to work through."

"I know. What I don't get, though, is how he doesn't seem to mind being around us at Mrs. Culpepper's house, or other places. What's the big deal about coming to our house and having a meal?"

"I don't know," Wanda Nell said. "But I'm gonna have to sit him down pretty soon and have a talk with him. It's really starting to bug me."

"If you find out what the problem is, let us know," Tuck said. "Maybe he's afraid of my cooking." He laughed, but the sound was strained.

"Who knows? Now, you stop worrying about it."

"Yes, ma'am. Now, y'all don't be late."

Wanda Nell assured him they would be leaving in a minute, then hung up the phone. She stood staring at it, thinking about her son-in-law. She really was going to have to have a talk with Teddy. This situation couldn't go on, because it was creating a strain in Miranda's relationship with her brother. Miranda had always adored T.J. and looked up to him, and she had quickly accepted Tuck as part of the family. But she was also loyal to her new husband, and that had caused some friction.

"I'm ready, love," Jack said from behind her.

Wanda Nell turned. "Juliet's already there."

"Good, then we don't have to worry about trying to get away from Belle without hurting her feelings." He wiggled an eyebrow at Wanda Nell.

"No we don't, thank goodness. Otherwise, we might not get over there until it's time for dessert."

They shared a smile for a moment. Belle was a dear, but as Wanda Nell's mama would have said, she could talk the horns off a billygoat, and his hind legs, too.

"I'll be ready to go in two minutes," Wanda Nell said.

Jack looked at his watch. "I'm timing you."

Wanda Nell punched his arm lightly.

"Ow, I thought you didn't hit."

"That was a love tap," Wanda Nell informed him. "Now let me get by, and I'll be ready to go, I promise."

Jack grinned as he stood aside. Wanda Nell hurried down the hall to their bathroom. She wanted to check her makeup and wash her hands.

Just under two minutes later she was back. Jack waited by the door. He opened it with a flourish. "After you, ma'am."

Wanda Nell picked up her purse and went out the door. The late afternoon heat was still oppressive, but not as bad as it had been at midday.

The drive to Tuck and T.J.'s house was a short one. Several years ago Tuck had bought a house in one of the upscale subdivisions in Tullahoma, only a few miles from Wanda Nell's trailer park. All the houses in the development were two-story, with two- or three-car garages, large lots, and expensive landscaping. Wanda Nell had no idea how much money Tuck made with his law practice, but he seemed pretty comfortable. He came from a family with money, too.

An unfamiliar pickup was in the drive when they pulled in. "Must be Elmer Lee's," Jack said.

"I guess so," Wanda Nell replied. "You know, I don't think I've ever seen him in anything but a Sheriff's Department car."

"Just as well he didn't show up in one of those," Jack said, putting the car in Park and switching off the ignition. "What would the neighbors think?" His tone made a joke of it.

"In this neighborhood," Wanda Nell said, "who knows? Thank goodness, they don't seem to have much problem with two men living together."

"It's nice to know there's at least one enlightened part of town." Jack got out of the car and came around to Wanda Nell's side to open the door.

Wanda Nell stepped out, and Jack shut the door behind her. She started walking toward the front door, Jack right behind her. His cell phone began to ring, and they both paused.

Jack pulled the phone from his jacket pocket and glanced at the number. "It's Sandra Baker's number," he said, a note of excitement in his voice.

Thirteen

Jack flipped open his phone and punched a button. The phone to his ear, he said, "This is Jack Pemberton." He listened.

Wanda Nell stood, her back to the evening sun, hoping that it was Sandra June calling, and not her scary husband.

"Yes, I see," Jack said, a slight frown on his face. "No, I understand. That's fine with me. How about the Kountry Kitchen? Do you know where that is?" He listened for a moment. "Sure, I'll be there around ten tomorrow morning. My wife will be there, too." After a few more reassuring words, he ended the call, folded his phone, and tucked it into his pocket.

"Well? What did she say?"

"She wants to meet me, but she doesn't want me coming back to their house." Jack took Wanda Nell's arm and steered her toward the front door. "Her husband allows her to go grocery shopping on Monday mornings, and she shops at the store right across the highway from the Kountry Kitchen."

"So she's going to meet you there at ten," Wanda Nell

said. They had reached the front door, and Jack pushed the doorbell.

"Yes. She won't be able to stay long. She didn't say why, though I can guess."

"Her husband probably times her." Wanda Nell grimaced. "That's horrible. Doesn't he have to go to work?"

"He'll be at work, according to Miz Baker. I don't know the details. Maybe she'll tell us tomorrow."

The door opened, and T.J. stood there, smiling. "Come on in." He stood aside to let them enter.

Wanda Nell smiled up at her son. He was such a handsome young man, and the older he got, the more he looked like his daddy. Bobby Ray had been very good-looking—way too much for his own good. Though he got his looks from Bobby Ray, T.J. took a lot of his temperament from her. After a few rough years, he had finally settled down, and Wanda Nell often gave thanks to see him so happy.

"Elmer Lee's already here," T.J. said as he shut the door. "He and Juliet are in the living room. Let me get you something to drink. How about a glass of wine?"

"Sounds fine," Jack said.

"Me, too," Wanda Nell added.

"Red okay?"

"Sure," Jack and Wanda Nell agreed.

"Y'all go on in the living room, and I'll be back in a minute with your wine." T.J. headed down the hall to the kitchen, a large room at the back of the house.

Jack and Wanda Nell stepped across the hall to the living room. Pausing on the threshold, Wanda Nell glanced around the room. She remembered the first time she had come to Tuck's house, right after T.J. had moved in with him. She hadn't known what to expect, being half afraid she'd find the place full of all kinds of frilly curtains and strange colors. She had been ashamed of herself for thinking that way, especially after she saw how tastefully the whole house was done. There were no frills anywhere, but neither were there animal heads, gun racks, and bearskin rugs. The furniture was comfortable, some of it antique, but overall the impression was one of ease and understated good taste.

Elmer Lee and Juliet sat on opposite ends of an old-fashioned, high-backed sofa. Elmer Lee sipped from a glass of wine, and Juliet cradled a glass of iced tea in her hands.

"Hi, Mama, hi, Jack. Mr. Johnson's just been telling me some stories about when you were in high school."

"I'm not sure I like the sound of that," Wanda Nell said. "I hope he's not been telling you any of the bad things I got up to."

"Now, you know you didn't get up to that much." Elmer Lee rose from his seat. "Except breaking a lot of hearts, that is."

Wanda Nell blushed. "I did not."

"Juliet's going to be doing the same," Elmer Lee said, and now it was Juliet's turn to blush. "She looks just like you did when you were that age."

"Thank you, Mr. Johnson. I hope I'm as pretty as Mama is when I'm her age."

Wanda Nell smiled at her younger daughter.

"She's not just pretty," Jack said, "she's beautiful." He beamed at his wife.

"Enough," Wanda Nell said. "Y'all are going to have me blushing again."

"Blushing? What for?" T.J. asked as he came into the room. He held a glass of red wine in each hand. Tuck came in right behind him, also bearing two glasses of red wine.

T.J. offered a glass each to Wanda Nell and Jack, then took his own glass from his partner. Tuck slipped his arm around T.J.'s waist and raised his glass. "To family and good friends."

They all responded to the toast, and when they had done,

Tuck said, "Glad you could be here. I hope you'll like what we've made for dinner."

"I'm sure it will be delicious, as always," Jack said. "You've never disappointed us yet." He smacked his lips, and the others laughed.

"There's always a first time," Tuck said in a self-deprecating manner.

"Don't listen to him," T.J. said fondly. "If he wasn't such a great lawyer, he could open his own gourmet restaurant. You wouldn't believe how much I have to exercise because of his cooking. If I didn't, I'd be as big as the side of a barn."

"I don't see how you have time to do all the things you do." Elmer Lee's tone betrayed his envy. "And cook, too. Heck, I eat out of a can most of the time at home, or else heat up a frozen dinner in the microwave."

"I love to cook," Tuck said. "It's a good way for me to relax." He grinned. "And it doesn't hurt to have someone to clean up after me, either."

T.J. sighed and shook his head. "Now you hear the truth. He just keeps me around to clean up the mess he makes in the kitchen."

"Yeah, right," Juliet said amidst the laughter her brother's remark had evoked. She held up her right hand, rubbing her thumb and index finger together. "You see this? This is the world's tiniest violin, and it's playing "My Heart Bleeds for You.' "

T.J. turned to Tuck. "Are you sure that's just iced tea in her glass? She's sounding pretty big for her britches."

Juliet giggled, and the others laughed with her.

"Let's eat," Tuck said. He turned to lead the way to the dining room. "Juliet set the table for us, so if everything's in the wrong place, you'll know who to blame." He turned to grin over his shoulder. Juliet retaliated by sticking out her tongue at him.

In the dining room Tuck stood at the head of the table and directed everyone to his or her seat. T.J. sat at the foot, Wanda Nell on his left and Jack on his right. Elmer Lee took the chair to the left of Tuck, and Juliet was on Tuck's right. "Help yourselves to the bread and butter," Tuck said. "T.J. actually made the bread. I'll be back with the salad."

"I'll help you." T.J. followed Tuck out of the room.

"T.J. actually made bread?" Wanda Nell asked, impressed. "I didn't know he could do that."

"He used the bread machine," Juliet said.

"It looks delicious." Elmer Lee picked up the basket and parted the linen cloth to peek inside. "And it smells great." He served himself a piece before offering the basket to Juliet.

Tuck and T.J. returned moments later, bearing trays. They served the salad, and Wanda Nell inspected hers with interest. There was no lettuce. She had never had a salad like this before. It consisted of at least three kinds of peppers, with onions, olives, and tomatoes mixed in. There was also some kind of cheese. And she thought she detected a smell of vinegar.

"What kind of salad is it?" Elmer Lee asked. He appeared as fascinated by it as Wanda Nell.

"It's a Greek salad," Tuck said. "The dressing is red wine vinegar mixed with olive oil. There's feta cheese, onion, cucumber, tomato, and three kinds of peppers in it."

"It's really good," T.J. added.

"It looks delicious," Wanda Nell said. "And so does the bread."

T.J. grinned. "This isn't my first attempt, so it should be okay."

Over the salad they chatted in desultory fashion. No one had yet broached the subject of murder, and Wanda Nell was enjoying a break from talking about, or even thinking about, the case.

The salad course finished, T.J. and Tuck cleared away the remains. They returned several minutes later, again bearing trays, this time loaded with pasta and fragrant meat sauce. Once T.J. had emptied his tray, he returned to the kitchen for more bread. Tuck refilled glasses before passing around a bowl of grated Parmesan.

"This is great," Elmer Lee said after his first taste of the meat sauce. "And what kind of spaghetti is this? It tastes different."

"It's whole-grain linguini," T.J. said. "The whole grain is better for you, and that's about all we eat."

"It's good," Wanda Nell said. "It's got a real nice texture to it. But this meat sauce is what makes it so wonderful."

Tuck smiled at them, obviously pleased with their response. "This is one of my favorites. I'm glad you're all enjoying it. And we have a special treat for dessert. At least I hope it will be a treat. Does everybody like homemade peach ice cream?"

Jack and Elmer Lee groaned at the same time. Startled, they looked at each other. Elmer Lee grinned. "It's about my favorite thing in the world, that's all."

"I love it, too," Jack added. "I hope you made a lot of it."

Laughing, T.J. said, "Don't worry, there's plenty."

They took their time over the pasta, savoring the rich flavor, again talking of things other than murder. Finally, when all the plates and the bread basket were empty, Tuck pushed back from the table. "Is everyone ready for dessert?"

"I am," Elmer Lee said.

"You sound just like a little boy, Elmer Lee," T.J. said teasingly.

Elmer Lee grinned. "Can't help it. I love peach ice cream."

"Y'all go on into the living room," Tuck said. "We'll have dessert in there. Would anyone like some coffee?"

"I would," Jack said, and Wanda Nell and Elmer Lee

said they would, too. Tuck nodded as he headed for the kitchen.

"Can I help clear the table?" Wanda Nell asked, standing and starting to gather up plates.

"No, you cannot," T.J. replied. He took the plates from her. "We'll have plenty of time to clear up later, Mama. Y'all go on to the living room, and don't worry about this."

"Okay, honey. I'm not going to argue with you. I'm too full of good food." Wanda Nell kissed his cheek.

Ten minutes later they were all seated in the living room, enjoying the freshly made ice cream, along with coffee.

"We've waited long enough," Tuck said, setting aside an empty bowl. "I know we're all curious about what's been going on."

Elmer Lee nodded. "I sure am. I want to hear all about what you two have managed to find out."

Wanda Nell glanced at Juliet. She was sixteen now, and old enough to be a part of this discussion if she wanted to be. "Honey," she said, "do you want to hear about all this?"

Juliet nodded. "I guess I ought to. If Jack's going to write a book about it, I'd like to know about it ahead of time." She shrugged. "And who knows? There may be some way I can help."

"Okay, then," Wanda Nell said. "But if anything bothers you about any of this, I want you to talk to me about it, okay?"

"I will, Mama."

Reassured, Wanda Nell nodded at Jack. He set aside his empty bowl and took a sip of coffee before he started.

Jack gave them a quick rundown of what had happened since Saturday morning. Wanda Nell occasionally chipped in with a detail or two, but Jack gave a very clear picture of the case. The others sat, very attentive, until he had finished. At some point, Elmer Lee had pulled a pen and a small notebook from his pocket and started jotting down notes.

"Just as we were coming up the walk to the front door," Jack said, concluding his summary, "my phone rang, and it was Sandra June Baker. She's going to meet me tomorrow to talk. And I hope she'll tell me where her brother is."

"So you're pretty sure he's still alive?" Tuck asked.

"We think so," Wanda Nell said. "She didn't tell us he wasn't. All she would say was that he was gone."

"If she was as drugged up as you say," Elmer Lee said, "that's probably about as clear as she was going to get."

"That's what we thought," Jack said. "The fact that she's willing to talk to me tomorrow is a good sign. She's obviously got something to say."

"And if she tells you where her brother is, what then?" T.J. asked.

"I want to find him and talk to him. I'm just hoping that he's somewhere not too far away. If he's several thousand miles away, or in another country, I might not be able to find him."

"I'll bet you he didn't go that far away," Tuck said. "More than likely he went to some big city, like Atlanta or Memphis, or maybe Houston."

"I hope so," Jack said. "I can afford to get to one of them without much trouble."

"What will you do if she doesn't tell you where he is, or if she doesn't even know?" Juliet asked.

"We'll have to go to Plan B," Jack replied with a rueful laugh. "Not that I have a Plan B right this minute."

"We'll figure out something," Wanda Nell said. "If she can't lead us to him, we'll find him some other way. Can't you get on the computer and try to find him that way?"

Jack shrugged. "That was what I was doing this afternoon after we got home. I wasn't having much luck, but that's not to say there might not be traces of him somewhere. The problem is, he probably changed his name. That makes it a whole lot harder."

"I hadn't thought about that," Wanda Nell said.

"It's pretty common," Elmer Lee explained. "But pretty often you'll find it's something similar. Like they'll use the same initials, or maybe some variation of their name. Most people don't have a lot of imagination when it comes to making up names for themselves." He smiled. "And I bet you Roscoe Lee Bates is one of them without a lot of imagination."

"I hope you're right," Jack said. "We'll know more tomorrow."

"What about Grandmama?" T.J. asked. "It sure sounds like she knows something."

"It's very likely," Wanda Nell replied. "Otherwise, I don't think she would have reacted like that."

"Would you like me to try talking to her about it?" T.J. asked. "She might tell me something."

Though she had come to love her two granddaughters, Mrs. Culpepper still made it pretty clear that T.J. was her favorite grandchild. Sometimes she even forgot and called him Bobby Ray. T.J. was very good with her, and his attention to her was one of the reasons she had mellowed so noticeably over the last year or so. At least, that was Wanda Nell's theory.

"If she really knows something that could help us," Jack said, "of course I'd love to know what it is. But I don't want to make her ill over this. We may be able to find out what we need to without asking her about it again."

"I'll feel her out a little," T.J. offered. "She's a lot tougher than you think she is. But I don't want to see her upset any more than you do. I promise I'll be careful if I talk to her about it."

"Well, you know her better, really, than any of us," Wanda Nell said. "I know you'll use good judgment."

T.J. nodded.

Elmer Lee stood. "I got to be going. I sure have enjoyed this evening." He faced T.J. and Tuck. "Thanks for inviting me. The food was great, and the company was even better." He smiled.

Tuck and T.J. stood to shake Elmer Lee's hand. "We're glad you could come," Tuck said.

"Wanda Nell, Jack, Miss Juliet," Elmer Lee said, "I'll be talking to you. Call me"—he looked at Jack—"after you've talked to Miz Baker."

"I will," Jack said, standing to shake his hand.

"I guess we ought to be getting home, too," Wanda Nell said. "Now are you sure you don't want some help cleaning up? It won't take us but a few minutes, and we can get it all done."

Tuck shook his head. "No, we'll do just fine. Y'all go on home and get some rest. You've had a busy couple of days. It won't take me and T.J. long to get everything put away."

After a few minutes of more thank yous and goodbyes, Wanda Nell, Jack, and Juliet left. The ride home was quiet, and all three of them were yawning by the time they walked in the front door of the trailer.

Mayrene's trailer was dark and quiet. Only her car was parked beside it, and Wanda Nell hoped her friend had been able to patch things up with Vance. If that was what she wanted, of course. Sometimes she wasn't quite sure just what Mayrene really wanted.

Monday morning dawned clear and hot, and after a leisurely breakfast around eight, Jack and Juliet cleared up while Wanda Nell got ready for work. She headed off to the Kountry Kitchen at nine. Jack would be there by ten, and Juliet was going to spend the day at home.

At the Kountry Kitchen, Wanda Nell greeted her boss,

Melvin Arbuckle, and the two morning-shift waitresses, Betsy Estes and Patsy Ferris. They were both new, both in their late twenties, and both good-looking. Melvin's breakfast and lunch business had grown, once word had got around about the two pretty new waitresses.

Wanda Nell enjoyed working with both of them. Neither one of them shied away from hard work, and they treated her with friendly respect as the more experienced worker.

The breakfast crowd was thinning out, and Wanda Nell helped the two girls get the place ready for the lunch crowd. Many of their regulars started coming back for lunch around eleven-thirty, and they would stay busy until at least two.

Wanda Nell kept an eye on the clock as she worked, watching for her husband to come through the door. At ten minutes to ten, he did.

He took a seat at the counter, and Wanda Nell brought him a cup of coffee. They chatted for a moment before Wanda Nell went back to work.

The clock hit ten, and both Wanda Nell and Jack had anxious eyes on the front door. Five minutes ticked by, then ten, and Jack's shoulders slumped. Wanda Nell commiserated with him.

"She could still be planning to come," she told her husband. "Give her a few more minutes."

"I'll have to," Jack said. "I don't really dare go back to her house. I don't want to cause her any trouble with her husband."

The front door opened then, and they both turned to look. Jack sighed with relief.

Sandra June Baker stood there, staring at them.

Fourteen

While Sandra June Baker continued to hesitate in the doorway, Wanda Nell moved quickly to greet her. She eyed the woman's faded, worn dress and old shoes with pity. The man wouldn't even allow her to dress decently. Surely he could afford better clothes than this for her.

"Good morning, Miz Baker," she said, pulling the door open farther. "Come on in. Can I get you something to drink?"

Mrs. Baker seemed to collect herself with an effort. "I sure would like a Coke," she said. "I don't get to drink them at home."

The wistful tone of those words made Wanda Nell's heart ache for the poor woman. "Of course you can have a Coke," she said, laying a gentle hand on the woman's arm. "Come on in. Jack's here to meet you. We'll find y'all a quiet place to talk, and I'll bring you as many Cokes as you want."

A brief smile hovered on Mrs. Baker's lips, and she allowed Wanda Nell to lead her into the restaurant. Jack came up to them, and when he spoke, his voice was soft. "Good morning, Miz Baker. Thanks for coming to talk to me."

Sandra Baker stared into his face for a moment. "I

didn't take my pills last night or this morning," she said, sounding almost surprised. "My head is clearer today."

"That's good," Jack said. He took over from Wanda Nell and led Mrs. Baker to the back room of the restaurant, where there were a number of empty tables. He selected one well away from any occupied ones, and they waited until Wanda Nell came back with Sandra June's drink.

"I'm going to be busy back there for a few minutes," Wanda Nell told Betsy Estes. "Do you mind covering for me?"

"Sure."

Smiling her thanks, Wanda Nell took a glass of ice and a can of Coke back to the table where Jack and Mrs. Baker sat.

"Thank you," Sandra June said as Wanda Nell poured the soft drink into the glass for her. "That sure looks good."

Wanda Nell and Jack exchanged quick glances. Though she still appeared timid, at least Mrs. Baker seemed a little more alert today.

"I know you don't have much time, Miz Baker," Jack said. "I don't want to rush you, but I don't want to cause any trouble for you, either."

"Call me Sandra," she said, her voice a little stronger now. "I really hate the name Miz Baker."

Wanda Nell wanted to wrap her arms around the woman to comfort her. She pulled out a chair and sat down beside her.

"Sandra, then," Jack said. His smile was gentle as he continued. "You remember we were asking about your brother yesterday, and you told us he was gone."

Sandra nodded. "I remember." She took another sip from her drink. "I didn't mean he was dead. He's alive."

"Do you know where he is?" Jack asked, and Wanda Nell found herself holding her breath, waiting for an answer.

Sandra nodded. "My husband don't know about this—about Roscoe, I mean. I never told him any of that."

"We certainly won't tell him anything," Wanda Nell said.

"I don't want Roscoe to get in no trouble." Sandra's face became more animated. "He was a good boy. He tried to look after Mama and me after Daddy ran out on us, but it was hard."

"We don't want to cause trouble for your brother," Jack said. "But we're hoping he has some information that can help us find out more about the dead girl. Do you know her name?"

"I used to, but my memory ain't that good these days. I tried to think of it, but I couldn't."

"That's okay," Wanda Nell said. "As long as your brother can remember it."

"I don't imagine he ever forgot it. He thought she was the prettiest girl he ever saw. He was real upset about her getting killed. And I swear he didn't do it."

"We both think you're right," Jack said, "and we want to find out who did. And maybe if we can do that, your brother can come back here."

For the first time Sandra's face shone with a bit of hope. "That would be good." The light faded after a moment. "I'd love to see him again." She hung her head. "Though I surely would hate for him to see me like this."

Wanda Nell stretched a consoling arm around her shoulders. "You don't worry about that. He'd be so happy to see you, I'm sure." *And help you get away from that awful husband*, she added silently.

"Is he very far away?" Jack asked.

Sandra shook her head. "He's in Memphis, but he don't go by his name no more. He changed it."

Jack and Wanda Nell exchanged another glance, this time one of relief. Memphis was only about ninety miles north of Tullahoma, an easy drive.

"What's his name now?" Jack asked.

"He calls himself Rocky Lee. He's a mechanic at one of them big car dealerships in Memphis."

"How often do you hear from him?" Wanda Nell kept her arm around Sandra.

"He sends me cards from time to time. I'm at home when the mail comes, and after I get them, I get rid of them so my husband never sees them."

At that point, Wanda Nell was having a hard time holding back the tears. No woman should have to live like this. They had to find a way to help her. Maybe proving that her brother was not a murderer was the first step. Wanda Nell prayed right then that Roscoe Bates truly was innocent. His sister needed a savior, and he might be her best hope.

"Do you know which dealership it is?" Jack asked.

Sandra gave them the name of it. "I don't know where it is. I ain't never been to Memphis."

"We'll be able to find it," Jack said. "Do you think he'll be willing to talk to us?"

"Tell him I said he should." Sandra fumbled in her shabby purse for a moment. "And give him this. Then he'll know it's okay." She held out a small, very worn stuffed dolphin. "He won this for me once, when I was about ten. He always said he'd take me to see a real one, but we never got to go."

"I'll take very good care of it," Jack said, his voice husky. "And we'll bring it back to you."

"Thank you. Well, I guess I'd better be going. I need to get on over to the grocery store and do my shopping."

"Thanks for talking to us," Wanda Nell said around the lump still lodged in her throat. "Are you going to be okay? Because of the time and everything?"

Sandra gave her a faint smile. "I'll come up with something to tell him. He won't be mad, so don't worry about me."

Jack escorted Sandra to the front door with Wanda Nell

walking behind them. Once Sandra was safely in her car, Jack came back in the restaurant and sat down at the counter.

"I'd like to take a horsewhip to that husband of hers," Jack said, his face dark with anger. "There has got to be something we can do to help her get away from that man."

"If her brother didn't kill that girl, and we can prove it," Wanda Nell said, patting his hand, "then maybe he can get her to leave her husband. She can disappear along with her brother, and nobody ever needs to know about it."

"Sounds good to me. And the sooner the better."

"Amen to that." Are you going to Memphis today?"

Jack glanced at his watch. "It's just a little past ten-thirty. I could be there around noon, and hopefully he'll be at work. If I can get him to talk to me, I could be home by four or five."

"Do you know where this dealership is?"

"I'm pretty sure I do. We had cousins in Memphis when I was growing up, and we used to visit them a couple times a year. And I've been up there a few times in the last three or four years."

"This wasn't Lisa, was it?" Wanda Nell asked, speaking of his cousin who had been going through some rough times recently. She was doing much better now, thanks to the work of a local therapist.

"No, not Lisa's family. These were cousins on my mother's side. Her first cousin and his family."

"Okay," Wanda Nell said. "Promise me you'll be real careful."

"Why don't you see if you can come with me?" Jack asked. "I'd sure rather you were there, too. He might find it easier to talk with you there. You seem to have that effect on people."

Wanda Nell really wanted to go, but she demurred. "I don't like asking Melvin for any more time off right now. He was so nice about giving me time for our honeymoon."

"In all the years you've worked for him, you've never asked for hardly any time off. Come on, it can't hurt to ask."

"Okay," Wanda Nell said with a sigh. "I'll go ask him. I'll tell him I should be back in time for the evening shift, at least."

Jack grinned.

Wanda Nell walked through the kitchen and down the short hall to Melvin's office. He was sitting at his desk, looking over some bills, making notes on a pad. He glanced up.

"What can I do for you, Wanda Nell? I recognize that look on your face. I know you're about to ask me for something."

"I guess we've worked together too long. You can read me too easy."

"I reckon you want some more time off," Melvin said. "I saw you and Jack talking to that woman. Are you mixed up in another murder? I haven't heard about one."

"Well, sort of. I can't really tell you about it now, but I will later, I promise. It's important, or I wouldn't ask you. And I should be back in time for the evening shift."

Melvin stared at her a moment, his craggy face stern. Then he grinned. "Aw, Wanda Nell, you know I have a hard time saying no to you." He waved a hand at her. "Go check with Betsy and Patsy. I don't think they'll mind. I'll call Ruby. She's not taking any classes this summer, and she can use the extra money."

Ruby Garner was going to the local community college, and she usually worked the evenings with Wanda Nell.

"Thanks, Melvin. I really owe you one. And Ruby, too."

"Nah," he said, pointing at the door. "Now get outta here."

Wanda Nell grabbed her purse out of the small closet the waitresses shared, and she heard Melvin on the phone to Ruby as she headed down the hall.

She had a quick word with Patsy and Betsy, saying she had some business she needed to take care of with her husband. After assuring them that Ruby would probably be there to help through the lunch rush, she hit the bathroom before going back to where Jack sat at the counter.

"I'm ready."

"Great. We'll just leave your car here, okay?"

Wanda Nell nodded as she followed him out of the restaurant. Once they were headed for the highway that would take them to Memphis, she pulled out her cell phone to make a couple of calls. The first was to Juliet, to let her know where they were going, and why.

"I'll be okay, Mama. Actually, Miranda just called a little while ago to say she and Lavon are coming over for a visit."

"I'm glad you'll have some company," Wanda Nell said. "But don't let Miranda talk you into baby-sitting just so she can go running off somewhere with one of her friends."

"No, Mama. Y'all be careful."

Wanda Nell shook her head as she ended the call. She knew darn well that Juliet would end up baby-sitting for Miranda. It never failed. Teddy was going to have to put his foot down about Miranda doing that, especially with her being five months' pregnant now.

Next Wanda Nell called T.J. He listened to her rapid explanation. "Y'all be careful, Mama," he said. "And I'll check on Juliet in a little while. Tuck's in Oxford this morning, and I might run over there with some lunch. Don't you worry about her."

"Thanks, honey, I appreciate that."

Wanda Nell tucked her cell phone back in her purse, noting, to her surprise, that they were now on the highway, headed north.

"Everybody taken care of?" Jack asked, a hint of humor in his voice.

"Yes. You know how I am. I just can't go off without making sure they're all okay."

"I know, honey." Jack reached over to squeeze her hand. "I'm glad you called them."

They were quiet for a while as Jack concentrated on driving. Wanda Nell watched the scenery flow by, her mind on the forthcoming meeting with Roscoe Bates, or Rocky Lee, as he called himself now. What would they do if he wasn't at work today? Would they be able to find his home if they had to?

She decided she was thinking too far ahead and coming up with problems. They would just have to see what happened when they got there. Maybe they could get Roscoe to go to lunch with them. She knew both she and Jack would be hungry by then, and maybe talking over lunch would make things a little more friendly.

She mentioned her idea to Jack, and he agreed. "I know a good place close to the dealership," he said. "Let's try talking to him first, and if he'll go with us, fine. If not, we'll just go afterward."

Wanda Nell settled in for the rest of the ride, looking forward to seeing Memphis again. She hadn't been there since before her mama died, a little over seven years ago. She used to go to the one of the malls there with her mother every year to do Christmas shopping. They had always had such a good time together, and thinking about it now made Wanda Nell a little sad. She missed her mother, and her daddy, too, though he had died many years ago.

The time passed quickly, and soon they had reached the outskirts of Memphis. Jack pulled off the highway to stop at a service station. "We might as well fill up the car," he said, parking at a pump. "I also figured we could both use a bathroom break about now."

"Thanks, honey," Wanda Nell said. "I'll be back in a few minutes."

By the time Wanda Nell returned to the car, Jack had finished at the gas pump and with the restroom. He held the door open for her, and soon they were on their way again.

From that point, the drive to the dealership took about fifteen minutes. Jack drove with confidence, and Wanda Nell was relieved they didn't have to worry about getting directions.

At the dealership, Jack found a place to park the car near the service entrance. "We're going to have to avoid looking like a couple who's here to buy a car," he said as he opened Wanda Nell's door. "Otherwise, we'll get waylaid."

"Maybe back here they won't try to sell us anything," Wanda Nell said. "They sure do look busy, though."

The service area was a beehive of activity, and they paused for a moment to get their bearings.

"That looks like the place to ask," Jack said, pointing to a counter.

They had to wait a few minutes. When their turn came, Jack stepped up to the desk.

"How can I help you?" the young woman asked. She smiled brightly at them. Her name tag said Jessica.

"We need to talk to one of the mechanics," Jack said. "His name is Rocky Lee. It's on a personal matter."

The young woman frowned. "Well, let me see. Rocky's here today. They don't really like us doing personal stuff at work, though. I'm not sure he'll have time to talk to you." Her hand hovered over a phone.

"He does get a lunch break, doesn't he?" Wanda Nell asked, her tone polite but firm.

"Sure." Jessica shrugged. "I guess it's up to him. Let me call back there."

Jack and Wanda Nell waited while Jessica punched in a number. When someone answered, she said, "Hey, Bobby. There's a couple people here who need to talk to Rocky. They say it's personal. He had his lunch yet?" She listened for a moment. "Thanks." She hung up the phone. "He'll be out in a minute. He was just about to go on his lunch break."

"Thank you, Jessica," Wanda Nell said. "We appreciate your help."

"You're welcome." The girl turned to the next person in line, and Wanda Nell and Jack stepped out of the way.

They waited near the door, and about two minutes later, a tall, thin man about fifty came through the door. He wore an oil-stained uniform, but his appearance overall was neat. The name tag on his shirt read Rocky. He looked around for a moment before he spotted Wanda Nell and Jack.

"Are you the folks looking for me?" His voice was soft and deep.

Jack nodded. "We are. I'm Jack Pemberton, and this is my wife, Wanda Nell." He offered his hand, and the man took it after a brief hesitation.

"Don't want to go getting any oil or grease on anybody."

"That's fine," Jack responded. "We'd like to talk to you for a few minutes. Privately."

Rocky frowned, looking slightly alarmed. "What is this about? Is everything okay with Judy? Nothing happened at school, did it?"

Jack was quick to reassure him. "No, we're not from the school. Judy is your daughter?"

Rocky nodded, obviously relieved. "So what is this about?"

"Could we step outside for a moment?" Jack tilted his head toward the door.

Shrugging, Rocky agreed. He followed them outside, and Jack moved to a spot that afforded a little privacy from the people going in and out of the service area.

"We're from Tullahoma," Jack said, and Rocky tensed. "We need to talk to you about something that happened there."

Rocky started backing away. "Look, you got the wrong person. I never been to this Tullahoma. I don't even know where it is."

"Please, Roscoe," Wanda Nell said, deliberately using his real name. "We talked to your sister. She was the one who told us how to find you."

Rocky stopped, staring at them uncertainly. Jack reached inside his coat and pulled out the stuffed dolphin. He held it out to Rocky. "She said we should show you this."

Rocky took the toy into his hands, cradling it gently. He stared at it for a long moment, and when he raised his eyes to Wanda Nell and Jack, there were tears in them.

"I'll talk to you," he said.

Fifteen

"How about we do it over lunch?" Jack asked. "I know a good place nearby."

"How long can you take for lunch?" Wanda Nell asked when Rocky didn't respond. He held the toy dolphin in one hand and stroked it with the other.

"I can take an hour. Let me go tell my supervisor." He handed the dolphin back to Jack. "You better take this back to Sandra."

Jack accepted the toy and tucked it in his pocket as Rocky ambled off.

"You don't think he's going to try to skip out on us, do you?" Wanda Nell asked.

"No, I don't think so. I believe he meant it when he said he would talk to us."

Rocky returned in a couple of minutes. "Come on," Jack said. "We'll take our car."

Rocky followed them, opening the door for Wanda Nell and closing it before getting into the backseat. Wanda Nell turned to look at him, struck by his sad expression. "We know this is going to be hard for you," she said. "But we think maybe we can help you."

"I didn't kill her," Rocky said, his eyes on her.

Wanda Nell believed him, maybe because of the simple way he had spoken. "I don't believe you did," she responded, and he gave her a faint, brief smile. "If we can find out who really did, we want to. She deserves justice, and so do you. Your name should be cleared."

"Here we are," Jack said, pulling into one of the few vacant spaces in the parking lot of a steak house. "I hope this is okay."

"Sure," Rocky said. "The food's good here." He got out and opened Wanda Nell's door for her. Wanda Nell smiled her thanks. She already liked this gentle man. She could see the resemblance to his sister in his face, though Sandra looked quite a bit older instead of four years younger.

They had to wait about ten minutes for a table, and during that time they didn't talk. When their turn came, the hostess showed them to a booth near a window. Wanda Nell slid into it, with Jack after her. Rocky sat down across from them.

Once the preliminaries were out of the way and their waiter had brought their drinks, Rocky stirred his tea. "I guess we'd better start. Y'all just tell me what you want to know, and I'll tell you, if I know it."

"Okay," Jack said. "I guess the first thing is, what was her name? Your sister couldn't remember it."

"Jenna Rae Howell. They never found out who she was? Even after all this time?"

"No, not as far as we know," Wanda Nell said. "From what we've been able to find out, the whole thing got hushed up as soon as you left town."

"I'm not surprised, I guess." Rocky paused for a drink of his tea. "The way they was treating me down at the Sheriff's Department, I figured I was going to end up going to jail. So I ran, though I sure hated to leave my mama and Sandra June that way."

"I know they understood," Wanda Nell said. "They wanted you to be safe."

Rocky nodded. "I got a friend to drive me to Greenville, and from there I caught a bus. I ended up in Oklahoma City. I knew a guy out there, he used to live in Tullahoma. He didn't ask no questions, just helped me find a job and gave me a place to stay until I could earn some money."

"How long did you stay there?" Jack asked.

"About eight years, I guess. Didn't look like nobody was trying to find me, or else they just couldn't. So I moved back closer to home. Memphis was as close I'd get, though."

"So you've been here a long time?" Wanda Nell asked.

"Seventeen years. I been with the dealership for twelve now. It's a good job."

"And nobody has come looking for you here?" Jack asked.

Rocky shook his head. "Naw. You're the first people, far as I know. Now that I think about it, that is kinda strange."

"Once you disappeared," Jack said, "we figure the Sheriff's Department, and whoever else was behind the cover-up, used that as an excuse to ignore the case. They didn't really try to search for you, I'm willing to bet, because your running away actually worked to their benefit."

"They probably figured you wouldn't come back, either," Wanda Nell said.

"I never have. I didn't even go back for my mama's funeral, and that like to've killed me." His right hand moved restlessly on the table.

Impulsively, Wanda Nell reached over and squeezed his hand. "I'm sure your mama understood."

Rocky shrugged. "Wasn't nothing much I could do about it."

"Do you have any idea who might have been behind the cover-up?" Jack asked after a brief pause.

"Naw, all I saw was the inside of the Sheriff's Department, and him and some of his men. I never heard them talking about anybody else. They just kept me there for about eighteen hours, going over and over it all. And me telling them what I knew, and that wasn't much."

"How did you meet Jenna Rae?" Wanda Nell asked. "She was a stranger in Tullahoma, right?"

"Yeah, she was. I was working a couple of jobs back then, trying to help my mama out. One of them was working at a little motel out on the highway, not far from where you turn off to go out to the lake. It was a pretty sleazy kind of place. It's probably not there anymore."

"I know where you're talking about," Wanda Nell said. "They tore it down about fifteen years ago, something like that."

"It was a real cheap place to stay," Rocky continued. "I worked there in the afternoons and evenings. I did some cleaning, and I was kind of the night clerk, too. Jenna Rae was renting a room there."

"How long had she been there before she was murdered?" Jack asked.

Rocky looked up and frowned. Their waiter was approaching with their food, Wanda Nell saw when she turned her head. They waited until they had been served before continuing the conversation.

"She was only there about three days," Rocky said.

"Did she tell you why she was there?" Wanda Nell asked.

"She wouldn't say much, though I tried to talk to her as much as I could." He paused for a moment. "She was the prettiest girl I ever seen, and she was sweet. But she was also real determined about something."

"Did she tell you anything?" Jack asked.

"All she'd tell me was that she was in Tullahoma looking for her daddy. She was adopted when she was a baby, and she was trying to find her real daddy."

Wanda Nell set down her knife and fork. "Did she know who he was?"

"She seemed to, but she wouldn't tell me who he was. She said she had to be real careful about how she approached him. I figured he must be somebody pretty well off, and that maybe he wouldn't be too happy about her turning up all of a sudden."

"You're right about that," Jack said. "Especially if he was married to someone who wasn't her mother. Did she say anything about her mother?"

"Naw, she didn't talk about her, so I figured she must already know who her mama was."

They ate in silence for a few minutes, Wanda Nell and Jack both lost in thought. Rocky ate steadily, not speaking unless to answer a question.

"Can you tell us about the night before her body was found?"

Rocky nodded at Jack. "Yeah, I had to go over it and over it a lot of times for the sheriff." He set down his knife and fork to take a long drink of his tea. "I was working that evening, and I saw her come back about seven. I followed her to her room to talk to her. I couldn't help myself, she was so pretty. But she didn't seem to mind too much.

"She was kind of excited. She was going to talk to somebody that evening. She didn't tell me who, but she seemed real pleased about it. Said she'd be meeting her daddy soon. She left about nine, and that was the last time I saw her."

"How was she getting around?" Wanda Nell asked, as the thought suddenly struck her. "Did she have a car?"

"Naw, she came to town on the bus. But I let her use my car in the afternoons and evenings while I was at work. She was always back with it by the time I got off work, and she put some gas in it."

"Did she have your car the night she was murdered?" Jack asked.

"Yeah, and that was what was so strange about it. I usually left there around one in the morning, because I had another job at a garage in town from seven to three. I didn't see her come back, but my car was where it always was, and the keys were in it. I didn't think nothing of it at the time." He stared down at his hands for a long moment. "And then we heard next day about the girl found dead on the football field over at the high school. I didn't want to believe it was her."

"She really made an impression on you," Wanda Nell said, her voice soft.

"Yeah, she did. She was so pretty, and she was young, about my age, nineteen or twenty. I couldn't imagine why someone would want to hurt her." His fingers toyed with his steak knife. "But I reckon she must've stirred up something that somebody didn't want stirred up."

"You're probably right," Jack said. "That's sure what it sounds like."

"What happened to her things?" Rocky asked. "Surely somebody come and took all that? And they would have known who she was. She had a driver's license."

"We don't know," Jack said. "The only accounts we've able to find say that she was unknown. My guess is that whoever killed her destroyed everything she brought with her, to make it harder to trace her."

"I see. I thought it was pretty strange they found her without any clothes on."

"That's why," Wanda Nell said. "But at least we know her name now. You've given her that much."

Rocky smiled sadly. "I hope you can find out who killed her, and if they're still alive, see that they pay for it. She didn't deserve to die like that."

"No, she didn't," Jack said. "And we're going to try our best for her."

"Is there anything else she might have told you?" Wanda Nell asked. "Like where she came from?"

"I saw her driver's license when she registered. She was from Hattiesburg."

"Good, that gives us something else to go on," Jack said, relieved. "Did she happen to say anything about any family there? Her adoptive parents, or anybody?"

"I don't remember her saying much about that, though I did ask her at some point." Rocky frowned, trying to remember. "Seems like she did say something, though. Now what was it?"

Wanda Nell and Jack waited in silence while Rocky tried to recall what Jenna Rae Howell had said to him. With her name and the fact that she came from Hattiesburg, they now had some solid leads to follow up. But if there was something more, they'd be happy to hear it.

"I was asking her how long she was going to stay in Tullahoma," Rocky said. "And she said 'maybe forever.' And then I asked her if she wasn't ever going back to Hattiesburg. She shook her head. She said 'never,' and then she said something kinda strange, or at least it sure sounded that way at the time." He paused again. "I think what she said was, 'I'm sick of the stink of death.' Or something like that. I never did get to ask her what she meant by that."

"We'll have to think about that one," Wanda Nell said. "That is kind of a strange thing to say."

By now they had finished their food, and Rocky glanced at his watch. "I gotta be getting back to work." His tone was apologetic.

"Of course," Jack said. "I can't tell you how much we appreciate you talking to us this way. I promise you we'll do our best to find out who killed her, and why."

"You know, it was kinda good to talk about it to somebody, after all these years. I ain't told anybody, not even my wife."

"You're married?" Wanda Nell asked. "You mentioned your daughter."

"My wife died about five years ago. She had cancer. It's just me and Judy now. She's fourteen."

Jack signaled the waiter to bring their check, and he refused to accept any money from Rocky for his share of the meal. "We invited you to lunch, so it's on us."

"Thank you, then," Rocky said.

On the brief drive back to the car dealership, Rocky asked them how his sister was doing. Wanda Nell didn't want to lie to him, but she really hated having to tell him the truth. After a deep breath, she said, "We don't think she's doing real well, to be honest. We think the man she's married to isn't treating her right. She seems pretty out of it most of the time. And he keeps an eye on everything she does."

Rocky absorbed this in silence. "Is he hitting her?"

"We're not sure," Wanda Nell said. "We couldn't see any signs of it, the two times we saw her. But he's trying every way he can to control her."

"That just don't sound like her. But I ain't seen her in thirty years, so what do I know? She's only sent me a few letters, and she never said nothing about any of that." He shook his head. "I need to do something about it. She shouldn't have to live like that."

"We'll be glad to help you," Wanda Nell said, and Jack echoed her.

"Thank you, I sure do appreciate that. You're good folks." They had reached the dealership, and Rocky opened his door to get out. He closed the door and stood by the driver's side window. Jack rolled down the window, and Rocky stuck his hand in. They shook.

"We'll be in touch," Jack said. "We'll let you know as soon as we find out anything."

"Thank you." Rocky pulled a business card from his pocket. "You can call me here if you need to. Just tell 'em you're calling from my daughter's school, and they won't make a fuss."

"We will," Jack said. "You take care."

Rocky turned and walked off.

Jack and Wanda Nell sat there for a moment. They glanced at each other.

"I don't think he killed her," Wanda Nell said.

Jack sighed. "I don't, either, though I'm only going on my instincts when I say it. I like him. He seems like a good man, despite all he's been through."

"I know," Wanda Nell said. "He didn't even sound bitter about any of it. He just got on with his life the best way he could, as far as I can tell."

Jack headed the car out of the parking lot and back toward home.

"So, are we going to Hattiesburg now?" Wanda Nell asked.

"Tomorrow," Jack said. "Let's go home first, and tomorrow we'll drive down there. You think you can talk Melvin into another day or two off? We might have to spend the night down there."

"We'll see. Maybe Ruby won't mind filling in for me at lunch, and Gladys is still working the evening shift. Betsy or Patsy might be willing to put in an extra shift."

"Good," Jack said. "I don't want to go without you."

Wanda Nell smiled and settled back in her seat for the drive home.

Sixteen

They reached Tullahoma in plenty of time for Wanda Nell to work her shift at the Kountry Kitchen. Jack dropped her off, and Wanda Nell promised to talk to Melvin right away about the time off. "If he says I can't, I'll tell him I'll work some extra Saturday nights. Okay?"

Jack grimaced. "I guess it's for a good cause, but I hate you not being home on Saturday night."

Wanda Nell kissed him again. "I hate it, too, but we'll see."

Inside the restaurant things were pretty quiet before the evening crowd started drifting in. Monday nights weren't usually too busy, but they were busy enough. Wanda Nell took advantage of the lull to talk to Melvin.

During the drive back from Memphis, she and Jack had discussed how much they should tell Melvin about what they were doing. "He's a good man," Wanda Nell said. "And I think if we tell him the whole story, he'll be willing to help by letting me take the time off. Plus, it's early in the week. The evenings aren't as busy, and he'll have enough help at lunchtime."

"I guess you ought to tell him," Jack said. "I just don't

want what we're doing to get to be general knowledge. We're going to be stirring up something pretty nasty, and the more we can find out before the you-know-what hits the fan, the better."

"Melvin won't talk to anybody about it. We can trust him."

"I know. I guess I'm just being a little paranoid."

Melvin was at the register, talking to a customer, when Wanda Nell entered the restaurant. She waited until the customer was on his way out the door before saying, "Can I talk to you a minute? Back in your office?"

Melvin's eyes narrowed. "I'm not sure I like the sound of that. Sounds like you're going to ask me for some more time off, or some other favor. I know that tone."

Wanda Nell gave him a sweet smile. "Come on back, and I'll tell you."

Melvin rolled his eyes, but he followed her. "Let's stop here," he said when they reached the back door. "I need a smoke break." He opened the door and stepped outside.

"Okay." Wanda Nell watched as he lit a cigarette, and she sniffed the air appreciatively, watching the smoke drift into the hot evening air. She had quit smoking when Miranda was pregnant with Lavon, and she still missed it sometimes.

"So what's going on?" Melvin asked. "Do you want some more time off?"

"Yes, but it's for a real good reason." Wanda Nell launched into an explanation, and Melvin listened without interruption. By the time she finished, he had smoked two more cigarettes. He flicked the butt of the last one toward the Dumpster; where it hit the side and bounced onto the pavement below.

"That poor kid," Melvin said. "I remember it now. I guess if you think you can find out who killed her, you ought to go ahead with this." He shook his head. "But you might be stirring up something mighty nasty. Have y'all thought about that?"

Wanda Nell nodded. "Of course. That's why Jack wants to keep this as quiet as we can until we have something pretty concrete. And since Elmer Lee knows about it, well, he's there if we need him."

"That's good," Melvin said. He ushered her back inside and shut the door. "I guess you can take the next couple of days off, then."

"But not with pay. You were real sweet to pay me while I was on my honeymoon, but I don't expect it now."

"Good. Business is slower in the evenings right now. I guess it's just too hot for folks to get out."

"I know how they feel." Wanda Nell was looking forward to a glass of water after standing outside. "I'll let you know how it goes when we get back from Hattiesburg."

By the time the Kountry Kitchen closed at ten, Wanda Nell had earned some decent tips, but Melvin was right. People just weren't coming out to eat in the evenings. Or at least, not to the Kountry Kitchen. Her car was still warm inside when she left the restaurant.

She drove home with the windows down, and when she pulled her car into the driveway behind Jack's, she glanced over at Mayrene's trailer. The lights were out, and there was no sign of Dixon Vance's pickup. She wondered how things were going with her best friend, and resolved to call her tomorrow before they left for Hattiesburg.

Jack met her at the door with a kiss. "I sure do like coming home," Wanda Nell said, smiling, as he released her. "It makes going to work even better, knowing I'm coming home to you."

Jack grinned. "Glad to be of service, ma'am."

"Is Juliet home?"

"Yeah, I picked her up. I think she's probably still up, reading, if you want to say good night to her."

"I'll do that. And then we'll talk about tomorrow. Melvin's letting me take the time off."

"Good."

She walked down the hallway toward Juliet's bedroom. The door was slightly ajar, and there was a glow from the bedside lamp. Wanda Nell knocked on the door.

"Come in, Mama," Juliet called. Laying aside her book, she sat up on the bed as her mother came into the room.

Wanda Nell sat down on the bed, glancing over at the book her daughter was reading. "I've never heard of Georgette Heyer," she said, reading the author's name and the title, *The Grand Sophy*.

"She's wonderful, Mama." Juliet's eyes were alight with enthusiasm. "They're historical novels, and I really love them. You'll have to read her."

"I'll give her a try," Wanda Nell promised. "Now, did Jack tell you we're going to Hattiesburg tomorrow?"

Juliet nodded. "He told me what y'all found out in Memphis. I'm so glad you found out what her name is. I kept thinking about her, and how awful it was that we didn't even know who she was."

"I'm glad, too, baby," Wanda Nell said. "And I'm so glad you understand what we're doing, and why."

"It's important." Juliet's face clouded. "What I don't understand, though, is why somebody didn't come looking for her. Do you think she didn't have any family, Mama? Like maybe her adoptive parents were dead, or something?"

"That's possible. It bothers me, too. Maybe we'll be able to find out more about that in Hattiesburg tomorrow. Now, what are we going to do with you tomorrow? And the next day, if we end up staying overnight?"

Smiling, Juliet said, "Jack and I already worked that out. I called Belle, and she and Grandmama said I could stay with them."

"Are you sure that's okay, baby?" Wanda Nell frowned. "There can't be much for you to do over there."

"It's okay, Mama," Juliet said, placing a hand on her mother's arm. "I really don't mind. Belle and Grandmama like having me there, and I can go up to my room and read whenever I want to."

Juliet loved to read. Wanda Nell sometimes worried that she spent more time reading than doing anything else, like hanging out with friends her own age. Her youngest child had always been shy, though, and she hadn't really pushed her into being more sociable. She didn't know if that had been a mistake, but Juliet seemed happy enough with a couple of friends and spending a lot of time reading, or sitting at the computer.

"Then I guess it's all right." Wanda Nell kissed her daughter's forehead. "Now, you turn out that light soon, and get to sleep, okay? I don't want you hurting your eyes by reading till all hours of the night."

Juliet smiled, but she didn't promise she wouldn't. Wanda Nell paused at the doorway, looking back. Juliet was already absorbed in her book. Suppressing a sigh, Wanda Nell pulled the door nearly closed.

Jack was in their bedroom, already in bed. He put aside a book when Wanda Nell entered. "Everything okay, love?"

Wanda Nell nodded. "Juliet said y'all have already talked about her going over to Miz Culpepper's while we're gone."

"It was her idea. I really do think she likes spending time over there." He watched as Wanda Nell began to undress.

"Thank goodness," Wanda Nell said. "But I do worry about her spending so much time with adults, instead of with kids her own age." She put aside her blouse and jeans and, barefoot, padded into the bathroom.

Now clad in her nightgown, she returned to the bedroom. "Don't worry so much about her," Jack said. "She's a very bright girl, and reading makes her happy. It wouldn't surprise me one bit if she turned out to be a writer. She spends a lot of time in her head, and that's not such a bad place to be."

"I hope you're right." Wanda Nell slid into bed beside him. "What about tomorrow? What time to do you want to leave?"

Jack reached over and turned off the bedside lamp. "We can talk about that in the morning." He moved closer and kissed her.

Wanda Nell didn't argue.

The next morning, Jack went over to the high school to run. While he was gone, Wanda Nell did a bit of laundry and packed a few things for them, in case they did stay the night in Hattiesburg. She tried calling Mayrene, hoping for a chat to see how her friend was doing, but Mayrene had already left for work. Since she didn't want to bother her friend at the beauty parlor, Wanda Nell decided she would try calling her at home that night.

Finally they were ready to set out for Hattiesburg a little after ten. After a quick detour to drop Juliet off at Mrs. Culpepper's house, Jack headed for the highway, turning south.

"We ought to hit Jackson around lunchtime," Jack said. "Shall we stop and get something to eat there?"

"How far is it to Hattiesburg?" Wanda Nell asked.

"A couple hundred miles. About a four-hour drive, depending on how many times we stop along the way."

"Let's see how hungry we are when we get to Jackson," Wanda Nell said. "We had a pretty big breakfast."

"That's true." Jack grinned. "I'm really spoiled now. I used to have just some cereal and a piece of fruit. I hardly ever cooked eggs and bacon for myself."

"I probably shouldn't be cooking them for you every morning," Wanda Nell said in a slightly rueful tone. "I don't want to make you have a heart attack."

"Maybe we can compromise. As much as I'd love to have that every morning, you're right." He sighed. "Aging is no fun, but I guess the alternative is worse."

"Then we're going to start having cold cereal or oatmeal for breakfast during the week. And we can have the bad stuff on the weekends for a treat."

Jack agreed, and conversation lapsed for a while.

"We didn't have much time to talk this morning," Wanda Nell said, turning the volume down on the Reba McEntire CD they had put into the player. "So what are we going to do when we get to Hattiesburg?"

"No, I guess we didn't have much time. Especially last night." Jack flashed a wicked grin at Wanda Nell, and she could feel herself blushing.

Wanda Nell repeated her question, and Jack sobered. "After Juliet and I got home last night," he said, "I spent some time on the computer. I looked up the name Howell in Hattiesburg, and I found about twenty-five of them."

"Did you call any of them?" Wanda Nell asked, her heart sinking. Twenty-five of them was a lot, and it might take a long time to track them all down.

"No. I made a list of them, and their phone numbers and addresses. But then I had another idea. You remember what Rocky told us about the strange remark Jenna Rae made about going back to Hattiesburg?"

Wanda Nell thought back to yesterday's conversation. "Yeah. Something about how she was tired of the stink of death."

"Yes. And what do you think she meant by that?"

"I can think of two things right away. One of them's a funeral parlor, and the other's a slaughterhouse." She shivered suddenly. "I sure wouldn't want to work in either one, and I can imagine they both have a stink of death about them."

"Exactly," Jack said in a tone of grim satisfaction. "Those are the same two things that occurred to me. So I looked through businesses in Hattiesburg and the surrounding area. Guess what I found?"

"What?"

"There's a funeral home named Duckworth–Howell. I figure we ought to start there."

"Good thinking. Did you find out anything more about the place? Like who owns it?"

"Yeah, I found quite a few items about it on the Internet. It must be a very successful business, because I got lots of hits through obituaries."

"Was that all?"

"No. There were some articles about their support of various charities, among a few other pieces. They mentioned a Jackson Howell a number of times, and I figured he's as good a candidate as any for being Jenna Rae's adoptive father."

"So we're going straight to the funeral home when we get to Hattiesburg?"

"Might as well. And if we're lucky, we find her family right away. If not, we keep trying. Surely there's still someone in town named Howell who was connected to her."

"Or somebody who will remember her, even after thirty-one years."

"That's what I'm counting on."

They reached Jackson around a quarter to noon, but they decided not to stop for lunch. Neither of them was hungry, and they both felt an urgency to reach Hattiesburg. Wanda Nell confessed as much, and Jack agreed.

"I know how you feel," he said. "I'm so curious, and nervous, too, I guess. To think we might find someone there who knew her."

They ended up stopping briefly in Mendenhall for a quick bite to eat. Jack spotted a sandwich shop just off Highway 49, and they ordered their food to go.

Something over an hour later they were approaching Hattiesburg. Jack said, "Honey, can you grab my jacket out of the back seat? I stuck the directions in my pocket, and I forgot to get them out when we stopped for lunch."

Wanda Nell twisted around in her seat and reached back for the jacket. She felt in the pocket and pulled out the folded papers.

Facing forward again, she opened the papers and scanned them. The top page had a map of their route from Tullahoma to Hattiesburg, with directions right to the funeral home.

"You got all this off the Internet?" Wanda Nell asked.

"I know, pretty amazing, isn't it?" Jack smiled. "Will you read the directions out to me?"

Wanda Nell did as he asked, and she helped him look for the appropriate turns and street signs. In another fifteen minutes they pulled up in front of Duckworth–Howell Funeral Home. Jack parked the car in front of an impressive, old three-story house with a broad porch across the front and along one side.

"I wonder if anybody lives there," Wanda Nell said. "As big as that place is, it looks like somebody could."

They sat staring at the house for a moment longer. "Guess we might as well go in," Jack said. "Come on."

He got out of the car, went around to Wanda Nell's door, and held it open while she stepped onto the sidewalk. He tucked her hand around his arm as they headed up the walk to the porch, up the steps to the front door. Jack pulled open the screen door and twisted the knob on the main door. Wanda Nell pushed it open, and they stepped inside the funeral home.

The air inside was chilly, and there was a pervasive smell of flowers. Wanda Nell wasn't very fond of funeral homes. They brought back the sad memories of her parents' deaths, and that of her ex-husband, Bobby Ray.

She and Jack glanced around the foyer. Ahead of them a grand staircase led to the second floor. On either side were doors with signs over them, and just ahead of them, near the stairs, stood a lectern with a book on it. Jack stepped forward to glance at it, and as he did, one of the doors to their right opened. A man in a dark suit walked toward them.

"Good afternoon," he said, his voice quiet. "I'm Delbert Duckworth. How can I help you? Are you here for the Ferris viewing?" He extended his hand to Jack.

Jack shook the proffered hand. "No, we're not. Actually, we were hoping to talk to Mr. Howell. It's a personal matter."

Duckworth frowned. "I'm afraid that's going to be rather difficult," he said. "Mr. Howell is in Chicago on business at the moment, and he won't be back until sometime next week."

Seventeen

Wanda Nell and Jack exchanged glances of dismay.

Seeing the expressions on their faces, Mr. Duckworth said, "I'm surely sorry he's not here. Are you sure it's not something I can help you with?"

Wanda Nell turned her head to look at him again. She judged him to be in his mid-to-late fifties. He surely ought to be able to remember someone from three decades ago. She left it to Jack to decide, though.

"You might be able to," Jack said. "Would you mind if I asked you how long you've been here?"

Duckworth smiled. "Not at all. This is a family business. Or I guess I should say, a two-family business. My father owned it, and his father before him. Same thing on the Howell side. The first two owners were brothers-in-law, way back when."

"So you've been part of it all your life," Wanda Nell said.

"Yes, ma'am, I surely have. Started working here as a teenager, and I don't want to tell you how long ago that was." He laughed. "Probably before you were even born, ma'am."

Wanda Nell smiled. "Thank you." She glanced at Jack.

He grimaced slightly but turned a bland face to Duckworth. "Sounds like you ought to be able to help us, then. We're looking for the family of a young woman from Hattiesburg, who left here about thirty-one years ago."

Duckworth frowned. "Sorry, but I'm not sure I follow you. How is she connected with Mr. Howell?"

"We're not entirely sure she is," Jack said. "But her name was Jenna Rae Howell." He watched the man's face for any sign of recognition. There didn't seem to be any.

"My partner, Mr. Howell, doesn't have any children," he said, still frowning. "In fact, he's never married. You've got the wrong Howell."

"Yes, I can see that," Jack said, the disappointment obvious in his voice.

Duckworth thought a moment, his brow wrinkled. Then his face cleared. "But I know who you need to talk to. The man you want to talk to is my partner's uncle, Mr. Parnell Howell."

"Did he have a daughter?" Wanda Nell asked.

"Yes, ma'am, he did. And as I recall, her name was Jenna Rae. She was a very pretty girl. She used to come with her daddy here to the parlor and help him." He shook his head. "I haven't thought about her in a long, long time. I'd pretty much forgotten her until you mentioned her."

"What did Mr. Howell do here?" Wanda Nell asked. For Jenna Rae's sake, she hoped he wasn't a mortician.

"He was our janitor until he retired, about seven years ago." Duckworth had an odd look on his face. "Once upon a time, he was one of the partners in the business. I shouldn't be telling you this, but his brother, my partner's father, had to buy him out. They kept him on, though. He couldn't hold down a job anywhere else." He mimed lifting a glass repeatedly to his mouth, and Wanda Nell and Jack nodded to show they understood.

"Do you know where we can find him?" Jack asked. "We surely would like to talk to him about his daughter."

"We have his address on file. He still gets a pension from us. If you'll wait just a moment, I'll get you that information."

"We're getting closer," Wanda Nell said, her voice low. "Let's just hope he's in decent enough shape to talk to us. It doesn't sound like he ever got over his drinking problem."

Duckworth came back, holding an index card. He proffered it to Jack and gave them directions on how to find the place.

When Jack thanked him, he said, "You're welcome. I reckon Mr. Howell will be glad to have some news of his daughter. I hope she's doing fine."

When neither Jack nor Wanda Nell responded to that, he went on, "Now that I've thought about it, I remember her running off. It was right after her mama died, and I guess she didn't want to stay with her daddy." He shook his head. "Can't say that I blamed her for that."

"So her mother died before Jenna Rae left town?" Jack said.

"Yes. I don't remember the exact timing now, it's been so long ago. Must be thirty years or more." He shook his head. "Where does the time go? Anyway, it wasn't too long after Miz Howell passed away that the girl just up and ran off."

"We sure do appreciate your help, Mr. Duckworth," Jack said. He offered his hand.

Duckworth shook it. "You're mighty welcome, and if there's anything I can ever do for you, just give us a call." He pulled a card from his inside jacket pocket and handed it to Jack.

"Thank you," Wanda Nell said, smiling. "We sure will." Jack held the door open, and she walked outside. For a mo-

ment she welcomed the heat. The air inside the funeral
home had chilled her.

Jack tucked Duckworth's business card into his pocket.
"You never know," he said. "I might need to talk to him
again at some point." He laughed. "But I bet you he sells a
lot of really expensive caskets."

"I'm sure he does," Wanda Nell said.

Inside the car, the air conditioning blasting, Jack repeated
the directions Duckworth had given them. When he was
satisfied he had them down, he put the car in gear and drove
off.

Duckworth's directions proved to be accurate, and they
found the street about twenty minutes later. The neighborhood was shabby, the houses rundown, and many of the
lawns brown with neglect. Jack pulled the car in front of
the house that matched the number the funeral director had
given them. He put the car in Park but left the engine running.

He and Wanda Nell gazed at the house. It was a small,
one-story frame house. The front porch sagged, and the
paint was almost gone, the boards weathered to a dull gray.
There were no flower beds and only two old trees, neither
of which appeared very healthy. There was an air of neglect about the place, a lack of care that had existed for a
very long time.

"How awful," Wanda Nell said. "I hope it wasn't this
way when Jenna Rae lived here."

"If it was, it's no wonder she ran off when her mother
died." Jack shut the car off and opened his door. "We
shouldn't put this off any longer." He got out and shut his
door.

Wanda Nell opened her door and stepped out before
Jack reached her. She took his arm as they made their way
along the broken walk to the dilapidated porch.

"Watch your step, honey," Jack said, navigating the rot-

ting steps with care. "It's a wonder somebody hasn't broken a leg, or worse, on these things."

Gingerly Wanda Nell followed her husband up the steps.
The porch was little better, but at least the area in front of the
door appeared stable. Jack rapped on the door and waited.

When there was no response after about thirty seconds,
he rapped again, harder this time.

He was just about to knock again when they could hear
the sounds of shuffling feet approaching the door. Jack
stepped back a pace.

The door swung open, and Wanda Nell had to stifle a
gasp of shock at the sight of the man standing before them.
What little hair he had left stood out at odd angles from his
scalp, and didn't look very clean. His clothes had obviously
been slept in for more than a few days, and the odor emanating from him made Wanda Nell's eyes water. It was all
she could do not to clap a hand over her nose and mouth.
She stole a glance at Jack and could see that he was simi-
larly affected.

"Mr. Howell?" Jack asked, his voice strained.

Bleary eyes regarded them. Wanda Nell thought he was
over eighty, but years of drinking had taken such a toll on
him, he might be more than a decade younger.

The man continued to stare at them.

"Mr. Howell," Jack said, raising his voice slightly, "we'd
like to talk to you."

"Ain't got no money to buy anything," Howell replied,
his voice rusty, as if from disuse. He shuffled back a couple
of steps and started to close the door. "Get the hell off my
porch."

Jack stuck his foot in the door, and Wanda Nell was glad
he was wearing his boots. Howell shoved the door hard.

Jack winced, but he didn't move his foot. "We're not
trying to sell you anything, Mr. Howell. We want to talk to
you about something else, something personal."

Howell paused, his hand still on the door. Trying to focus on them again, he said, "This ain't about my food stamps again, is it? I done tole y'all I ain't using 'em to buy anything to drink." His voice had taken on an unpleasant whine.

"No, it's not about your food stamps," Jack said. "It's not about anything to do with them, I promise you."

"Then what the hell is it?" Howell's anger gave his voice strength. "I ain't got time to stand here in the dad-blamed door all day."

"We came to talk to you about Jenna Rae," Wanda Nell said.

Howell regarded them in stony silence for a moment. "Who the hell is she?"

Wanda Nell wasn't taken in. She had seen the flash of recognition in those bloodshot eyes. "Your daughter, Jenna Rae," she said, her voice kind but firm. "We want to talk to you about her."

"Ain't got nothing to say." Howell tried once again to shut the door, but Jack held firm, and Howell gave up after a moment.

"It's important," Jack said. "We don't want to bother you, Mr. Howell. But this is something very important. May we come in and talk to you?"

Without a word, Howell turned and walked away, his feet in worn slippers rubbing against the floor. Jack shrugged and held the door for Wanda Nell.

Not sure she really wanted to go inside this particular house, Wanda Nell hesitated for a moment.

"I know," Jack said. "It's going to be awful. But we've got to talk to him."

"I know." Wanda Nell stepped inside, and the smell took her breath away for a moment. Then, trying to breathe shallowly through her mouth, she followed in the direction Howell had taken. Jack came behind her.

The house was hot, the air stifling and laden with un-pleasant smells. Wanda Nell did her best not to identify them, but she knew one of them was stale urine. They found Howell sitting in an old recliner, his feet up, sipping from a beer can. Nearby stood an old box fan, whirring gently, providing a slight breeze.

Wanda Nell figured they were in the living room, but it looked more like a garbage dump. There were piles of news-papers, many of them yellowed with age, all over the room. Beer cans littered the floor, and Wanda Nell didn't even want to acknowledge the bugs she saw scuttling out of their way. She followed Jack to a ratty old sofa. He pushed some of the piles of paper out of the way, leaving a few for them to sit on.

Wanda Nell sat down, taking care to keep the newspaper under her. It might be dusty and smelly, but she figured it was better to have that against her clothes than whatever was on the fabric of the couch.

Howell continued to drink his beer as if they weren't in the room with him.

"Mr. Howell," Jack said, "we really need to talk to you about your daughter. Can you hear me?" He raised his voice.

Howell grunted. He didn't look at them.

"When Jenna Rae ran off," Jack said, "she ended up in a place called Tullahoma, up north of here, in Tullahoma County. Do you know where that is?" He waited a moment for a response, but Howell continued to ignore him.

Wanda Nell could tell her husband was getting exasper-ated, but to his credit, he didn't make it obvious. "Jenna Rae came to Tullahoma, and she was there for about three days." Jack paused. "We know she was adopted, Mr. How-ell. And someone who knew her in Tullahoma told us she came there to find her biological father."

"Damn ungrateful little bitch." Howell crumpled his beer can and dropped it on the floor. It made a metallic sound as it landed on other beer cans.

"You didn't want her going up there?" Wanda Nell asked. Maybe he would respond better to her. It was worth a try. Jack nodded at her. "Did she know who her biological father was?"

"Told her to leave well enough alone," Howell said. "But I wasn't good enough for her. The minute her mama was dead, she was ready to take off. Damn ungrateful little bitch." He muttered that last phrase several times until his voice faded away.

The venom of his words shocked Wanda Nell. How could he talk about his daughter that way? Had Jenna Rae hurt him that badly?

"Where did you adopt her, Mr. Howell?" Jack asked, when Wanda Nell failed to continue. "Was it in Tullahoma?"

"Never been there," Howell said, a shifty look in his eyes. "Don't remember where we got her. Wish I'd never married her mother, and I wouldn't have got stuck with that brat."

"Was your wife Jenna Rae's biological mother?" Wanda Nell asked, struck by his words and their possible meaning.

"Naw." Howell looked away from them.

Wanda Nell thought he was lying, both about never having been in Tullahoma and about his wife being Jenna Rae's biological mother.

"What was your wife's name?" Jack asked.

Howell didn't say anything. Jack asked again, but when Howell still didn't respond, he gave up on that question for the moment.

Wanda Nell could feel the sweat building all over her body. The room was stifling, and the fan couldn't do enough to alleviate that. She desperately wanted some water, but she would be afraid to drink anything in this house.

She moistened her lips, and after another glance at Jack, she spoke to Howell again. "I'm afraid we have some bad news for you, Mr. Howell."

Howell grunted again.

"Jenna Rae died, Mr. Howell. After she was in Tulla-homa for only three days, she was murdered." Wanda Nell winced inwardly at her own words, but there didn't seem to be any other way to get through to this man.

Either Howell already knew Jenna Rae was dead, Wanda Nell concluded from his lack of reaction, or else he was so far gone in drink he didn't understand her.

"Served the little bitch right. Should have left well enough alone."

"How can you say such a thing?" Wanda Nell was so horrified by the man's words, she spoke before she thought.

"What the hell do you care? Why're you asking me all these questions? It don't matter anymore."

"It does matter, Mr. Howell," Jack said. "It matters, be-cause no one ever figured out who killed Jenna Rae. In fact, someone did everything possible to cover it up, blaming an innocent young man for the crime. They even took away her name. They weren't able to identify her, or so they claimed."

Wanda Nell watched Howell closely for a reaction while Jack spoke. She could tell that he took in what Jack was saying, because he stirred in his chair. Something Jack had said had gotten through to him.

"Are you sure there isn't anything you want to tell us?" Wanda Nell asked.

"Naw," Howell said. "Go away, and leave me alone." Slowly he got out of his chair and started shuffling away. "I want some more beer."

Wanda Nell and Jack watched him go.

"What do we do now?" Wanda Nell asked.

"I think we should go away and come back tomorrow," Jack said with a sigh. "If we give him some time to think about it all, maybe in the morning we can get him to talk more freely."

"I guess it's worth a shot," Wanda Nell said. She stood. "Come on, then, let's get out of here. I want to go somewhere and take a long bath."

Jack stood beside her. "I'm with you on that."

They made their way to the front door. Stepping outside, they both breathed deeply. As they made their way with care down the walk, Wanda Nell glanced at the house next door. She spotted the face of an elderly woman peering out a window, regarding them with frank curiosity.

On a hunch, when she and Jack reached the street, instead of following Jack to the car, she turned to approach the old woman's house.

"Where are you going?" Jack asked.

"Following my instincts. I think we might be able to find out something from Mr. Howell's neighbor." She headed up the walk, and Jack came along behind her, muttering under his breath.

Eighteen

Before Wanda Nell could knock on the front door, it opened, and a small woman of about seventy-five stood there with a beaming smile. "What on earth are two nice young people like you doing over there, talking to that nasty man?" she said, her voice light and high as a child's. "Somebody needs to take him away and put him in a home. You didn't come to do that, did you?"

Wanda Nell smiled at her. "No, ma'am, we didn't. We came to talk to him about something important, though."

The little woman's gaze was shrewd and sad. "But he didn't talk much, did he? I'm surprised he could even open the door." She shook her head. "Now what am I doing, just standing here chattering away like I don't have any manners at all? Y'all just come on in. You're probably dying for something to drink, aren't you?"

"Thank you, ma'am," Wanda Nell said, stepping through the door, Jack right behind her. "Actually, we would appreciate some water, if that wouldn't be too much trouble. It sure is hot out there today, and that house next door is like a steam bath."

Their hostess beamed at them. "My goodness, you two

are tall, but what a lovely couple you are." She assessed them for a moment. "Newlyweds, aren't you?"

Startled, Jack and Wanda Nell glanced at each other. "Yes, ma'am, we are," Jack said with a smile. "How could you tell?"

"Just something about you," their hostess said smugly. "Now y'all come on into the parlor and sit yourselves down. I'll be right back with some water. Are you sure that's all you want?"

"That will be fine, thank you," Jack said.

Their hostess disappeared down the hall, and Wanda Nell and Jack walked through the doorway she had indicated. They found themselves in a room completely unlike what they had seen next door. The furniture, the curtains, and the rugs had all obviously seen better days, but the air of genteel shabbiness only added to the charm. The air was blessedly clean and fresh-smelling—and above all, cool. A window unit purred, emitting blasts of chilled air. Wanda Nell and Jack sat on a sofa near a small wingback chair that appeared to be just the right size for their diminutive hostess.

Soon she came bustling back with a pitcher of ice water and three glasses on a tray. She set the tray on the coffee table in front of the sofa and began to pour. After handing her guests their glasses, she poured one for herself before sitting down in her chair. Bright eyes regarded Wanda Nell and Jack over the rim of the glass. Suddenly, she laughed, a light, silvery sound. "My goodness, my manners are all mixed up today. I forgot to introduce myself."

"We haven't introduced ourselves either," Wanda Nell said. It was impossible not to smile. "I'm Wanda Nell Pemberton, and this is my husband, Jack."

"It's a pleasure to meet you, Wanda Nell, Jack. I'm Lyda Fehrenbach. *Miss* Lyda Fehrenbach." She beamed at them. "There was no man ever lucky enough to choose me for his bride, though in my day I surely had my chances."

Jack chuckled. "I'll bet you were a firecracker, Miss Fehrenbach." He paused. "And you still are."

Miss Fehrenbach laughed. "Young man, Wanda Nell had better watch out, or I might not let you leave."

"I'm not done with him just yet," Wanda Nell said. "You'll have to be mighty careful yourself." She grinned at Miss Fehrenbach.

Their impish hostess winked at her. "I will be." She laughed again. "Now, let's get serious here. You said you had something to talk about with Mr. Howell. I've lived in this house all my life, all eighty-eight years of it."

Seeing the startled looks on the faces of her guests, Miss Fehrenbach smiled. "You thought I was younger than that, didn't you?"

"We certainly did," Jack said. "I thought you might be seventy, tops."

"He is a charmer," Miss Fehrenbach said. "I can't take any credit myself. Just good genes. My mother lived to be ninety-nine, and she didn't look a day over eighty. She lived here with me until her death ten years ago."

"My goodness," Wanda Nell said. "Those are some mighty good genes."

"Thank you. Back to Mr. Howell. May I be so impertinent as to ask why you came to see him? He hasn't had any visitors in years, except his nephew." The tone of her voice indicated what she thought of the nephew. "If he really cared about his uncle, he would have him out of that cesspit and in some nice place where he could be looked after."

"Since you've always lived here," Wanda Nell said, "you must have known Mr. Howell and his wife and daughter."

"Oh, my, yes. Margaret was a very sweet woman, but she didn't have the gumption to take a rolling pin to the side of that man's head the way she should have. I can't tell you how many times I advised her to do just that. He really is a coward, you know, and if she had simply been firm with him, he wouldn't have wasted so much of his life drunk."

"That is too bad," Jack said. "Did Miz Howell talk much to you about personal things?"

"Some. The poor girl needed a shoulder to cry on, and I was very glad I could do that for her. In many ways, she was such a sad girl."

"You say 'girl,'" Wanda Nell said. "Do you mean she was a lot younger than her husband?"

"Oh, my, yes." Miss Fehrenbach took a sip of her water. She thought for a moment before continuing. "Margaret would only be in her late sixties now, probably sixty-seven."

"She was a young mother, then," Jack said. "And of course you knew their daughter, Jenna Rae."

Miss Fehrenbach's face grew sad. "Yes, she was such a beautiful child, and such a sweet disposition, despite her terrible father. She grew up to be a beautiful girl. I can't really say as I blame her for running off the way she did, though I sure wish she had kept in touch with me." She sighed. "I was her history teacher in high school, and she was a bright girl. I had such hopes for her."

Wanda Nell and Jack exchanged uneasy glances.

"Go ahead and tell me," Miss Fehrenbach said. "Not much shocks me these days."

"I hate to have to tell you this," Wanda Nell said. "Jenna Rae is dead."

"How did it happen?" Miss Fehrenbach asked after a moment.

"She was murdered, probably not long after she left here," Jack told her. "The case was never solved, and Wanda Nell and I are trying to solve it. We think she deserves that much."

Miss Fehrenbach wiped away a few tears. "Excuse me a moment. I'll be right back."

Wanda Nell and Jack sat and finished their water. "I

hope she's okay," Wanda Nell said in an undertone. "I don't care what she said about nothing shocking her. That obviously upset her."

"We'll see when she comes back," Jack said. "She sure is a game little thing, isn't she?"

Wanda Nell nodded. "I hate it that we had to give her such awful news."

Miss Fehrenbach came back shortly after that, carrying a framed picture. She handed it to Wanda Nell and Jack before she resumed her seat.

Wanda Nell held the portrait while she and Jack examined it. It looked like a senior portrait, the kind found in high school yearbooks, and its subject was a beautiful young woman. Her shoulder-length wavy blond hair shone, and her blue eyes sparkled with intelligence and determination. The angle of her head in the photograph showed off her elegantly shaped nose and high cheekbones to perfection. Wanda Nell's heart contracted. This was Jenna Rae Howell.

She handed the portrait to Jack and picked up her purse, looking through it for a tissue. She found one, wiped her eyes, and looked at their hostess. She saw the same sadness in Miss Fehrenbach's face. "Such a waste," Miss Fehrenbach said. "Such a lovely girl. She didn't deserve what happened."

"No, she didn't." Jack's voice was gruff. He set the portrait on the coffee table. Clearing his throat, he continued, "I think you can understand why we're doing what we're doing, Miss Fehrenbach."

"I certainly can," their hostess replied. "I'm glad someone is doing it. Now, tell me what happened."

Jack gave her a summary of what they knew about the case. He concluded by saying, "We know why she came to Tullahoma. We just don't know exactly who she was looking for."

"If we could figure that out, I think we'd be a lot closer to knowing who killed her," Wanda Nell said. "Did Jenna Rae's mama ever talk to you about Tullahoma?"

"Not precisely," Miss Fehrenbach replied. "She was reticent about some things, and all she ever told me was that she came from the northern part of the state. I don't believe I ever heard her mention Tullahoma."

"What about Mr. Howell?" Jack asked. "According to him, he's never been there."

"I'm sure it will come as no surprise to you that he's lying about that," Miss Fehrenbach said, a touch of asperity in her voice. "He must have been there, because when he came back to Hattiesburg, he brought Margaret and the baby with him."

"So he hasn't always lived here?" Jack asked.

"No, he was gone for a number of years. First in Vietnam, and that might explain a lot about the drinking." She sighed. "After the war he didn't come home for several years, but when he did, as I said, he had Margaret and the baby with him. That's when his brother gave him a job at the funeral parlor."

"If Miz Howell didn't talk about where she really came from, did she say what she did before she moved down here?" Wanda Nell asked.

"She worked as a maid for somebody. She did that here, too, when Jenna Rae was old enough to go to school. She cleaned for several families here in Hattiesburg. I could give you some of the names, if you need them."

"We might," Jack said. "Thank you."

"Did she tell you what her name was before she married?" Wanda Nell asked.

"No, I don't believe she ever did," Miss Fehrenbach said after a few moments' thought. "Now that I come to think of it, I don't believe Margaret ever really talked about her family at all. I assumed it was because she either didn't have any to speak of, or they were so awful she was glad to be away from them." She shook her head. "Whatever it was, it must have been pretty bad for her to take up with a man like Howell."

"Okay, so we know that she probably worked as a maid for some family in Tullahoma," Jack said. "And when she moved here, she was married, and she and Howell had adopted the baby. It seems to me that the family she worked for probably has some connection to Jenna Rae."

"I would say you're probably right," Miss Fehrenbach said. "But I do have to correct you on one thing."

"What's that?" Wanda Nell asked, slightly puzzled.

"Howell was Jenna Rae's adoptive father, but Margaret was her mother. There's no doubt about that."

Nineteen

"I guess I shouldn't be surprised at that," Wanda Nell said after a moment. "It really makes more sense in a way."

Jack nodded. "It sure does. Did Jenna Rae know that Margaret was really her mother?"

"Margaret had a long talk with her a day or two before she died, and I think that's when she told Jenna Rae a number of things," Miss Fehrenbach said. "I always thought that was mighty strange. When Howell first brought them here, he put out the story that he and Margaret had adopted the baby after they were married. Not that he was all that chatty about it, you understand." She shrugged. "I had no reason, at least not then, not to believe what he said."

"But at some point you began to suspect the truth," Wanda Nell said.

Miss Fehrenbach nodded. "Oh my, yes. By the time Jenna Rae was six or seven, her resemblance to Margaret was undeniable. I asked Margaret about that one day, and she admitted it. I asked her why they had pretended otherwise for so long, and she didn't have a very good answer.

Just something to the effect that Howell wanted it that way. It was an odd situation, for sure."

"Surely Jenna Rae could see the resemblance for herself," Jack said.

"She probably did. She was a bright girl, like I told you before. But if she did, she kept her own counsel about it. She didn't confide in me. I wish she had." She sighed, twisting her hands in her lap. "If only she had, maybe I would know enough to help you now."

Jack and Wanda Nell protested that she had already been of help, but Miss Fehrenbach gave them a sad smile. "Thank you, my dears. But what we all really need to know is who Jenna Rae's biological father was. That seems to be the key to the whole terrible mess."

"Exactly," Jack said. "If we could find out who Margaret worked for in Tullahoma, that would be a start."

"Since Jenna Rae was Margaret's own daughter," Wanda Nell added, "it seems reasonable to think that some married man got her pregnant, then fobbed her off on somebody to get her out of Tullahoma."

Miss Fehrenbach nodded. "I'd say you're right about that. The question is, though, was that married man her employer? Or someone else?"

"Good point," Jack said. He shook his head in irritation. "And the one person who could answer these questions is right next door."

"Do you want to go back over there and tackle him about it?" Wanda Nell asked. "I might have to ask Miss Fehrenbach to lend me a clothespin for my nose, but I'll go with you."

Both Jack and Miss Fehrenbach smiled at Wanda Nell's attempt to lighten the mood.

"That's not such a bad idea," Miss Fehrenbach said. "About going back to talk to him, that is. If you wait much

later in the day, he'll probably be passed out for the night."
She shook her head, a doleful expression on her face.
"Once he's that far gone, not even the Last Trump would
wake him up."

"I suppose it's worth a shot," Jack said. He stood. "You
don't have to come, honey. Why don't you stay here, where
it's cool and pleasant?"

Wanda Nell was torn. She wanted to be there in case
Jack needed her for anything, but she remembered all too
well the horror of the inside of that house. "Then I'll stay
here," she said, with a quick glance at Miss Fehrenbach.
"I'll keep Miss Fehrenbach company, if that's okay with
her."

"Of course, my dear." Miss Fehrenbach beamed at
them. "I don't get that many visitors these days, and you'd
be doing an old woman a service to visit longer."

"Since that's settled," Jack said, "I guess I'll go and get
it over with. Keep your fingers crossed that I can get him to
talk to me again."

He turned to leave the room, insisting that he could see
himself out. Miss Fehrenbach instructed him on how to set
the latch so he could come back in when he was done. Jack
thanked her and departed.

Moments later they could hear him knocking hard on
Howell's door.

"Good luck to him," Miss Howell said. Wanda Nell nodded. "Now tell me, my dear, while Jack is gone, how long
have you two been married?"

With a smile Wanda Nell responded to Miss Fehrenbach's query, telling her a bit more about Jack and herself.
They conversed for several minutes, and Wanda Nell told
her hostess about her children.

"Sounds to me like you've done a lovely job raising
them," Miss Fehrenbach commented. "And since you

didn't mention their father, I guess he must have bowed out of the picture not long after Juliet was born."

Wanda Nell had to laugh at that, and at the tone of censure in her hostess's voice. She told her a little bit about Bobby Ray, and was just about to tell her about his murder when they heard Jack coming up the porch.

When he came into the room, he was scowling. He sat down by Wanda Nell. "That was pretty much a waste of time. He opened the door to me, but he wouldn't answer my questions."

"Oh, dear, I was afraid of that," Miss Fehrenbach said. "That man could outstubborn a dozen mules any day."

"He didn't say anything?" Wanda Nell asked. "What, exactly, did you ask him?"

Jack had a long drink of water before he responded. Setting his glass on the table, he said, "I was very direct with him. I told him we knew he wasn't telling the truth about Tullahoma. He just grunted at me."

"Was that all?" Wanda Nell asked when he failed to continue.

"No. Next I asked him to tell me who his wife had worked for in Tullahoma. That at least got more than a grunt out of him. He asked me why I wanted to know something like that." Jack glanced at Miss Fehrenbach. "But he didn't ask it in words that polite."

"I've lived next to him a long time," Miss Fehrenbach said, her tone dry. "It's been quite educational sometimes, but not in the best way."

"I can imagine." Jack's tone matched hers. "When I told him that knowing who she worked for might help us find out who killed Jenna Rae, he just stared at me. Then he said he couldn't remember, and I should get the hell out of his face."

"I don't believe him," Wanda Nell said. "But maybe all

the years of drinking have affected his memory." She turned to their hostess. "What do you think? You know him a lot better than we do."

Miss Fehrenbach considered the question for a moment. "It's entirely possible that he doesn't remember. Goodness knows, his brain is probably more like a pickled peach than anything else by now." She shook her head. "But he could very well be lying. Since the whole matter of Margaret and the baby is very shady, I'd be willing to bet he does remember. Or certainly could, if he exerted himself a bit."

"What should we do now?" Jack asked. "I don't think it will do any good to go back again this afternoon."

"No, it wouldn't," Miss Fehrenbach said. "I think your best strategy would be to wait and talk to him again in the morning. Around ten. He's usually up and moving around by then, and he hasn't had time to get hard drunk yet."

"Maybe we'll have better luck in the morning, honey," Wanda Nell offered hopefully. "We thought we might have to spend the night here, anyway."

"That's fine with me," Jack said. "But we do need to find somewhere to stay. Miss Fehrenbach, are there any motels or hotels nearby?"

"Yes, but you're overlooking the most obvious solution. You can stay here with me. I have a lovely extra bedroom, and you'd be most welcome to it. The only thing is, there's only one bathroom, but that wouldn't be a problem."

"That's very kind of you." Wanda Nell was touched by their hostess's generosity. "But we don't want to impose on you."

"What imposition?" Miss Fehrenbach beamed at her guests. "I wouldn't have asked if I didn't mean it. Besides, having the pleasure of your company would be such a treat."

Neither Wanda Nell nor Jack could hold out against the wistful appeal in Miss Fehrenbach's voice. "Then we'd be delighted to accept, and very grateful," Jack said. "But I do insist that you let us take you out to dinner tonight as a way of expressing our thanks."

Miss Fehrenbach clapped her hands together. "Why, thank you, Jack. What a sweet notion. I won't argue with you. I don't get to eat out in restaurants all that often these days. Now, you go get your things and bring them in, while I show Wanda Nell your room."

"Yes, ma'am. I'll do that."

While Jack went out to the car to retrieve their luggage, Wanda Nell followed Miss Fehrenbach down the hall. The house was bigger than it looked from the street, because it extended pretty far back on what was actually a large lot. There was a small dining room next to the front parlor, with the kitchen next. The two bedrooms were on the other side of the hall with the bathroom between them, and the front room on that side of the house was a study. There were shelves bulging with books, a couple of comfortable chairs with reading lamps, and a small desk.

"This looks very comfortable." Wanda Nell smiled at Miss Fehrenbach. "I bet you spend a lot of time in here."

"I do. I do love to read, and I'm blessed with good eyesight. Mother's eyes didn't give out until about a year before she died, and I'm counting on mine lasting at least that long, too." She waved a hand at the shelves. "I love rereading, and I'm determined to reread my favorites often. Not to mention the new books I get from the library."

Jack came back with their things, and Miss Fehrenbach left Wanda Nell to show him the way to their room. Once they were inside, Jack closed the door behind them. He set the bag down and surveyed the room. He stepped closer to examine an old but sturdy four-poster bed with a canopy. The top of the mattress came up to his waist.

"Looks very comfortable," he said. "I haven't slept in a bed like that since I used to stay with my dad's mother." He grinned. "Back then I had to take a running jump to get up on it. I was only five."

Wanda Nell had to laugh at the thought. "I bet you were so cute when you were little. You're even cuter now."

"Shucks, I could say the same about you." Jack gave her a quick kiss. "So, what do you think of all this?" He leaned against the side of the bed.

"The room, you mean, or the situation?"

"Both."

"It's a very nice room," Wanda Nell said. "A lot nicer than the kind of motel we could afford. I wonder how she manages to keep everything so clean." Indeed, the room appeared to be in apple-pie order, with not a speck of dust to be found.

"She's such a little dynamo, I wouldn't be surprised if she does it all herself," Jack said admiringly. "But I'll bet she gets some help, probably from ladies at her church."

"You're probably right. Now, about the situation. We've got to find some way to get Mr. Howell to talk to us. But what?"

"I'm not sure," Jack said. "But I'm hoping Miss Fehrenbach's right. Maybe he'll be easier to talk to in the morning, if we can catch him before he's had a chance to drink very much."

"I guess. If we don't, though, what's our next step?"

"I already thought of one. Since we know Howell's name, but not Margaret's maiden name, I put in a call to T.J. and Tuck while I was outside. I asked them to see if they could find a marriage license for the Howells in Tullahoma or any of the nearby counties." He shrugged. "It might be a long shot in some ways, because we can't be sure they were actually married. This whole setup stinks to high heaven."

"I bet they *were* married," Wanda Nell said, after thinking about it for a moment. "I'll bet Jenna Rae's real father would have insisted on it, because he would have wanted to get Margaret and the baby permanently out of the way. At least, that's what I think he would want in a situation like this."

"You're right. I hadn't thought about it like that." Jack paused. "The other thing I wonder about is how much money, if any, was involved."

"Do you mean the real father paid Howell to marry Margaret and go away?"

"It seems logical. I think I'll ask Miss Fehrenbach a few questions about it. For example, did Howell seem to have more money than he ought to, given that he was a janitor at a funeral parlor?"

"And if anybody would have noticed something like that," Wanda Nell said, "I'm sure she would have."

There was a light knock at the door. "Come in," Jack called.

Miss Fehrenbach opened the door and peered in. "Is there anything y'all need?"

"Everything's fine," Wanda Nell assured her. "It's a lovely room. I was telling Jack this is a lot nicer than any motel we would have stayed at. You're so sweet to have us stay with you tonight."

Their hostess beamed. "I'm so glad you like it. Now, if either of you would like to freshen up next door before dinner, you just go right ahead. I've set out some extra towels and so on, so you just make yourselves right at home."

"Thank you," Jack said. He glanced at his watch. "I've totally lost track of the time. It's almost five-thirty." He looked at Miss Fehrenbach. "What time would you like to go to dinner?"

"How about seven? That will give us all time to relax a bit and refresh ourselves. Besides, I have to decide what to wear. I haven't put on my party clothes in quite a while."

"That sounds fine," Jack said, "but don't outshine us too

badly. Wanda Nell and I didn't bring any party clothes." He winked at Miss Fehrenbach.

She laughed. "Now, never you mind. Just let me know if you need anything. I promise I'll be ready to go when you are." She smiled and left, shutting the door behind her.

They were ready to go by a quarter to seven. Jack escorted Miss Fehrenbach—or Miss Lyda, as she now insisted they call her—to the car. He insisted that she sit in the front seat beside him, and Wanda Nell assured her she would be just fine in the back seat.

As Jack prepared to drive away, Wanda Nell glanced next door at Mr. Howell's house. There was no sign of life anywhere. It wouldn't be dark for a while yet, and she couldn't spot any lights burning inside the house. She thought about what Miss Lyda had said. He was probably passed out drunk somewhere. How sad that was.

Miss Lyda directed Jack to a favorite restaurant, and during the meal she regaled them with tidbits of local history. Wanda Nell and Jack were touched by the story of Hattiesburg's founding and the origin of the town's name.

"In August of 1880, Captain William Harris Hardy was on his way from Meridian to New Orleans on a surveying trip," Miss Lyda said, in her best history teacher manner. "He stopped along the way to have lunch, and the spot he chose was on the north side of Gordon Creek, amidst a large oak and several hickory trees." She paused for a sip of her iced tea. "That spot is now in downtown Hattiesburg, across from the post office.

"While he was resting after his lunch, the captain spread out one of his survey maps, looking at the line of one of the railroads. He thought that a rail line from Jackson to Gulfport would help develop the southern part of the state. When he drew the lines to connect this new rail line with the existing one, it was right through this area. He decided to name the train station after his beloved second wife, Hattie."

"What a charming story," Wanda Nell said. "I'm sure Miss Hattie loved having a town named after her."

"No doubt she did," Miss Lyda said. "But sadly, she never lived to see it in person. She died in 1895."

"That is sad," Jack commented.

Through the rest of the meal Miss Lyda kept them entertained with somewhat less sedate stories about historic citizens of the town. By the time they had finished their dessert and coffee, it was almost nine-thirty.

"My goodness, look at the time," Miss Lyda said as they were leaving the restaurant. "I'm sure you two must be tired and ready to rest, after all the driving and everything today."

Once they were home again, Miss Lyda firmly bade them good night, insisting that they rest. "I'm going to have a little nap," she said. "I'm a bit of a night owl. I don't need much sleep, but I won't wake you, I promise."

Jack and Wanda Nell kissed her on either cheek, and Miss Lyda's face turned pink. "And thank you again for such a lovely dinner, my dears. I can't think when I've had such a delightful time, or more charming companions."

Wanda Nell and Jack made their preparations for bed, and they were soon snuggled down in the old four-poster. It was very comfortable, and they were both very tired. Neither of them had any trouble dropping off to sleep.

At some point Wanda Nell woke to the sound of a firm knock on their door. She squinted at the window, trying to figure out what time it was. There was some light, so it must be morning.

Jack woke, yawning, and sat up in bed. Wanda Nell got up and went to the door. Miss Lyda was there, already dressed for the day.

"My apologies for waking you." Her tone betrayed her distress. "Ordinarily I would have let you sleep, but I'm worried."

Now wide awake, Wanda Nell said, "What's wrong?"

"I think perhaps Jack should go next door and check on Mr. Howell. I'm afraid something has happened to him."

Twenty

A moment later, his pants now on, Jack stood beside Wanda Nell. "What do you think has happened?"

"I'm not sure. Maybe I'm just being a silly old woman, but I think something may have happened to him."

"Something must have triggered this feeling," Jack said in a gentle voice. He and Wanda Nell exchanged quick glances. They were both worried about Miss Lyda. She was far too pale.

Wanda Nell took Miss Lyda's hand and led her into the room, to an armchair by the dressing table. Miss Lyda sat, her hands twisting in her lap. "It may be nothing," she said, looking up at them. "I told you I'm a night owl."

Wanda Nell and Jack nodded. "So did you see something during the night?" Wanda Nell asked.

"I did. It was about one in the morning. I had slept for a bit, and then I got up and tiptoed into the study to read for a while. I usually read for a couple of hours and then go back to bed. I don't need that much sleep most of the time." She stilled her hands. "Anyway, as I was sitting there in my chair, about to open my book, I heard a car pull up out front."

"And was that unusual?" Jack asked.

"At that time of the morning, yes. I know this neighborhood doesn't look like much, but it is actually pretty quiet here at night. So when I heard the car, I got up and looked out the window. By the time I got to the window, whoever was in the car was already out of it and on the way up the walk to Mr. Howell's front door."

"Was it anyone you recognized?" Jack asked.

"No, it wasn't. The lights out there aren't that strong, and I'm afraid my night vision isn't very good. I could see that whoever it was wasn't very tall and was wrapped up. Maybe to disguise his identity."

"You got the impression that it was a man?" Wanda Nell asked. "At least that's something."

Miss Lyda frowned. "That was my first reaction. But when I think back over it, I can't really say for certain. There was something slightly odd about the person's gait. Of course, whoever it was seemed to be in a dreadful hurry, so maybe that's all it was."

"What happened once this person was at Mr. Howell's door?" Jack asked. "Were you able to see that?" He frowned. "No, you couldn't see that from your study, because it's on the other side of the house."

Miss Lyda offered a slight smile. "Well, curiosity got the better of me, so I hurried into the front parlor and peeked out the side window. I got there in time to see the door open and the person step inside. I didn't see Howell, but who else would have opened the door?"

Jack nodded. "Did you keep watching?"

"I watched for a few minutes, but everything was very quiet. As curious as I was, I was getting a bit bored just standing there." She blushed slightly. "Plus I needed to visit the ladies' room. And by the time I came back, the car was gone."

"Did you happen to notice what kind of car it was?" Jack asked. "Two-door, four-door, SUV, for example?"

Miss Lyda shook her head. "It was small, that's all I remember. Oh, and it must have been pretty dark-colored. Maybe black. I'm sorry, I'm not very good when it comes to knowing much about cars."

"That's at least something," Jack said.

"How long do you think the person was in Mr. Howell's house?" Wanda Nell asked.

Miss Lyda frowned in concentration. "I'd say at least twenty minutes, maybe a little longer. I must have stood there a good ten minutes, watching to see what would happen. And then I was probably in the bathroom for about the same length of time."

"Were you worried then?" Wanda Nell asked. "You could have gotten us up then if you were concerned. We wouldn't have minded a bit."

"I really wasn't that worried at first. I went back to reading my book, and to tell the truth, I got so wrapped up in it, I forgot about it. I must have dozed off in my chair, because I woke up there a little while ago. Then I remembered what had happened, and the more I thought about it, the stranger I realized it was."

"So you don't think it could have been someone delivering a late-night bottle of whisky, or something?" Jack asked.

"No, I don't think so. In all the time since Margaret died and Jenna Rae left, he's had very few visitors at night. He used to have some drinking buddies who'd come over, and they would have a right rowdy time. But I don't think this was one of them. I haven't seen hide nor hair of them in at least a year."

While Jack and Miss Lyda talked, Wanda Nell dressed as quickly as she could. She pulled on her jeans, then exchanged her nightgown for a blouse.

"I'll go have a look, just in case, to make sure he's okay," Jack said. He went for his shoes and then pulled a shirt on over his T-shirt. "Y'all wait here, and I'll see what's going on."

As Jack left, Wanda Nell focused her attention on Miss Lyda. She was still pale. "Why don't we go in the kitchen and fix some hot coffee, or maybe some hot tea?" She held out a hand to her hostess.

"Thank you, dear. I think I'd like some hot coffee," Miss Lyda said, accepting Wanda Nell's hand.

In the kitchen Miss Lyda directed Wanda Nell to the coffee and the filters for the coffeemaker. Soon Wanda Nell had the machine going, and she was about to pour the first cup for Miss Lyda when Jack returned.

Wanda Nell took one look at his face and knew something really bad had happened. "Miss Lyda," he said, "I'm afraid we need to call the police. Where's your phone?"

Mutely, Miss Lyda pointed to the wall nearby. Her hand was shaking, and Wanda Nell quickly poured her coffee and added a couple of spoons of sugar to it. While Jack punched in a number, Wanda Nell urged Miss Lyda to drink her coffee. She pulled a chair next to her hostess and kept an arm around her small, trembling shoulders.

Jack spoke tersely, and Wanda Nell could feel Miss Lyda continue to shake as they listened to Jack's side of the conversation.

After a moment Jack hung up the phone and turned to them. "I'm sorry, Miss Lyda, but you were right."

Miss Lyda nodded. "That person in the night killed him." Wanda Nell had to steady the hand holding the coffee cup. "Perhaps if I had done something earlier. . . ." Her voice trailed off.

"No, ma'am," Jack said, his voice very gentle. "There's nothing you could have done for him. I'll spare you the details, but believe me, nothing you could have done would have helped him."

"Drink some more coffee, Miss Lyda," Wanda Nell

urged. She was terrified that the shock might prove too
much for their hostess, but Miss Lyda rallied. "I'm sorry
that something like this happened. He was an awful man in
so many ways, but he surely didn't deserve this."

"No, he didn't," Jack said. His own face had paled, and
without a word, Wanda Nell left Miss Lyda's side to pour
some coffee for her husband. The sight must have been
pretty grim, because Jack was obviously very shaken.

Jack accepted the hot coffee with a grateful look.
"Thanks, honey." Wanda Nell rubbed his arm, not liking
how cold it felt.

"Keep drinking," she said.

Moments later they heard a siren in the distance, and by
the time they all reached the front door, the sound was very
loud. Jack opened the door, and all three of them stepped
onto the porch. The morning heat was welcome. Wanda Nell
hadn't realized how cold she had been until she came outside.

Two officers got out of the squad car, and Jack went down
the walk to greet them. Wanda Nell and Miss Lyda remained
on the porch, sitting in the two chairs Miss Lyda kept there.
They couldn't hear the conversation, but after a quick con-
sultation with Jack, the officers headed to Howell's front
door. Jack came back to Wanda Nell and Miss Lyda.

In the next few minutes more vehicles arrived, and curious neighbors had started coming out of their homes. A
couple of patrol officers worked to keep them from crowd-
ing too close. One neighbor, a woman in her sixties, attempted to approach Miss Lyda's house, but a patrolman
stopped her. A vociferous argument ensued, but the officer
wouldn't budge. Finally the woman retired, casting furious
glances at him.

"Betsy Bobo," Miss Lyda told Wanda Nell and Jack in
an undertone. "The neighborhood busybody. She'll be beside herself because she doesn't know what's going on.
She'd rather gossip than eat any day."

"She'll have enough to keep her going for a while," Jack said. "As soon as the details of this leak out."

Miss Lyda placed a hand on his arm. "Please tell me at least a little. I promise I'm okay."

Jack stared at her. Wanda Nell caught his eye and nodded. He squatted next to Miss Lyda's chair. "He was beaten pretty badly, with a poker from the fireplace."

Miss Lyda clutched the arms of her chair for a moment. "How terrible. Someone must have been very angry to do something like that."

"The police will be coming to question all of us before too much longer," Jack said. "Will you be okay with that?"

"Of course," Miss Lyda said, her tone firmer. "I know my duty."

Wanda Nell clasped one of Miss Lyda's small hands in hers. "And we'll be here with you."

"Thank you. I think I'd like to go back inside."

"Good idea," Wanda Nell said. "Let's go have some more coffee. I know I could sure use some."

"I'll be along in a minute," Jack said. Wanda Nell nodded as she led Miss Lyda into the house.

Miss Lyda had finished her second cup of coffee, and Wanda Nell her first, by the time Jack came back to the kitchen. He brought with him a tall, heavyset black man in a rumpled suit. Jack started to speak, but Miss Lyda interrupted him.

"My goodness, Rufus King," she said, starting to rise from her chair. "Are you in charge of this investigation?"

King stepped forward to take Miss Lyda's hand and urge her to remain seated. "I sure am, Miss Lyda. How are you doing?" He smiled at her, and she beamed at him.

"Better, knowing that you're in charge." Miss Lyda turned to Wanda Nell. "Rufus was one of my students thirty years ago. He's always been a fine boy, and I'm so proud of him."

The fifty-something-year-old "boy" blushed. "Miss Lyda was always everyone's favorite teacher. No one worked us harder, but no one ever gave us more."

Wanda Nell was greatly touched by the affection and admiration in the policeman's voice. "Somehow I don't have any trouble believing that," she said.

"This is my wife," Jack said. "Wanda Nell Pemberton."

"How do you do, ma'am?" King turned his attention back to Miss Lyda. "Now, Miss Lyda, I sure hate to put you through all this, but I do need to ask you some questions."

"Of course, Rufus," she said. "I'm ready. Wanda Nell has been looking after me, and I'm feeling much stronger."

"Thank you. I'd rather talk to Miss Lyda alone. If y'all don't mind, I'll ask you to wait in another room."

"Of course," Jack said. Wanda Nell rose from her chair. "We'll be in our bedroom."

As they walked out of the room, King began. "Now tell me please, Miss Lyda, everything you saw or heard."

Back in their room, Wanda Nell sat down on the edge of the bed. "Are you okay, honey?"

Jack sat down beside her and pulled her close. She rested her head against his shoulder. "I hope I never have to see something like that again," he said.

"I'm sorry you had to. This sure is something I wouldn't have expected."

"Me either, though I guess we really shouldn't be surprised, after our visit. Howell saw a chance to blackmail somebody, and it went wrong."

"You thought he was lying about knowing who his wife worked for in Tullahoma," Wanda Nell said. "This proves it. Or that he knew who Jenna Rae's real father was."

"Something like that," Jack agreed. "He obviously called someone who was involved in the situation, and that person came rushing down here to make sure he stayed quiet about what he knew."

"And now we'll never know what he could have told us."

"Unless the police find something when they search his house. And I'm betting whoever killed him tried to make sure they wouldn't find anything."

"The house was such a mess, how would the killer be able to go through everything in the short time Miss Lyda says he was there?"

"You've got a point," Jack said. "We'll just have to hope the police will be able to find something. Anything."

Wanda Nell was struck by a terrible thought. "What if they think one of us did it?"

"They may very well think that," Jack said, shrugging. "I couldn't really blame them. After all, the coincidence is a bit much. We show up in Hattiesburg looking for this man, and in less than twenty-four hours, he's dead." He shook his head. "Miss Lyda will be able to give us an alibi. She ought to be a pretty credible witness, and King obviously has a great deal of respect for her."

"Thank goodness," Wanda Nell said.

They sat in silence for a while longer, waiting for a summons from King.

A knock came at the door at last, and Jack got up to answer it. King stood in the hall outside. "Would y'all mind coming into the kitchen with me?" He waited for Wanda Nell and Jack to leave the room and then followed them back to the kitchen.

Miss Lyda was still sitting in her chair. King indicated that Wanda Nell and Jack should sit down, and he took the remaining chair at the table.

"Now, according to Miss Lyda, you two are in the clear. Not that I don't believe her account of what she saw, you understand, but until I know more about the time of death, I'm keeping my options open."

"Certainly, officer," Jack said. "We can understand that. What do you want to know?"

"Why did you come here in the first place? What was your business with Howell?"

Jack began to explain, trying to give King a condensed version of the story. King wasn't interested in that, insisting on knowing everything. Jack began again, giving every detail of what he and Wanda Nell had done thus far. Wanda Nell chipped in occasionally, and King would nod at her.

At some point Miss Lyda got up and made a fresh pot of coffee. King accepted a cup with a quick nod of thanks, never taking his eyes off Jack. Wanda Nell sipped gratefully at hers and wished she didn't feel so hungry. She was surprised she could even feel hungry after what had happened, but she was. No doubt Jack and Miss Lyda were as well.

It took them nearly half an hour to share all the details with King. When Jack had finished, King sat staring at him for a full minute.

"That's a pretty complicated story you got there. Based on all that, I reckon you're thinking that the killer was somebody from Tullahoma—or at least connected to Tullahoma—who was involved in the murder of Howell's daughter thirty-one years ago."

"Adopted daughter," Miss Lyda said.

"Yes, ma'am," King responded with a slight smile. "His adopted daughter. Now, Miss Lyda has told me a lot about Howell and his habits. Considering the condition of that house, it's going to take us a while to go through everything, looking for some kind of evidence to tie this thing to someone in Tullahoma."

"Do we need to stay in Hattiesburg for a while?" Jack asked. "We can, if you need us to, but we don't want to impose too much on Miss Lyda."

Miss Lyda started to protest, but King shook his head. "I've already had a talk with the sheriff in Tullahoma." He looked at Jack. "He corroborated what you told me earlier,

Mr. Pemberton. He vouches for you, so I'm going to say it's okay for you to go back home. I'd rather you stay over one more night, though, just in case."

"And you will stay here with me," Miss Lyda said, her voice firm. "Don't you think of going anywhere else."

"Thank you, Miss Lyda." Wanda Nell gave a smile of gratitude. "We surely do appreciate it."

King rose. "Thank you, too, Miss Lyda." He nodded at Wanda Nell and Jack. "I might be back a little later with more questions."

"Of course," Jack said, rising from his chair. "I'll see you out." The two men left the kitchen, and Miss Lyda sighed.

"What a terrible situation. I'm embarrassed to admit it, but I'm more than a bit peckish. What about you, Wanda Nell?"

"I am, too. I know it's probably bad of me to be thinking of food at a time like this, but I was afraid my stomach was going to start growling any minute."

"Then we should definitely do something about that," Miss Lyda said. "I'm sure Jack must be hungry, too, though after what the poor boy has had to see, he might not want to eat." She shook her head.

"I know." Wanda Nell had been worrying about that very thing. Jack might have nightmares, and she wouldn't be surprised. It had sounded pretty grisly, even from the minimal details he had shared.

Miss Lyda stood. "Let's get cooking, then."

"I'll be happy to do the cooking," Wanda Nell said.

"Ordinarily I would insist on doing it myself," Miss Lyda replied with a sweet smile. "But I do get tired of my own cooking. So if you wouldn't mind, dear, I will take you up on your offer."

Jack came back a couple of minutes later to find his wife busy at the stove. He insisted on helping, and while they worked, they talked about other things. They all needed to think of something else for a while, and when the food was ready, they all ate. Jack ate less than usual, but Wanda Nell didn't say anything. She was just glad he felt like eating something. He would need it as the day went on.

They had finished breakfast, but were still sitting at the kitchen table, when a knock sounded at the front door. Jack went to answer it and came back with Rufus King.

King glanced at the table—wistfully, Wanda Nell thought—but then focused his attention on Miss Lyda.

"Please sit down, Rufus," she said before he could speak.

"Yes, ma'am." He took a seat across the table from her.

"How about some coffee?" Miss Lyda asked.

"Thank you, but I'm fine," King said with a brief smile. "Now, Miss Lyda, I have a few more questions I'm hoping you can answer. First, do you have any idea what kind of income the deceased had?"

Miss Lyda thought for a moment, her head cocked to one side. "Well, I know he received Social Security, but I doubt it was much, considering the kind of job he had. You don't make much being a janitor at a funeral home, I reckon." She paused. "I suppose his brother, and after he died, his nephew, might have given him money from time to time, maybe a pension. But I wouldn't think it was much. You saw how he lived."

King nodded. "That's exactly it. Some things just don't add up." He stared hard at Jack. "Now, I'm going to tell you something, and I don't want it going any further, understand?"

Jack nodded.

King looked at Miss Lyda again. "My men have been going over the place, and we found a couple drawers in the kitchen full of receipts of all kinds and bank statements. You're right about his Social Security. It wasn't very much. That was the only deposit we saw in the statements." He paused for a moment. "According to the receipts, though, he was spending hundreds of dollars a month on beer and alcohol. By the time you add up his utilities and what he was spending on food and medicine, he was spending way over his Social Security check every month."

"So he was getting money from somewhere every month," Jack said. "The question is, was he blackmailing someone?"

Twenty-one

"I suppose his nephew could have been giving him money every month," Miss Lyda said. "But it surely wouldn't have been enough for him to spend that much on liquor. His nephew's a teetotaler, that I do know."

"He was probably blackmailing whoever killed him," Wanda Nell added. "Maybe the person who killed Jenna Rae thirty-one years ago."

"Wanda Nell and I were talking about this earlier," Jack said. "We figure that Howell had been getting money from someone for years. But then we show up, asking questions, and he gets the idea that what he knows is worth a lot more money."

"And so he calls the person who's been paying him all this time, and he comes down and eliminates Howell," King said, continuing the train of thought.

Jack nodded. "Doesn't that sound reasonable?"

"It does," King replied. He stared at Wanda Nell and Jack for a moment, his expression serious. "Another thing I'm wondering is whether Howell had time to tell the killer about you two. The killer would certainly want to know exactly why Howell was wanting more money all of a sudden."

Jack turned to Wanda Nell in dismay. "I hadn't thought about that. We're going to have to be pretty careful when we get home." He turned back to King. "I did give Howell a note with my name and phone numbers on it, when I went back to talk to him the second time. I don't suppose you've found that piece of paper anywhere?"

"Not that I recall, but I'll be sure to tell them to look for it. Even if it does turn up next door, I think it's my duty to warn you that you might be in danger anyway. We have no way of knowing what Howell told the killer, or what the killer could have figured out from your car being on the street in front of this house."

Wanda Nell shuddered. "Maybe he was in too much of a hurry to notice our car. But what if he'd tried to break in here, looking for us?"

"He probably wanted to get in and out of here as quickly as he could, and he might have figured you were less of a threat than Howell," King said. "But we're just guessing at this point. When you do get home, though, I think you need to be on the lookout for anything strange."

"We certainly will," Jack said. "I hate to say it, but both of us have been in this position before." He shrugged. "One thing this whole situation tells me, though, is that we must be on the right track. Otherwise, why would Howell have been killed?"

"And were we responsible for getting him killed?" Wanda Nell asked, looking at Jack. He nodded in agreement. "That really bothers me."

"I can understand that," King said. "But you didn't force Howell to make the choices he made. It was his responsibility, not yours."

"Exactly, Rufus." Miss Lyda's tone was emphatic. "Don't you two go blaming yourselves for this. The seeds of this tragedy were sown long ago. I think it's terrible that Mr. Howell has died the way he did, but I'm convinced good will come of it yet. You're going to find out who murdered that beautiful child all those years ago, and that person will have to face up to it."

"Thank you, Miss Lyda," Wanda Nell said, clasping the little woman's hand in hers.

" 'Pride goeth before destruction, and an haughty spirit before a fall,' " Miss Lyda quoted. "That's what the Good Book tells us. Proverbs, chapter 16, verse 18. But it might as well say 'stupidity' instead of 'pride.' Howell was a stupid, venal man, and he brought destruction upon himself."

"Exactly, Miss Lyda," King said. Glancing at his watch, he rose from his seat. "Y'all will have to excuse me. I've got to go see Mr. Howell's grandnephew. I need to talk to the family, and apparently the nephew is away on business." He stared hard at Jack. "I may be back with more questions later, and I'll expect to find you here until tomorrow morning."

"We'll be here," Jack promised. King nodded and headed for the door.

Wanda Nell muttered "Excuse me" and followed him. She caught up with him in the hallway. "Mr. King," she said.

He stopped and turned to face her. "Yes, ma'am?"

"My husband and I won't leave until you tell us it's okay, but I was wondering if it would be okay for one of us to leave the house for a little while."

"To do what?"

Wanda Nell glanced over her shoulder before replying. "Well, I got to noticing this morning that Miss Lyda doesn't have a lot of food on hand, and I thought maybe Jack or I could go to the grocery store. We don't want to be a burden on her, but I'm afraid we will be."

King smiled briefly. "That's very kind of you. Miss Lyda has her pride, and she would never say a thing to you about it. But I'm sure she'd be grateful to you for thinking of it, and I know you'll do it in a way that won't embarrass her."

"Thank you," Wanda Nell said. "So it's okay if Jack or I go to the grocery store."

"I'll let my men know," King promised.

Wanda Nell went back to the kitchen feeling better. Having seen the contents of their hostess's refrigerator and her pantry, she had been concerned about the effect their continued presence would have on Miss Lyda's budget. It might be that Miss Lyda simply didn't keep much food on hand because she didn't eat a lot, but just in case, Wanda Nell didn't want to cause their hostess any hardship.

Once again in the kitchen, Wanda Nell asked, "Miss Lyda, do you like fried chicken and homemade biscuits?"

"I surely do. My mother used to make the best fried chicken, and her biscuits were so good, you could eat them by themselves and think you were having a special treat. I never learned how to make them as good as she could, though."

"Wanda Nell knows how to make them," Jack said. He nodded at Wanda Nell to show that he understood what she was doing. "And her fried chicken is something else, too."

"I was just thinking," Wanda Nell said, resuming her seat beside Miss Lyda, "that I sure would love to be doing something to help pass the time. And at home I usually cook. So if you don't mind, maybe I could cook our lunch, and our dinner tonight."

Miss Lyda smiled uncertainly. "That's very kind of you, dear, but I'm not sure I have what you need. I haven't been to the grocery store lately."

"That's not a problem," Jack said. "I can run to the grocery store and pick up whatever Wanda Nell wants, if you don't mind telling me how to find the grocery store around here."

Miss Lyda explained how to find the grocery store where she shopped, and Wanda Nell found a pencil and a piece of paper and made a list for Jack. He headed to the bathroom to take a shower, promising to be ready to go in a few minutes.

"It won't be long before we're all ready for lunch," Wanda Nell said, her list finally complete.

"It's very kind of you to do the cooking. I'm afraid I never was very good in the kitchen." She got to her feet. "Let me just get my purse so I can give Jack the money."

"Miss Lyda," Wanda Nell said, placing a hand gently on her hostess's arm, "considering all the trouble we've put you to, it would mean a lot to me if you'd let us do this. It's a small enough thing to do to thank you for your hospitality. Staying here with you has been so much nicer than staying in some motel where you don't know whether the sheets are really clean or not."

Miss Lyda protested once, but Wanda Nell soon overcame her objections, and she agreed to let Jack and Wanda Nell buy the groceries. By the time they had settled it between them, Jack came into the kitchen, freshly showered and dressed in clean clothes.

He accepted the list from Wanda Nell, repeated the directions to Miss Lyda, then left. Wanda Nell accompanied him to the front door.

"Did she fuss much about our paying for the food?" he asked.

"A little," Wanda Nell admitted. "But I got her to agree to it. She's such a sweet lady. I wish we could take her home with us. I hate to think of her living here all by herself."

"I know, honey." Jack gave her a quick kiss. "But she does have friends here, and her church, and from what she told us last night at dinner, they're pretty good about checking up on her."

"You're right," Wanda Nell said. "Now be careful, and if you think of anything I might have left off the list, go ahead and get it."

"Will do." After one more kiss, not quite as quick this time, Jack left.

While Jack was gone, Wanda Nell decided she would shower and change clothes, too. Seeing that Miss Lyda had a small washer and dryer in a utility closet in the kitchen, Wanda Nell asked if she could wash the clothes she and Jack had worn the day before. She had packed very lightly for this trip, not really expecting to be away two nights.

"Of course," Miss Lyda said. "Now you go on and have your shower, and as soon as you're done, we'll put your clothes in the washer."

Wanda Nell stood gratefully under the hot water of the shower. Her back was a little stiff from riding in the car the day before and from an unfamiliar bed, and she could feel the muscles relaxing thanks to the heat. As she showered, she thought about the events of the past few days. Had it really only been Sunday that Jack had come home to tell her about the poor dead girl on the football field?

They had made good progress very quickly, but she hated the fact that another person had died because of this. What was so important that someone had killed two people over it? Was it simply shame over a baby born out of wedlock? A prominent man has an affair with a maid, gets her pregnant, and when the child comes back looking for her father, someone kills her to keep the truth from coming out?

Wanda Nell shook her head over these thoughts as she dried herself. The second murder made more sense, because of course the killer didn't want to be exposed for the first murder. It all came down to the motive behind Jenna Rae's murder. Was shame at the root of it all? Or was there more to the story? Wanda Nell figured money had to be in-

volved somehow. Maybe Jenna Rae's biological father was
really rich, and someone hadn't wanted to share with an illegitimate half sister.

That made some sense, at least. People would do all
kinds of nasty things for the sake of the almighty dollar.
Wanda Nell had seen plenty of that in her forty-two years
on this earth.

By the time Wanda Nell was dressed and had freshened
her makeup, Jack had returned from the grocery store. He
and Miss Lyda were putting things away in the kitchen
when Wanda Nell came in with her hands full of the clothes
she wanted to wash.

Jack greeted her with a quick kiss. "I thought, since
you're going to cook your famous fried chicken and biscuits for dinner tonight, maybe I'd make a batch of chili for
lunch, and maybe some cornbread. How does that sound?"

"Sounds good," Wanda Nell said. "What do you think,
Miss Lyda?"

"It sounds good to me, too. Plus I think it will be fun to
watch a man cooking in this kitchen. My father, bless his
soul, never once in his life cooked anything."

Wanda Nell and Jack laughed, and while Jack got busy
with his preparations for lunch, Miss Lyda showed Wanda
Nell how to use her washing machine.

"It's getting pretty old, just like me," she said cheer-
fully, "but she's still got some miles in her. Just like me."

The three of them had a pleasant lunch, and by tacit
agreement, none of them spoke of either of the murders.
Instead, Miss Lyda continued to regale them with bits of
Hattiesburg history and stories from her many years as a
teacher in the public school system.

After lunch Miss Lyda confided that she always had a little "lie down" in the afternoon, and while she rested, Jack
and Wanda Nell got on their cell phones to bring family and
friends up to date on what had been going on in Hattiesburg.

Wanda Nell checked on Juliet first, and she was pleased to hear that Juliet was doing fine with her grandmother and Belle. Wanda Nell called Ernie Carpenter next, because she knew Ernie would be about to bust from curiosity by this point. She spent nearly half an hour on the phone with Ernie, and Ernie promised to do a little digging to see if she could find out anything about Howell's time in Tullahoma.

When Wanda Nell ended her call with Ernie, she looked across the table at Jack. He was busy scribbling something in his notebook.

"What did T.J. have to say?" Wanda Nell asked.

"He hasn't had any luck so far tracking down a marriage license for Howell and Margaret," Jack said with a frown. "You know, I'm beginning to wonder if they were actually married."

"Maybe they got married down here somewhere," Wanda Nell said. "We've been assuming they would have gotten married before they left Tullahoma, but maybe they didn't. Seems to me that someone didn't want any kind of record of them in Tullahoma, so maybe they waited till they got here to do it."

"Good point, I hadn't thought of that. I'll call T.J. back and ask him to check around here." Jack reached for his phone, but it started ringing as he picked it up. He looked at the screen to see the caller's number. "That's odd," he said as he answered the call.

"This is Jack Pemberton. Yes, sir, I'm actually out of town on business at the moment."

Jack listened, and Wanda Nell watched him. He was scowling, and that didn't bode well. He said "Yes, sir," a few more times before ending the call. He set his phone down and looked across the table at his wife.

"Who was that?" Wanda Nell asked, worried. "From the look on your face, it wasn't good news."

"No, it wasn't." Jack's voice was grim. "That was the superintendent of the school system. He wants to see me as soon as we get back home. Someone's been complaining about me, it seems. He's concerned that I'm engaging in activities not suitable for a teacher in his school district."

Twenty-two

"He actually had the nerve to say that to you?" Wanda Nell could feel her temper stirring, but she was also beginning to feel more than a little nervous.

"He did, so that means someone in Tullahoma knows what we're doing." Jack folded his arms across his chest and gazed at Wanda Nell. "I was hoping we could stay under the radar for a little bit longer."

"Do you think it was the person who killed Mr. Howell?"

"If it wasn't, it was someone connected to him who has influence with the superintendent. I'm not going to back down. There's no reason I can't do this. I'm going to call his bluff."

"Good for you, honey." Wanda Nell hated people who tried bullying other people. "But you better be real careful when you talk to him face to face. I don't know him, or what he's like, but if he's feeling pressured, no telling how he might react."

Jack shrugged, his arms still crossed. "He's never impressed me as having much of a spine, to be honest. If he had one, he'd stick up more for the teachers, but he pretty much leans whichever way the wind is blowing."

"In that case, you'd better see if Tuck can go with you when you talk to him. Maybe having a lawyer with you will make him back down."

"Not a bad idea. I'll call Tuck later on and ask his advice." He grinned. "Having a lawyer for a son-in-law can be a handy thing, can't it?"

Wanda Nell smiled. She loved the way Jack had fit so easily into her family. "It sure can. He's a good man to have on your side."

Jack agreed. "I think I'd better call Elmer Lee again and tell him about this latest little twist. This whole thing could blow up suddenly, and he needs to be prepared."

While Jack talked to Elmer Lee, Wanda Nell tidied the kitchen and finished her small load of laundry. Miss Lyda came into the kitchen while Wanda Nell was folding the clothes. She looked around the kitchen. "My goodness, Wanda Nell," she said. "You've gone and cleaned up everything. I was going to do that."

"Now, Miss Lyda," Wanda Nell said with a smile, "my mama didn't raise me to leave someone's kitchen a mess. It certainly didn't take me very long. Everything was so tidy to begin with. I don't know how you keep such a clean house."

Miss Lyda turned slightly pink. "Well, I do keep busy, but once a week I have some help. A dear girl who was one of my students comes in one day a week."

"Good. Now how about you sit down here and let me get you something to drink. Would you like me to make some coffee? Or something else?"

Miss Lyda sat down, smiling. "I declare, I'm going to be thoroughly spoiled by the time you have to leave tomorrow." Her smile disappeared. "I sure am going to miss having you here. But you have some important work to finish."

"We do, but just because we have to go back to Tullahoma doesn't mean you'll never hear from me again." She stooped to hug Miss Lyda. "Now, how about that drink?"

"I'd love a cup of hot tea." Miss Lyda directed Wanda Nell to the cabinet where her tea kettle and the canister of tea were stored.

Wanda Nell and Jack spent a companionable afternoon with their hostess, and by the time Wanda Nell started her preparations for supper, she felt completely at home in Miss Lyda's kitchen.

Jack had just helped her set everything on the table when a knock sounded at the front door. "I'll go," Jack said.

He came back moments later with Rufus King, who stared hungrily at the table full of fried chicken, cream gravy, green beans, creamed corn, and biscuits. Wanda Nell immediately invited him to join them. "We have plenty," she said, and Miss Lyda added her invitation to Wanda Nell's.

"Well, I really shouldn't." King ruefully patted his waistline. "My wife would have a fit. She's been trying to keep me eating healthy. I can't tell you how long it's been since I've seen food like that."

"We won't tell Adaline, I promise," Miss Lyda said. "I know we shouldn't tempt you like this, Rufus, but you're more than welcome."

Temptation won, and Rufus sat down at the fourth place at the table. No one spoke again until all four plates were served, and Miss Lyda offered a short blessing.

Wanda Nell couldn't help but smile at the expression on King's face after he stuck the first forkful of biscuit and gravy in his mouth. Miss Lyda looked pretty happy, too.

"Just as good as my dear mama's," she said.

Jack raised his glass of iced tea and proposed a toast. "To Miss Lyda." Wanda Nell and King joined in, and Miss Lyda turned pink as she shyly raised her own glass.

After a few minutes of silent enjoyment of the food, Miss Lyda spoke. "Rufus, is there anything new you can share with us?" She looked around the table. "I know we're all about as curious as we can be."

"There's not much to tell at this point." King set aside his fork for the moment. "We did find out from the grand-nephew that Howell received a small pension from the family business, but it wasn't much. Certainly not enough to account for the kind of spending we've uncovered."

"So it's looking like blackmail is more certain," Jack commented.

King nodded. "He was definitely getting extra cash from somewhere. We're working on getting access to his bank records, but that could take a little while. But for now I'm working on the theory that he was getting paid by who-ever killed him. Or by someone connected to the killer."

Wanda Nell glanced at Jack. "Something happened this afternoon that you ought to know."

"What's that?" King set his glass down.

"I had a call from the school superintendent," Jack said. "Evidently someone has gotten to him and complained about my current activities. He wants to see me to talk about what he thinks is unsuitable behavior of one of his teachers."

"Someone's not happy about all this," King said. "Pretty much what I expected. It was bound to break sooner or later. But you'd better be pretty careful when you get home."

"Speaking of which," Wanda Nell said, "are we going to be able to go home tomorrow?"

"Yes, ma'am. I know how to reach you. Now, you real-ize, when this thing comes to trial, you both might have to come back to testify."

"Of course," Jack said, "and we'll do what we need to."

"Would I have to testify, Rufus?" Miss Lyda asked.

King nodded. "Yes, ma'am, you might."

"Oh, dear. Considering the circumstances, I know I shouldn't be excited about that. But I've never testified in court before."

Wanda Nell could see that King was trying very hard

not to smile. "Don't you go worrying about that, Miss Lyda. When the time comes, you'll do just fine."

"Thank you."

Before long they had finished supper, but not until after King had second helpings of Wanda Nell's biscuits and gravy. He turned down an offer of dessert, saying reluctantly, "I've got to be going. Thank you all kindly for supper. I can't tell you when I've enjoyed myself more."

Miss Lyda escorted him to the front door while Jack and Wanda Nell began to clear the table.

"I'm glad we can go home tomorrow," Wanda Nell said. "Though I guess I'm a little nervous about what we'll have to face when we get there." She wrapped the two remaining biscuits in plastic and put them in the refrigerator.

Jack disposed of the chicken bones in the garbage can. "I know, honey, but we'll just have to be on our guard. We have to use the situation to our advantage. Somebody's nervous about what we're doing, so it means we've definitely made progress."

"I just don't want anybody else to die."

Jack came to Wanda Nell and pulled her into his arms. "I know, love. It wasn't anything I thought would happen, but I still believe we're doing the right thing, for Jenna Rae's sake."

"You're right." Wanda Nell laid her head against his shoulder. "Something good has to come of this."

"Something will," Jack said firmly before he released her.

Miss Lyda came back from seeing King out. "Thank you, Wanda Nell. That was such a delicious meal. I tell you, I feel like a Christmas turkey, I had so much good food."

"Thank you, Miss Lyda. I'm glad you enjoyed it. Now, would you like some dessert? Jack bought some ice cream."

"Oh, my goodness, no. I do love ice cream, but I don't think I could right now. Maybe later."

The ice cream stayed in the freezer, and for the rest of the evening the three of them chatted. Wanda Nell and Jack went to bed at ten, because Jack wanted to be up early for the drive back to Tullahoma.

They had a quick breakfast the next morning with Miss Lyda, and Wanda Nell had to hold back a few tears as they said goodbye to her around seven o'clock.

"We'll call you and let you know what's going on," Wanda Nell promised.

"We sure will," Jack added, giving Miss Lyda a kiss on the cheek.

"Take care of yourselves," Miss Lyda said. "I can't bear the thought of anything happening to you."

"Don't worry about us," Wanda Nell called. "You take care, and I'll call you soon."

As Jack drove away, Wanda Nell looked back at Miss Lyda. She was waving, and Wanda Nell waved back at her until she could no longer see her. When Jack turned the corner, Wanda Nell faced forward.

"It'll be good to get home," she said. "But despite everything that happened, I sure did like getting to know Miss Lyda."

"Me, too, honey. We'll go back to see her when this is all over, and maybe she could come to Tullahoma for a visit. Don't you think she and Belle would have a grand old time together?"

Wanda Nell had to laugh at that thought. "They sure would, and I'll bet Miz Culpepper would enjoy her. And Ernie, too. She and Ernie would get on together like a house on fire." She sobered. "Speaking of Miz Culpepper, what are we going to do about her?"

"I've been thinking about that," Jack said. "We've kind of hit a brick wall on digging up more about Howell and

Margaret during their time in Tullahoma. Miz Culpepper obviously knows something about all this, and we may have no choice but to talk to her about it again."

"And hope that she won't have another spell with her heart." Wanda Nell sighed heavily.

"We'll have to take that into account," Jack agreed. "But if the only way we can move forward is by finding out what she knows, we may have to. If nothing else, maybe T.J. can talk to her. She finds it hard to say no to him."

"That's true. He's real sweet with her, and he'll know how to talk to her."

The miles sped by, and they stopped once, in Jackson, for gas and a restroom break. They reached home around eleven-thirty, and Wanda Nell was relieved to see that everything was okay. After they brought their things in from the car, they went into the kitchen for something to drink.

"What time are you going to talk to the superintendent?" Wanda Nell asked. She poured water into two glasses and handed one to Jack.

Jack glanced at his watch. "I'll call his office in a few minutes and make an appointment. Tuck told me he had a light afternoon, so he should be able to go with me."

"Good."

"What will you do?" Jack asked.

"I'm going to call the Kountry Kitchen. Now that we're back, I need to get back to work. I don't want to push Melvin too far."

"He understands what you're doing." Jack grinned. "Besides, he has a soft spot for you, and you know it. I'm just glad he lets me in the front door."

Wanda Nell blushed. "Oh, he got over that ages ago. He likes you. Believe me, when Melvin don't like somebody, you know it."

"That's good. Then I don't have to worry about somebody slipping poison in the gravy when I eat there."

"You better call and make that appointment," Wanda Nell said, ignoring his teasing remark. "And I'm going to get on the phone, too."

"Yes, ma'am." Jack pulled his cell phone out of his pocket and punched in a number.

While he was involved in his call, Wanda Nell went to the kitchen phone and punched in the number of the Kountry Kitchen. Melvin answered after three rings, and Wanda Nell told him she was back and ready to work the afternoon and evening shifts.

"Good. Come on in as soon as you can. One of the girls ain't feeling so hot, so we sure could use the help."

"I'll be there in about twenty minutes." Wanda Nell hung up the phone and turned to face Jack.

"So you're going in right away?"

Wanda Nell nodded. "What about you?"

"I've got an appointment at two. I'm going to call Tuck now and see if he can meet me there."

"Call me as soon as you're done," Wanda Nell said. "I want to know how it goes."

"I will."

Wanda Nell gave Jack a quick kiss before she headed for the bathroom to freshen up. Ten minutes later she was ready to leave for work.

"Tuck will meet me there," Jack told her. "In the meantime, I'm going to do a bit of work on the computer."

After they shared a longer kiss, Jack moved his car out of the way so Wanda Nell could back hers out of the carport. She waved goodbye and drove toward the highway into Tullahoma.

She was actually looking forward to being back at work. She liked staying busy, and she knew if she'd stayed home the rest of the day, she would have been fidgeting and looking for housework to do. She had almost suggested going along with Jack and Tuck to the superintendent's office, but she knew it was better for her not to be there. Her unruly temper might make the situation worse. Better that Tuck was going. He wouldn't lose his cool the way she often did.

Her cell phone rang, startling her. She fumbled for it in her purse. She really didn't much like talking on it while she was driving.

Her fingers grasped the phone, and she pulled it out. A quick glance at the screen revealed a familiar number. She opened the phone and put it to her ear. "Hello, Ernie. How are you?"

"I'm doing fine, Wanda Nell." Ernie's voice boomed into Wanda Nell's ear. "Where are you? Are you and Jack home yet?"

"We are. In fact, I'm on my way to work. My boss said they need me, so I'm going to be at the Kountry Kitchen the rest of the day."

"I'll be on my way there in a few minutes. I need to come into town anyway, and I've managed to dig up something interesting. I'll see you in about thirty minutes."

Ernie ended the call before Wanda Nell could reply. Amused and slightly exasperated, she dropped her phone back in her purse. She'd just have to be patient until Ernie showed up at the Kountry Kitchen, but she couldn't help wondering what Ernie had dug up.

Twenty-three

Wanda Nell reached the Kountry Kitchen a few minutes later, and she met Betsy coming out the door, purse clutched to her stomach.

"Thanks, Wanda Nell." Betsy's face was pale and her voice strained. "I got some kind of stomach bug."

"You go on home, and take care of yourself," Wanda Nell said.

Betsy nodded, and Wanda Nell watched for a moment until Betsy made it to her car. She wasn't so sure Betsy should be driving herself home, but she lived only a couple of miles away. And she seemed to be driving okay.

Wanda Nell opened the door and walked into the restaurant. The front dining room was packed, and from what she could see of the back dining room, it was pretty full, too. She nodded at Melvin as she hurried by him and went in the back to put away her purse. Less than a minute later she was out front, ready to dive in. Patsy pointed out Betsy's tables, and Wanda Nell went to work.

She barely noticed when Ernie came in. Melvin escorted Ernie to a table in the back dining room, and it happened to be one of Wanda Nell's.

"Hello, Ernie," Wanda Nell said with a smile. "As you can see, it's still pretty busy, so I might not be able to talk for a while."

"I can see that." Ernie had a slightly sheepish expression on her face. "Sometimes I lose all track of time, now that I'm not working to a schedule anymore. I didn't really stop to think that it was still lunchtime."

"It's okay," Wanda Nell said. "Now, can I get you something?"

"I haven't had my lunch yet, so I might as well eat. I'm actually hungry. What's good today?"

Wanda Nell recited the day's specials, and Ernie chose the pot roast with carrots, English peas, and mashed potatoes. "And a glass of iced tea, sweetened."

"I'll be back with your tea," Wanda Nell promised. She headed for the kitchen to turn in Ernie's order and fetch the tea.

Forty minutes later the lunch crowd had thinned out to a few lingering over dessert, mostly in the front dining room. Wanda Nell came back to Ernie's table with the tea pitcher and refilled her glass. Ernie pushed away an empty dessert plate. "I don't know when I've had better apple pie."

"There's more," Wanda Nell said, and Ernie considered it for a moment.

"No, I'm going to be good." She wagged a finger at Wanda Nell. "And don't try tempting me any further. I'm going to need to walk the fifteen miles home as it is, just to work off that heavenly—and fattening—lunch."

Wanda Nell grinned. "Yes, ma'am."

"Do you have time now to sit down for a few minutes?"

"I do," Wanda Nell said, taking a seat at the table. "I just have to keep an eye open in case I'm needed. What did you dig up? I've been dying of curiosity ever since you called."

Ernie reached for her tote bag and pulled out a few pieces of paper. She held them while she answered Wanda

Nell. "I started thinking about ways to figure out just who this Margaret was, and I wondered if perhaps she had gone to school here in Tullahoma."

"Good idea. So far T.J. hasn't had any luck finding out where she and Mr. Howell got married. If they did."

"I would certainly hope they did." Ernie's tone was a bit severe. "I'm sure T.J. will find the record somewhere. In the meanwhile, though, I started my search for Margaret." She indicated the papers she held. "We have a collection of school yearbooks at the Historical Society, going back over seventy years. I figured if Margaret went to school here, I could perhaps find her in a yearbook."

"So you just looked for girls named Margaret? I'm sure there were a bunch of them."

"There were. But I narrowed down the time frame, given what we know about this particular Margaret. It's not much, of course, but it gave me a place to start. Jenna Rae would be about fifty by now, had she lived, so I started working backward from there."

"According to Miss Lyda—I told you about her—Margaret was pretty young when Jenna Rae was born."

"Probably not much more than sixteen or seventeen," Ernie said. "Based on that, I was looking especially for a Margaret who probably dropped out of school before graduating." She handed the papers she had been holding to Wanda Nell. "These are copies I made from the yearbooks. Take a look through them."

Wanda Nell took the pages and began glancing over them. Ernie had drawn rings around the Margarets on each page, and Wanda Nell matched them with the photographs.

"I also marked ones with names like Margie and Peggy. Any name that sounded like it could be a nickname for Margaret."

"I see that." Wanda Nell examined with great care each ˢ the girls whose name was marked. She had put aside three pieces of paper and was looking at the fourth one when she spotted a face that seemed familiar. She glanced at the name: Peggy Lewis.

"Have you found her?"

"I think maybe I have. I've seen only that one picture of Jenna Rae, but this girl, Peggy Lewis, reminds me of her. None of the others did." She handed the piece of paper back to Ernie.

Ernie glanced at it. "This is one of the girls who didn't graduate with her class. This is her junior class photo." She put the paper down.

"If Peggy Lewis was Jenna Rae's mother, how do we go about finding out who she worked for fifty years ago?"

"There's the rub, as Shakespeare would have said. But this gives us something to go on, and if your son can find a marriage license, that will confirm it."

"I'll call him and let him know." Wanda Nell stood. "I've got to get back to work."

"Of course," Ernie said. "I'll give this some more thought. Surely I know someone who could help us find out more about Peggy Lewis and who her family was." She grinned. "I was in about the fifth grade when she was a junior, so I wouldn't have known her."

Wanda Nell had to smile. Then she sobered as a thought struck her. "What would her family have done, do you think? Could they have thrown her out if she'd gotten pregnant?"

"Given the time this happened, I'd say yes. Having a baby out of wedlock fifty years ago was pretty shameful, and though it's hard to believe, some parents would refuse to have anything more to do with a daughter who shamed them in that way."

Thanks to Miranda, Wanda Nell knew all about it. She had been furious with her daughter, and maybe a little embarrassed, but she had never seriously considered throwin her daughter out and not having anything to do with her.

"I know, dear." Ernie patted her arm and stood to go. "Thank goodness, some things have changed. For some families, anyway."

Wanda Nell nodded. "I just can't help thinking about how sad all this is."

"It does you credit," Ernie said, gathering up her things. "But we're doing what we can, even though it's been a very long time." She gave Wanda Nell a quick hug.

Wanda Nell got back to work, somewhat comforted, and Ernie waved goodbye to her a few minutes later as she left the Kountry Kitchen.

A while later, when the lunch crowd was completely gone and the restaurant was quiet, Wanda Nell sat down for a few minutes to have her own lunch. After she ate, she went to get her cell phone out of her purse. She called T.J., and he answered right away.

"Hey, Mama," he said. "Y'all had quite a time down in Hattiesburg."

"We sure did." Wanda Nell glanced at her watch, surprised to note that it was nearly three o'clock. "Have you heard any word from Tuck or Jack yet?"

T.J. laughed. "Oh, yeah. They got back to the office about ten minutes ago. Sounds like Tuck put the fear of God into the superintendent. Tuck says the minute they walked into the guy's office and he spotted Tuck with Jack, the guy started sweating. He knew who Tuck was, and that made him nervous."

"Good," Wanda Nell said, mightily relieved. "Is Jack still there?"

"He is. I'll get him for you."

Wanda Nell waited a moment, and Jack came on the line. "Hey, honey, it's okay."

"That's what T.J. said. So he didn't cut up too rough ·ith Tuck there."

"He sure didn't. He backed down pretty quick, so I'm not

sure who scared him more, Tuck or whoever called to complain about me." He paused. "I'm glad he's off my back, at least for now. Who knows what will happen, though, once he reports back to whoever put him up to calling about me?"

"Then the faster we figure this all out, the better. Honey, Ernie called me when I was on the way to work, and she came by here for lunch. She did some digging in old yearbooks at the Historical Society, and I think we may have found Margaret."

"Great. Tell me about it."

Wanda Nell gave him a quick rundown on what Ernie had done. "A girl named Peggy Lewis didn't graduate. And from what I could see, Jenna Rae favored her."

"Full marks to Ernie for coming up with that. Sounds like y'all did find Margaret, or rather, Peggy. I'll tell T.J. He's still working on finding a marriage license for them. No luck on a birth certificate for Jenna Rae, either."

"How does T.J. go about looking for these things, anyway? Are they all on the computer somewhere?"

"I'll let him explain that to you, honey. I'm about to head home. I'll pick up Juliet from her grandmother's, and we'll stop at the grocery store on the way home. Can you think of anything in particular we need? I'll make a list."

Wanda Nell thought for a moment before rattling off a short list of items. "Got 'em," Jack said. "Now here's T.J."

"Hey, Mama. So you were wondering how I go about finding marriage licenses and birth certificates?"

"Yes, I was. Aren't they all on the computer now?"

"They probably are in most counties in the state, but the public can't access them. You still have to write to the appropriate county and request the information. And of course it costs money."

"That can take a while, can't it?" Wanda Nell was dismayed at the thought.

"It can," T.J. admitted. "But when you're doing it fo

lawyer, you can speed up the process a little. I just call the county clerk's office in whatever county and work out something with someone in that office. I can usually get the information back in a day or two. In fact, I should be hearing back sometime today from the Forrest County clerk's office, and Lamar County, too."

"I see. Well, I hope they call back soon. I think we've found out Margaret's name, though. Get Jack to tell you."

"I will," T.J. said. "Before you go, Mama, what about talking to Grandmama again? Jack said y'all are pretty certain she knows something about this."

"We think she does. But from the way she reacted the other day, we're a little worried about asking her again. It surely has to involve your grandfather, and she's always been touchy where he's concerned. She probably doesn't want us raking up anything bad about him."

"There's probably plenty to rake up." T.J. spoke wryly. "You ought to hear some of the stories I've heard since I've been working with Tuck." He paused. "Let me talk to her, Mama. I'll see what I can do."

"If you think it won't make her have a stroke or something."

"It won't," T.J. said confidently. "She's a lot stronger than she lets on. She's pretty tough."

"Okay. I got to get back to work. I'll talk to you later."

"Bye, Mama." Wanda Nell tucked her cell phone in her pocket, deciding to keep it with her, just in case. Normally she left it in her purse, because Melvin wasn't real happy about his waitresses getting personal calls during their shifts.

Back out front again, Wanda Nell got busy with the side work that had to be done before the evening regulars started drifting in around five or five-thirty. She had just finished refilling all the salt and pepper shakers when she looked up to see Mayrene coming in the front door.

Wanda Nell put away the canisters of salt and pepper she'd been using and went to greet her friend.

"Hey, girl," Mayrene said, taking a seat at the counter near the cash register. "What's been going on? Why weren't y'all home last night?"

Wanda Nell grimaced. She hadn't thought about calling Mayrene to let her know they wouldn't be home last night. She apologized, explaining that they had been detained in Hattiesburg. "I can't really tell you much more about it right now. I'll have to fill you in later."

Mayrene sighed. "Okay, but I'll be about to bust from curiosity. How about a glass of tea? And you got any of that apple pie today?"

"There's plenty of pie. Want a scoop of vanilla ice cream with it?"

"I sure do."

Wanda Nell served her tea. "I'll be right back with your pie."

Mayrene had almost emptied her glass when Wanda Nell returned to set down a dessert plate with hot apple pie and ice cream in front of her. "Let me refill that." Wanda Nell, turned to pick up the tea pitcher.

Mayrene had stuck the first forkful of pie and ice cream in her mouth, and the expression on her face made Wanda Nell smile.

"Pretty good, huh?" Wanda Nell asked, setting the pitcher on the counter.

Mayrene nodded, still chewing. After she swallowed, she said, "Like heaven on your tongue, girl. That's the best apple pie I've ever tasted."

"Glad you're enjoying it." Lately, Mayrene had been skimping on desserts, trying to shed a few pounds. But after her fights with Dixon Vance, maybe she had given u on that. Wanda Nell was about to ask her straight out wh Mayrene spoke.

"And before you ask, I'm still seeing Dixon." She stuck more pie and ice cream in her mouth, savoring it. "We had a long talk, and he's real apologetic about everything."

"You're satisfied with that?"

"Yeah, I am. We talked about some stuff we never talked about before, and I flat out told him if he wanted me, he was pretty damn much going to have to take me the way I am. I'm not changing for any man, no matter how I feel about him. It just ain't worth it, in the long run."

"Good for you." Wanda Nell had seen her friend go through some bad patches in the past, just because she had been trying to change her habits for the sake of a man. It had never worked out, and Wanda Nell was pleased to know Mayrene had finally come to this decision. "All I want is for you to be happy."

Mayrene grinned. "Well, I got to find me something else to do these days, you being all lovey-dovey with Jack all the time."

Wanda Nell blushed, and Mayrene cackled with laughter. "Girl, the way you blush, somebody'd think you'd never been married before."

"Oh, stop it. Can I help it if Jack's a lot more romantic than Bobby Ray ever thought about being?"

Mayrene laughed again, more quietly this time. "Jack is everything that jackass Bobby Ray never was, and you deserve the best, darling. You know that as well as I do."

"Thank you." Wanda Nell tried not to blush again. "You got a date tonight?"

Mayrene nodded, her mouth full of the last bit of pie and ice cream. After a moment she said, "Yeah, Dixon's coming over for dinner after his shift." She glanced at her watch. "Guess I'd better get a move on. I got to get by the grocery store and get cooking." She grabbed her purse from the stool beside her and rifled through it, looking for her wallet. She pulled out some money and put it on the counter. "That cover it?"

Wanda Nell pushed back two of the bills. "It's way more than enough, and you know it. How many times have I got to tell you, you're not going to leave me a tip, girl?"

Mayrene shook her head as she stuck the two dollars back in her purse. "I swear, you try to be nice, but some people. . . ." She grinned. "Later, girl. You got to tell me everything."

"I will," Wanda Nell promised. "Now get on out of here, and let me get back to work." Smiling, she took the money to the register and rang up Mayrene's ticket.

Business was slow that evening, and Melvin sent them home at nine-thirty, saying he would close up on his own. Wanda Nell and Ruby accepted with gratitude. "I've got a test tomorrow, and I really need to study for it some more," Ruby said as she and Wanda Nell walked out to their cars.

"Don't stay up too late, now," Wanda Nell said. "I know you'll do just fine. You always do."

Ruby's face shone from Wanda Nell's praise. "I sure hope so. Good night, Wanda Nell. Drive safely."

"You, too, honey."

The drive home was quiet, and she was looking forward to a little relaxation with Jack before bedtime. Jack met her at the door with a smile and a kiss.

He shut the door behind them and followed her into the kitchen. "Juliet's already gone to bed. I think Belle and Miz Culpepper wore her out. Not that she seemed to mind. There sure aren't many girls her age who'd willingly spend that kind of time with two elderly women."

"I know. I'm proud of her for it, but I do worry about it sometimes. She doesn't have that many friends her age."

"She's selective," Jack said, "and she doesn't go for these little cliques so many girls have. She just ignores them."

"Good for her." Wanda Nell opened the refrigerator door and was peering in. "Did you get some orange juice?"

"I did. It's there somewhere."

"I found it." Wanda Nell reached into the fridge. "Want some?"

"No, thanks." Jack retrieved a glass from the cupboard and took the orange juice from her. "You sit, and I'll serve. You've been on your feet, and I haven't."

Wanda Nell smiled up at him. She sipped at her juice while he replaced the carton in the fridge.

He sat down at the table, a big smile on his face. "I've got good news."

"We could use some." Wanda Nell rubbed the back of her neck with one hand. "What?"

"T.J. called a little while ago. He went by to see his grandmother this evening, and he had a little talk with her."

"And?" Wanda Nell prompted him. He was teasing her.

"And," Jack said, drawing out that one syllable, "she's going to talk to us tomorrow morning. She wouldn't tell T.J. what she knows, but there *is* something. We'll find out in the morning."

Twenty-four

During the night Jack had nightmares, and he woke Wanda Nell up twice, thrashing about in the bed. Both times she woke him as gently as she could, and they talked about his dreams until he was able to drop off to sleep again. The night before, at Miss Lyda's, the first night after he had discovered Howell's body, he had slept soundly. This night, however, he had very little restful sleep.

Wanda Nell and Jack awoke to a knock at their bedroom door. "Mama, are you awake?" Juliet called.

Jack stirred beside Wanda Nell. "What time is it?" he mumbled, pushing his tousled hair back from his forehead. He squinted at the bedside clock. It was almost nine.

Juliet called out again. "Mama? It's almost nine o'clock. And y'all are supposed to go over to Grandmama's house at ten."

"We're awake now, baby," Wanda Nell called out. "We'll be up in a minute. Thank you."

"You're welcome. I'll start breakfast."

Both Wanda Nell and Jack were sitting up in bed. "That was one lousy night," Jack said. "I'm sorry, love. I know you didn't get much rest, either."

"I'm okay. It's you I'm worried about. Those awful dreams you were having."

Jack shuddered. "Lord, I hope they go away soon. They were horrible."

Wanda Nell leaned toward him and kissed him. "I know. I'm praying that they go away soon, but don't you be worried about waking me up, honey."

Jack offered a wan smile. "From your mouth to God's ear, amen." He yawned. "I guess I managed to get some sleep. I don't feel as bad as I thought I would."

"It was about four when I woke you the second time. You were asleep again by five, so you had a good four hours of uninterrupted sleep."

"You, too, I hope."

"I did. We'd better get a move on, though. Miz Culpepper will be testy with us if we're late."

Jack took a quick shower, shaved, and dressed in their bathroom while Wanda Nell took her shower in the bathroom she used to share with Juliet. By the time they were both done, Juliet had hot coffee, scrambled eggs, bacon, and toast on the table.

"Thank you, baby," Wanda Nell said. "This was real sweet of you." She hugged Juliet.

"It sure is," Jack agreed, dropping a kiss on top of his stepdaughter's head.

Juliet turned pink with pleasure. "I like cooking. I don't mind."

"Then let's sit down and eat. I'm really hungry," Jack said.

They enjoyed their breakfast, but Wanda Nell kept an eye on the time. They finished at nine-forty-three. "We'll clean up later," she said. "Just leave everything as it is. We don't have time to bother with it now."

"Yes, ma'am," Juliet said. "But I can stay here and clean up if you like."

"No, we want you to go with us." Wanda Nell's tone brooked no argument. She and Jack had discussed this last night. Until the case was solved, neither one of them felt comfortable leaving Juliet on her own.

The sky was dark with impending rain, and the heat was oppressive. "Looks like we're in for some bad thunderstorms," Wanda Nell said as Jack headed the car out of the trailer park.

"That's what they said on the news this morning," Juliet agreed. "I was listening to the radio when I first got up. It's supposed to clear up by this evening."

"Good," Jack said. "Let's just hope it blows through quickly and doesn't do much damage while it's here. I don't like thunderstorms."

Wanda Nell wasn't too fond of them either, but she knew Jack had a particular dread of them. He had told her once that his mother had been terrified of storms, thanks to her own father, who had rushed them all into the storm cellar every time a cloud blew up. "My grandfather was the only man in the county who had a storm cellar," Jack had said. "He grew up in Kansas, and he built one first thing when he moved to Mississippi. Mama told me she spent a lot of time in that cellar."

Wanda Nell patted her husband's arm, and he smiled sheepishly.

There was little traffic to slow them, and Jack pulled his car up in front of Mrs. Culpepper's house on Main Street at three minutes to ten. Wanda Nell was pleased to see T.J.'s pickup parked in the driveway.

"Just in time," Wanda Nell said. "And just in time to get inside ahead of the rain." They could feel the change in the air as soon as they stepped out of the car.

Sure enough, the rain hit just as they reached the front door. Belle was there, waiting for them. "Y'all get on in here before you get wet. My goodness, we're really going to have a storm today. Of course, it's been so dry the past week or so, we surely can use some rain. The grass has been about to burn up in all this heat, and as for the state of the flower beds in the back yard—well, I just feel sorry for the flowers. They're drooping like lost children."

By this time, Wanda Nell, Jack, and Juliet were safely inside the house with the door shut behind them. Jack and Wanda Nell took turns giving Belle a quick hug and a kiss on the cheek, and she beamed with pleasure.

"Y'all come on in the parlor," she said. "T.J. and Lucretia are there, waiting for you. Juliet, I think maybe you and I should take ourselves off to the kitchen. What do you think? I pulled out one of my favorite cookbooks, and I found a recipe for some oatmeal raisin cookies that I'm just about having a fit to try."

Juliet's eyes lit up, Wanda Nell noticed with some surprise. She had really meant it earlier when she said she loved to cook. Belle did, too, and perhaps that explained why Juliet was willing to spend so much time here with her grandmother and Belle.

Jack had noticed, too. He shared a smile with Wanda Nell. "I think I'm going to let her start cooking more at home," Wanda Nell confided in an undertone as they watched Juliet and Belle head for the kitchen.

"Good idea," Jack said. "If it's something she's really getting into, we'll have to encourage her."

"Wanda Nell, don't just stand out there, come on in here." Mrs. Culpepper's voice, more ill-tempered than Wanda Nell had heard it in a long time, reached them from the parlor.

"Yes, ma'am," Wanda Nell called back. "We're coming."

"Morning, Mama, Jack." T.J. stood to greet them.

"Morning, son." Wanda Nell offered him a kiss.

After a nod to T.J., Jack went to stand in front of Mrs. Culpepper. "Good morning, Miz Culpepper. We didn't mean to keep you waiting." He smiled down at her, and Wanda Nell could see the old lady's expression soften. Mrs. Culpepper had always had a soft spot for a good-looking man, and she had taken to Jack surprisingly well.

"That's quite all right, young man," Mrs. Culpepper said in softer tones. "I know it was that fool Belle's fault, anyway. We could hear her rattling on all the way in here. I can't believe she took Juliet off to the kitchen." She shook her head. "She's bound and determined to turn that child into Betty Crocker, I do declare. And if she's not careful, Belle will have Juliet as fat as she is."

"It seems like Juliet's really enjoying herself," T.J. said, his tone mild. "And you always say a girl should know how to cook."

Mrs. Culpepper sniffed. "That's certainly true. Every girl should learn how. Juliet is a very good girl. In fact, she's a very nice young lady." She fixed Wanda Nell with a basilisk gaze. "I certainly wish I could say the same thing about Miranda."

Though her first instinct when hearing remarks like this was to speak up for her daughter, Wanda Nell decided not to take offense at the remark. Besides, she reflected wryly, Mrs. Culpepper was right. Miranda had few, if any, domestic skills, though the good Lord knew Wanda Nell had tried hard enough to teach her.

"She's learning more now that she's married," T.J. said, again calming the waters. "But you know Randa, she's not in too big a hurry to learn." He grinned. He loved his sister, and he seemed to understand and tolerate her better than anyone else. Except, perhaps, her new husband. Wanda Nell was thankful for that.

"Do sit down." Mrs. Culpepper was starting to sound

testy again. "I declare, I'm going to get a crick in my neck if I have to keep staring up at all of you."

"Sorry, Grandmama," T.J. said. "Jack, why don't you and Mama sit here on the sofa by Grandmama, and I'll take that chair over there."

Wanda Nell and Jack complied with this suggestion, and once they were seated, Wanda Nell gazed with some apprehension at Mrs. Culpepper. The old lady seemed fine this morning, but Wanda Nell had to wonder how long she was going to be that way. She offered up a quick prayer.

"Now, Jack," Mrs. Culpepper said, "I'm not going to beat around the bush any longer. I had a talk with T.J. last night, and he told me the whole story." She paused for a moment, looking away. When she turned back to face Wanda Nell and Jack, her face was set in grim lines. "I can't pretend I'm happy to be raking up all this terrible business, but it has to be done. That poor girl deserves at least that much."

Jack said, "Thank you, ma'am. The last thing we want to do is cause you any distress. But we think you may be able to help us get to the truth more quickly by sharing anything you know."

"Then I'll help you. I regret that I wasn't helpful the first time you came to me."

"We understand," Wanda Nell said. Mrs. Culpepper nodded.

"T.J., would you pour me some water?" Mrs. Culpepper asked, picking up a glass from the table beside her chair.

Wanda Nell could feel Jack's tension while they waited for T.J. to refill his grandmother's glass. Mrs. Culpepper would tell them what she knew in her own time, and they couldn't do anything to hurry her along, no matter how anxious they were to hear what she had to say.

"Thank you," Mrs. Culpepper said. T.J. took her left

hand in his and squeezed it gently. She smiled at him. "I know, I should just get on with it." She sipped at her water when T.J. let go of her hand. She held the glass for a moment longer before setting it down on the table.

"My late husband," she began, "was not the most ethical of men, though it pains me deeply to have to say that. He learned that from his own father, and sadly, he passed it down to his only son. I'm grateful that it ended there." She smiled at T.J.

Wanda Nell was deeply touched. She could imagine what this was costing the old lady, and she had renewed respect for her former mother-in-law.

"Thaddeus wasn't above accepting money to look the other way now and again," Mrs. Culpepper continued. "He had some expensive habits"—her face twisted in a moue of distaste—"and the less said about those, the better. He earned a good living, of course, but he always wanted more."

She paused for a drink of water. "He had his cronies in town, and he always did what he could to help them. They were, you understand, some of the richest men in Tullahoma. Thaddeus didn't waste much time on men without money, unless they had some other kind of influence.

"One morning thirty-one years ago, Thaddeus got a phone call before he left for his office, and I overheard his part of the conversation. This was before I heard about a body being found at the high school, and it was only later that I connected the phone call with that girl's death." She paused for a moment. "Thaddeus tried to shield me from as much of his sorry doings as he could, but he didn't know that I was in the hallway outside his study when the phone rang that day. You'd be surprised what I learned over the years, just standing in that hall."

The bleak note in Mrs. Culpepper's voice cut Wanda Nell to the heart. She hadn't cared much for her father-in-law while he was alive, and she had even less respect for him now. She hated what he had done to his wife and son.

After another drink of water, Mrs. Culpepper continued. "I'm not sure who it was on the phone that morning, because I never heard Thaddeus call him by name. But from what happened later, I knew it had to be one of two men."

"Can you be certain of that?" Jack asked in a quiet tone. "How could you narrow it down to just two men?"

"The sheriff came to our house that evening. It was very late, and Thaddeus thought I was safely in bed, as he often did," Mrs. Culpepper said, a rebellious gleam in her eye. "But I heard someone come in, oh, it must have been almost midnight. I was curious, so I tiptoed down the stairs. Bobby Ray was sound asleep, didn't hear a thing.

"When I got downstairs, I saw Thaddeus hadn't closed the door properly. I got as close as I could and listened. He was telling the sheriff just what he had to do. The sheriff was even worse than Thaddeus. He was one of the crookedest men I ever heard tell of."

"That's what I've heard," Wanda Nell said when Mrs. Culpepper fell silent.

"His own family despised him," Mrs. Culpepper continued. "And they had a right to. I heard Thaddeus instruct the sheriff about interrogating some poor young man. Thaddeus said he was from a no-account family, and there wouldn't be any problem with them."

For the sake of Roscoe Bates and his family, Wanda Nell wished heartily that the old judge was roasting in hell where he belonged, right that very minute. How could he have done something like that to a poor family? Any family?

"You see why it shames me to tell you all this." Mrs. Culpepper looked right at Wanda Nell. It was almost as if she had been reading Wanda Nell's mind.

"I understand," Wanda Nell said. "I can only imagine how hard this all was for you."

"I was powerless. I knew if I spoke out against any of this, Thaddeus would beat me within an inch of my life."

At Wanda Nell's horrified protest and the men's expressions of outrage, Mrs. Culpepper smiled sadly. "He didn't do it very often, only when he thought I needed to learn a lesson. By the time this happened, he had me pretty well cowed. I didn't dare tell anybody." She shrugged. "Even if I had, who would have believed me? Not in those days, anyway."

Wanda Nell had no idea what to say, and apparently neither did T.J. or Jack. Mrs. Culpepper finally spoke again. "I'm not telling you this because I want your sympathy. I just want you to understand why I acted as I did."

"We understand, Grandmama," T.J. said, his voice rough. "I'm sorry we're putting you through this. Are you going to be okay?"

Mrs. Culpepper nodded. "Surprisingly, I think I am. Talking about it isn't as bad as I thought it would be. I can say anything about the bastard I want to, and nobody's going to stop me." She paused for a moment. "I suppose the truth will set me free—at least a little."

The others waited for her to speak again. There was very little they could offer in the way of comfort at the moment.

"The sheriff asked Thaddeus who had put him up to this, but Thaddeus wouldn't say. He just promised the sheriff that he'd be well rewarded, and he mentioned a figure that shocked me. Twenty thousand dollars." She shook her head. "Thirty-one years ago that was such a lot of money. And if Thaddeus was willing to give the sheriff that much to cooperate, then Thaddeus had to be getting at least three times that much for his part in it."

"That *was* a lot of money." Jack shook his head in wonder. "Whoever was willing to pay it had to have pretty deep pockets."

"Exactly," Mrs. Culpepper said. "Thirty-one years ago, there were only two men in Tullahoma who had that kind of money: Atwell Connor and Jackson Dewberry."

Wanda Nell vaguely recognized both of the names, but neither one meant much to her husband or her son. She waited for Mrs. Culpepper to explain.

"Both their families had money from way back, a lot of it from plantations in the Delta, and a lot more of it from real estate all over the South."

"Are they both still alive?" Jack asked.

"No. Connor died some years ago, but Dewberry is still alive, as far as I know. Last I heard, he was living in the nursing home here. He has his own apartment there. His family paid a lot of money for it. As soon as he started failing, they got him out of the house and into the nursing home."

"Doesn't sound like a very nice family," Wanda Nell said.

"It isn't," Mrs. Culpepper replied. "Atwell's family isn't much better, and that's the Lord's honest truth." She shook her head. "I've never known a family yet, with that kind of money, where any one of them was happy." Her mouth twisted in what seemed to Wanda Nell an expression of self-mockery. "Thaddeus left me a very wealthy woman when he died, thanks to his greedy, grasping ways. The happiest day of my marriage was when I buried him." She looked at her grandson. "I'm sorry if that shocks you, T.J. I never thought I'd talk that way about him, but I can't go on pretending any longer. Can you understand?"

"Of course, Grandmama." From the strained sound of his voice, Wanda Nell knew T.J. was having a hard time controlling his emotions. She knew exactly how he felt.

"Don't shed any tears over me, any of you," Mrs. Culpepper said, her tone suddenly fierce. "I won't have it. Save them for someone who needs them more." She leaned forward in her chair. "I think I'd like to rest now. T.J., would you help me upstairs?"

T.J. sprang to his feet, reaching her in three strides of his long legs. He slipped one arm around her as she rose from her chair. She stood for a moment, facing Wanda Nell and Jack, who had also stood.

"You know where to look now," she said. "I think the person you're looking for has to be a member of one of those two families. I'll leave it to you to figure out just who, because I have no idea which one of them could be the murderer."

Jack held out his hand to her. She took it, and he said, "Thank you." Mrs. Culpepper nodded as Jack released her hand.

Wanda Nell stepped forward and kissed Mrs. Culpepper on the cheek. She hoped her eyes would tell Mrs. Culpepper what her words couldn't. Mrs. Culpepper smiled at her for a moment, then brought up a hand to caress her cheek. Wanda Nell blinked back her tears.

T.J. led his grandmother out of the room and up the stairs.

Twenty-five

Wanda Nell and Jack sat down again, and neither of them spoke until T.J. came back some minutes later. "She's resting," he said. He sat down and leaned back in his chair. "I don't know about y'all, but I'm exhausted after hearing all that."

"Pretty extraordinary," Jack said. "Just goes to show, you never know what someone's life is really like."

"Mama, you okay?" T.J. asked when Wanda Nell didn't speak.

Wanda Nell nodded. "I'm fine. There's just a lot I'm going to have to think about."

"I know what you mean," T.J. said with a grimace. "Is it too late to change my name? I sure hate knowing I'm named after that old so-and-so." He tried to make a joke of it, but Wanda Nell could tell it was bothering him.

"Don't think about it like that," she urged. "He might not have been a good man, but you *are*. And that's all that counts."

"Thanks, Mama. I'll have to think some more about that, I guess." He stood. "I'd better be getting back to work.

It's getting close to lunchtime, and Tuck and I were planning to have it together."

"Oh, Lord!" Wanda Nell jumped to her feet. "I've got to get to work, too, before Melvin fires me. Come on, honey."

Jack stood. "It's okay, love, it's only ten after eleven, believe it or not. We'll get you there in time."

"I'm going to say goodbye to Belle," T.J. said. "And I'll tell Juliet you're ready to go."

"No, we'll go, too," Wanda Nell said. "I'd like to say goodbye to Belle myself."

She and Jack followed T.J. out of the room and down the hall to the back of the house. The tantalizing aroma of baking cookies reached them as they drew close.

In the kitchen Belle was chattering away to Juliet, who listened raptly. Belle broke off upon seeing the newcomers. "Hello, there. Is everything okay? How is Lucretia? I do hope she didn't wear herself out. I know this must have been hard for her, having to talk about all that. But she's tough, always has been. Always had to be." She shot a knowing look to Wanda Nell, Jack, and T.J.

"Grandmama's upstairs resting," T.J. said. "She'll let you know if she needs something, she said."

Belle nodded. "Oh, yes, she will. That bell she keeps by her bed will start ringing, and it won't stop until I get myself up those stairs to find out what she wants. She calls it Belle's bell." She laughed. "Isn't that sweet? Now, are y'all about to leave and take Juliet? I wish y'all would stay for lunch. It wouldn't take me five minutes to have something ready for all of us."

"We'd love to, Belle," Wanda Nell said, and she meant it. Belle was a wonderful cook. "But I have to get to work, and so does T.J. If Juliet wants to stay, and you don't mind having her, she can."

"Of course I don't mind. I can't tell you how much I enjoy talking cooking with her. She picks up everything so fast. I declare, she's going to be able to open her own restaurant before long."

Juliet flushed at the praise. "I would like to stay, Mama, if you and Jack don't mind."

"It's fine with us," Jack said, smiling. "I can pick you up later, when you're ready to come home."

"We'd better get going, then." Wanda Nell gave Belle and Juliet quick kisses, and after both the men had hugged Belle and said goodbye to Juliet, the three of them departed.

On the way to the Kountry Kitchen, Wanda Nell asked, "What are you going to do next? I don't know much about either of those families, except I recognize the names. I don't know that I've ever met any of them. Not people with that kind of money. They don't eat at the Kountry Kitchen."

"Probably not." Jack grinned. "But they're missing some mighty good food, not to mention first-rate service. Or do you save that only for me?"

Wanda Nell punched him lightly on the arm. "Behave yourself. Now what are you going to do?"

"We need to talk to someone who knows more about both families. At least, more about the younger generation of each of them. What do you think?"

"You're right. You could go to the library or get on the computer, but you can do that later if you have to. We need to talk to someone who knows the kinds of things you can't find in either of those places."

"So I'm thinking Ernie Carpenter," Jack said.

"Exactly," Wanda Nell replied. "She'd be hurt if we didn't include her. She's bound to know something about these people."

"Why don't you call her now? We'll be at the restaurant in about five minutes. Maybe she can come there, and we can talk after the lunch rush is over."

Wanda Nell was already reaching for her phone. Ernie answered on the third ring.

"Hello, Wanda Nell. How are you? Anything new?"

"There certainly is." Wanda Nell explained briefly and asked whether Ernie could come into town to confer with them.

"I certainly can." Wanda Nell had to smile at the enthusiasm in the older woman's voice. "I've managed to find out something about Howell, and I think it could be significant."

"That's great," Wanda Nell said. "You are amazing."

"I know." Ernie chuckled. "I'll see you about two. Will things be quiet enough by then?"

"They should be. We'll see you then." Wanda Nell ended the call and dropped her phone back in her purse.

"So she's coming?" Jack asked. "What time?"

"Two," Wanda Nell replied. "She says she's found out something about Howell, too."

"Even better," Jack said. "Maybe things are really coming together." They had reached the restaurant, and he pulled his car into a parking space around the side. The lot was filling up rapidly.

"You want to come in for some lunch?" Wanda Nell asked.

"No, I'm going home to do some work. You don't mind?"

"Of course not." Wanda Nell gave him a quick kiss before opening her door. "You go on home, and I'll see you at two."

"Will do," Jack said. "Don't work too hard."

Wanda Nell watched and waved as he backed the car out and headed down the street.

Melvin looked up from the cash register when she walked in the door. "Glad you could join us," he said, his eyebrows raised.

Wanda Nell could tell by his tone that he wasn't annoyed, just picking at her. She grinned. "Nice to see you, too." She went behind the counter and headed for the door into the kitchen. "I'll be right back," she said.

The next couple of hours passed quickly. By one-thirty the lunch crowd had thinned out to only four tables, and Wanda Nell was able to take a few minutes to have her own lunch. She finished it quickly, knowing that she shouldn't be eating so fast, but it was hard to break the habit.

She was doing side work in preparation for the evening dinner crowd when Jack arrived a little before two. Ernie came hard on his heels, and Wanda Nell took them to a table in the back dining room. "Would y'all like something to drink?" she asked as her husband and her friend sat down.

"I'd love a cup of coffee and some of that delicious apple pie," Ernie said. "With a big scoop of vanilla ice cream." She sighed. "I shouldn't, but I can't help myself."

"I'll have the same," Jack said, a twinkle in his eye. "Just so Ernie doesn't feel so bad, of course."

"Of course." Wanda Nell rolled her eyes at him. "Two coffees, two apple pies. I'll be back in a minute. Why don't you tell Ernie what we found out?"

"Will do." Ernie turned to Jack eagerly, and he was giving her a short version of the morning's interview with Mrs. Culpepper as Wanda Nell walked away.

She turned in the order for the pie, but before she poured the coffee, she wanted to make sure she would have some time to spend with Ernie and Jack without interruption. Patsy was busy flirting with the one customer sitting at the counter.

"Hey, Junior," Wanda Nell said as she approached, "mind if I borrow Patsy a minute?"

Junior Farley, one of the Kountry Kitchen's most faithful regulars, grinned. "You know I'd do anything for you, Wanda Nell. But don't keep her long, okay?" He winked.

Wanda Nell had to smile. Junior had sure perked up since Patsy had started to work at the restaurant. He had even lost a little weight, and it was all on account of Patsy,

Wanda Nell figured. Patsy seemed interested in Junior, so it wasn't just wishful thinking on Junior's part.

"What's up, Wanda Nell?" Patsy asked. She turned to Junior. "I'll be back, honey. Don't you wander off."

"No, ma'am."

Wanda Nell had moved away a few steps, and Patsy came closer. "I just need a little while to talk over something with my husband and my friend back there," Wanda Nell explained. "You mind?"

"Course not. It's pretty dead in here, and besides, Junior's here to keep me company. Melvin's probably taking a nap in his office. Go on, and if I really need you, I'll holler."

"Thanks." Patsy went back to flirting with Junior, and Wanda Nell prepared the coffee and a glass of tea for herself, and retrieved the pie from the kitchen. She carried the tray to the back and set it down on the table.

Ernie accepted her piece of pie with a happy sigh. "This is so good."

Smiling, Wanda Nell served Jack his pie and coffee and set her glass of tea on the table.

"Have you told Ernie what we found out?" Wanda Nell asked before sipping at her tea.

"We're all up to date," Jack said. "We were just waiting for you." He grinned. "Ernie knows all about both families, the way we figured she would."

"My father knew both Atwell Connor and Jackson Dewberry," Ernie said. "He served on the hospital board with both of them." She sniffed. "He didn't have a very high opinion of either one of them. Too much money and not enough morals, he always said."

"Miz Culpepper said Connor is dead, but that Dewberry is living in a nursing home here in town," Wanda Nell said.

"Yes," Ernie agreed. "So is Mrs. Connor. Mrs. Dewberry died a number of years ago."

"What family do Connor and Dewberry have, besides Mrs. Connor?" Jack asked. He had his notebook out, ready to jot down names.

"Dewberry had three children," Ernie replied. "Two sons and a daughter. The daughter was the youngest. There was a gap between her and the brothers. I believe the parents were both over forty when she was born."

"So she'd be about my age, or a little older," Wanda Nell said. "I don't know her, and I don't guess I know her brothers, either."

"The two brothers were just ahead of me in school," Ernie said with a smile. "So there's no reason you should know them."

"Did you actually know them?" Wanda Nell asked.

"Not really. Of course, everyone knew who they were. They were both very handsome, as I recall, and every mama in town wanted one of them to marry her daughter." She laughed. "Thank the Lord my mama was smarter than that."

"Where are they now?" Jack asked.

"The younger brother left town many years ago. I believe he went to New York. He had some ambitions of being an actor, but whether he ever achieved them, I don't know. I certainly have never seen him in anything. He's rarely come back." She grinned. "The last time he did, about twenty years ago, as I recall, he caused quite a sensation. He brought his boyfriend with him. And you can imagine how that set tongues to wagging."

Wanda Nell laughed. "I'm sure it did."

"The people in Tullahoma didn't know what to think," Ernie said. "Of course, he was a Dewberry, and no one dared say anything openly."

"What about the older brother?" Jack asked. "What does he do?"

"He lives in the Delta, running one of the plantations

they still own. He does come to Tullahoma, though. He still has business interests here, and the family home is here. His sister lives here. Mousy little thing and not very attractive. She was obviously an afterthought, if not a total surprise, to her parents. All their attention went to the two boys." She looked at Jack. "You actually know her. She teaches at the high school."

Twenty-six

"She teaches at the high school?" Jack shook his head. "I don't recall a teacher named Dewberry."

Ernie smiled. "She doesn't use that name. She got married while she was at Ole Miss, to some boy who probably thought he'd found himself a meal ticket." She shook her head. "Her father made it clear he wasn't going to support them, and the boy took off after a couple of years."

"So what *is* her name?" Wanda Nell asked. "I'm surprised she kept her husband's name if he ran off and left her like that."

"It's Avenel. Marysue Avenel. She teaches math."

"Do you know her?" Wanda Nell asked Jack.

"Only to say hello to if I see her in the hall," Jack said with a frown. "She doesn't mix much with the other teachers." He shrugged. "Usually when I see her, she has her head down. It's a wonder she doesn't run into people or walls all the time."

"Sounds pretty pathetic," Wanda Nell said. "Like she has no friends at all." She couldn't help feeling sorry for the woman, after all she had heard.

"It sounds like her parents are to blame," Jack said. "If

they gave all their attention to their two sons, it's no wonder she's the way she is."

"Yes," Ernie agreed. "They certainly did, from everything I ever saw and heard. The two boys were both handsome and outgoing, with many friends. Everything poor Marysue never has been. They're both a good bit older, both in college by the time she was born. Everyone knew them, but people tended to forget all about her."

"That's very sad." Wanda Nell's heart went out to that neglected child.

"She's not quite as bad as she sounds," Ernie said. "I think she just finds it very difficult to make friends. I used to chat with her some in the teachers' lounge, but much of the time she sat in a corner by herself." She sighed. "I would have loved to knock her parents upside the head a time or two, though, for what they surely did to her."

"So, getting back to the family as a whole," Wanda Nell said, "what do you think, Ernie? Could one of them be the killer?"

Ernie thought about it for a moment. "Jackson Dewberry was ruthless when it came to business, but I don't know that he would have killed his own daughter. If indeed that poor dead girl *was* his daughter. We still don't know that for sure."

"No, we don't," Jack conceded. "But I think we have to consider him a good candidate for being her father after what Miz Culpepper told us."

Ernie nodded. "I agree he could very well be her father. I just don't think he would have killed a child of his, and he certainly couldn't have killed that man in Hattiesburg. He isn't capable of leaving the nursing home, from what I hear tell." She shuddered. "I could certainly see him paying someone to take his an unwanted child off his hands and off his conscience, fifty years ago."

"What about his sons?" Wanda Nell asked. "Or Mary-sue? Do you think one of them could be the murderer?"

Ernie shrugged. "The oldest son without a doubt. He's as ruthless as his father ever was, from what I've heard. The other son you have to rule out because he simply hasn't been around."

"And Marysue?" Wanda Nell prompted.

"I would say she didn't have the gumption to say boo to a goose," Ernie replied. "But many a worm has turned. She could have done it, I suppose, though she would have been a bit young thirty-one years ago." She frowned. "Only about fifteen, perhaps."

"She sure doesn't seem to have much spunk," Jack said. "But I could see a teenager lashing out at someone in anger, not realizing what could happen."

"Especially an unattractive, unhappy girl confronted with a beautiful half sister she never knew about," Wanda Nell added. "Jenna Rae was a beautiful girl. I hate the thought of a girl killing another girl like that, but it does make sense, doesn't it?"

"You could certainly make a case for it," Ernie agreed. "You also have to consider Jackson Dewberry Junior. Thirty-one years ago he would have been in his thirties, and he might have seen an illegitimate half sister as some kind of threat. At least, financially."

"Okay, so we have two potential suspects there, Jackson Junior and Marysue Avenel." Jack paused in thought. "What about Connor's family?"

"You said his widow is living in the nursing home, too," Wanda Nell said. "I guess that rules her out."

"Physically, at least," Ernie replied. "Evangeline is in her late eighties, I'd reckon. She can't walk, has to use a wheel-chair. Mentally, though, I'd say she was tough enough to pay someone else to do her dirty work for her."

"A big fan of hers, are you?" Jack asked.

Ernie laughed, but there was no amusement in the sound. "Evangeline Connor is one of the meanest women I ever had the misfortune to meet. My parents loathed her *and* her husband. You'd think she's the Queen of England's cousin, the way she carries on sometimes, but she was just plain Evangeline Thibodeaux before Atwell Connor dug her out of some swamp in Louisiana."

"You really don't like her." Wanda Nell was faintly shocked. "I don't think I've ever heard you use that tone talking about somebody."

"I surely don't." Ernie grimaced. "I knew the Connors's daughter, Sarabeth, and she was a sweet, dear girl. Evangeline made her life an absolute hell, and her father did nothing to stop it. They forced her to marry some business crony of Connor's who was a good twenty years older than Sarabeth. All for the sake of business." Her face darkened.

"What happened to her?" Jack asked. From Ernie's demeanor, the answer must be terrible.

"She committed suicide on their first anniversary. She begged her parents to help her get away from her husband, but they wouldn't do it. She felt absolutely abandoned, I'm sure, and she must have figured death was the only way out." She paused for a moment. "I was away at college by then, and I had no idea what was going on. By the time I came home again, Sarabeth was dead."

"That's appalling," Jack said. "What kind of monsters would do that to a child?"

Wanda Nell was sick to her stomach.

Seeing her face, Jack said, "Honey, what's wrong? You've gone white as a sheet." He reached out to her, the worry evident in his expression.

"I'm okay." Wanda Nell clasped his hand, but her voice shook. "That poor girl. Those poor girls," she added, thinking of Jenna Rae. "No one was there to protect them. Things like that shouldn't happen."

Jack pulled his chair next to hers, slipping an arm around her shoulders, and Wanda Nell drew comfort from him.

"No, they shouldn't," Ernie said. Neither Wanda Nell nor Jack had ever seen her look so grim, like an avenging angel. "But Evangeline paid a heavy price for what she let happen to Sarabeth. Everyone in town knew what happened, and people started shunning her. The only woman in town who'd have anything to do with her after that was Ramona Dewberry, and that was probably because Jackson didn't give her any choice. He and Connor had too many business interests at stake."

"Why didn't they just move away?" Jack asked. "Surely they had enough money to do that."

"Of course they did," Ernie replied. "But Connor didn't give a damn about what people thought. They traveled a fair amount, so they weren't here as much as they might have been. But I think he and Evangeline both got some perverse kind of satisfaction out of it, knowing that they weren't going to be driven away."

"That just sounds sick to me," Wanda Nell said. "Are there really people like that?" She shuddered. "I don't think I've ever known anybody that . . . twisted."

"Twisted is a good word for them," Ernie agreed.

"Did they have any children besides their daughter?" Jack asked.

"Yes, a son. Cameron Connor."

"Where have I heard that name before?" Jack asked. "It sure sounds familiar."

"He was a football player," Ernie said. "Star of the team when he was in high school. He went on to play for Alabama, and he was even drafted by the NFL. I can't remember what team he played for. But he didn't last very long. He was badly injured during a game, and he had to give up playing football."

"I remember him now," Jack said. "He used to do the sports for some TV station."

"Yes, that's right," Ernie said.

"What does he do now?" Wanda Nell asked. "He's not still on TV, is he?"

Ernie shook her head. "No, he lost that job eventually. Took to drinking, and he showed up on the set one day, drunk as Cooter Brown. From what I heard, they'd already had enough of him at the station, but that was the final nail in his coffin. He was fired, and he came back to Tullahoma."

"What's he been doing since then?" Jack asked.

"Living off his mother." Ernie gave a sniff of contempt. "His father died a few years after he came back here, and for a while Cameron tried his hand at managing his father's holdings and business interests, but he apparently wasn't very good at it. So Evangeline stepped in. As far as I know, she's still in charge, even though she lives at the nursing home."

"With that kind of money, you'd think she'd prefer to live at home," Jack said. "Surely she could afford as much help as she needed."

"She certainly can, but she was having a hard time finding anyone willing to work for her. I told you she was a mean woman."

"If she's that mean," Wanda Nell said, "it's a wonder they haven't thrown her out of the nursing home."

Ernie shrugged. "I'm sure there are times when they'd like to, but no doubt she pays well to live there. And the staff there aren't her responsibility. The poor man who runs the place has to handle all that. She probably makes his life a living hell."

"Charming woman," Jack muttered. "Now, what about Cameron? Can you see him as a murderer? He doesn't sound like much, frankly."

"He isn't," Ernie agreed. "He's big and dumb, and enough like his mother to be nasty. It wouldn't surprise me a bit if he had killed somebody, especially if Evangeline put him up to it."

Wanda Nell looked at Jack. "I don't think it's a good idea for us to try to talk to him or his mother. I think if anybody's going to, it had better be Elmer Lee."

Jack sighed. "You're probably right. He needs to be told about all this, anyway. I'll see if I can go over and talk to him this afternoon."

"Good plan," Ernie said. "Someone with some real authority is going to have to deal with these people. Besides, if you just went over there and asked to speak to Evangeline, I doubt you'd get very far."

"What about Mr. Dewberry?" Wanda Nell asked. "Would it be just as hard getting in to talk to him? Somebody besides Elmer Lee, I mean."

"Maybe," Ernie said. "I'm not really sure."

"Will y'all excuse me a minute while I call Elmer Lee?" Jack asked, standing. He pulled out his cell phone.

"Sure, honey," Wanda Nell said. Jack walked a few feet away and punched in a number.

"This sure is a mess," Wanda Nell commented to Ernie. "Those people just sound so terrible. How can people like that live with themselves?"

"If you don't have a conscience, it's a lot easier," Ernie said, a cynical note in her voice.

Jack was back in a moment. "Elmer Lee has some time to talk to me now, so I'm going on over to the Sheriff's Department. I'll let you know how it goes." He bent to kiss Wanda Nell.

"Okay, honey."

"Ernie, thanks for all the information," Jack said. "You're amazing."

Ernie grinned, clasping his proffered hand and pumping

it with vigor. "You're welcome. I like knowing I might have done something to help bring this to a close. I've been thinking a lot about that poor girl the last couple of days, and she deserves some justice."

"She sure does," Jack said. "I'll see y'all later."

Wanda Nell turned back to Ernie. "Well, I guess I'd better get back to work. Even though it don't look like there's any customers to take care of at the moment."

"Yeah, I'd better be going, too." Ernie started to rise, then sat down again. "You know, I completely forgot what I was going to tell you and Jack. About what I found out."

"That's right," Wanda Nell said. "You found out something about Mr. Howell, didn't you?"

"I sure did. I didn't remember him, of course. He was before my time, but when I was going through some of the old high school yearbooks, I found something."

"What?" Wanda Nell asked.

"He worked briefly as a custodian at the high school," Ernie said with a triumphant gleam in her eye. "Fifty years ago."

Twenty-seven

"You're sure it's him?" Wanda Nell asked.

Ernie nodded. "Oh, yes, it has to be. How many Parnell Howells could there be?" She reached into her bag. "Just to be certain, though, I brought the yearbook with me. Careful, now, it's a bit tattered." She placed the book in Wanda Nell's hands.

A strip of paper marked the page in the yearbook where Howell's photograph was. Wanda Nell parted the pages with gentle fingers and gazed at the page with pictures of staff members at the high school. She stared at Howell's picture.

"He was handsome, but he also looks a bit cruel. Something about his mouth, the way he's holding it. It's like what I remember of Howell when I met him." She shut the book and handed it back to Ernie. "So now we know he was in Tullahoma fifty years ago." She shook her head. "It's hard to think that Jenna Rae would be around fifty now."

"We'll find out who took all those years away from her," Ernie promised. "We're getting very close, I'm sure. I just feel it in my bones."

Wanda Nell had to smile at that. For a moment she imagined Ernie dressed like a Gypsy fortuneteller, uttering predictions about the future. "I hope you're right."

"Maybe all it will take is Elmer Lee and Jack confronting Jackson Dewberry and Evangeline Connor," Ernie said. "Maybe they can rattle them enough to let something slip."

"I suppose," Wanda Nell said. "They're both pretty old, though."

"They are," Ernie agreed. "But if you're feeling some qualms of conscience about that, I wouldn't, if I were you. Neither one of them deserves much consideration, as far as I'm concerned. Especially Evangeline. After what she did to her own daughter." She shook her head, and Wanda Nell could see how angry Ernie was about what had happened, even after all these years.

"I guess you're right. Bad things ought to come home to roost. I can't help wondering, though, if even Elmer Lee, going in there as the sheriff, will be able to get them to talk if they don't want to."

"They might not admit anything," Ernie said. "You're right about that. But rattling their cages, as they say, might get some kind of reaction."

"I'm just wondering if there isn't another way to get into the nursing home and try to talk to them." Wanda Nell stared off into space for a moment. She smiled. "You remember my friend Mayrene Lancaster?"

"Of course."

"Well, you know she's a beautician, and she works for the best beauty salon in town. Mayrene doesn't do it herself all the time, just fills in for the girl who does it on a regular basis, but she sometimes goes to the nursing home to do hair for the ladies, and to cut the men's hair if they want a trim."

Ernie grinned. "I see the glimmerings of a plan, I do believe. Mayrene can get in there and ask a few questions, stir things up a little bit."

"Yes," Wanda Nell said, "but I was thinking maybe she didn't have to go by herself. I could go with her, and between the two of us we might be able to talk to both Miz Connor and Mr. Dewberry. It might be less threatening if I was to do it, rather than the sheriff and Jack."

"It's certainly worth a try," Ernie said. "Are you going to suggest it to Jack and Elmer Lee?"

"All they can do is say no," Wanda Nell replied.

"Whatever happens, good luck. And let me know as soon as you know something more." Ernie started gathering her things together. "This time I really do have to get going, and you probably have to get back to work." She rose from her chair.

"I sure do," Wanda Nell said with a guilty start. The restaurant was still quiet, with only a couple of customers, but she really needed to get ready for the dinner crowd. She gave Ernie a quick hug and followed her to the front of the restaurant.

After Ernie was gone, Wanda Nell got started on what her mama would have called her "busywork"—checking the sugar dispensers, salt and pepper shakers, and the supply of napkins and clean cutlery. While her hands did the tasks, her mind was occupied elsewhere. She kept thinking about her idea of going to the nursing home in the guise of beautician's assistant. She knew Mayrene would go along with the idea. Mayrene was always up for something like that. The question was, what would Jack and Elmer Lee say?

Wanda Nell decided she had better find out. Excusing herself for a few minutes, she went into the restroom and locked the door. Pulling out her cell phone, she speed-dialed Jack. He answered on the third ring.

"Hey, darling, what's up? I'm still here at the Sheriff's Department."

"How's it going?" Wanda Nell asked. "What does Elmer Lee think?"

"He thinks we're on the right track. He trusts Ernie's information and her take on the people involved. But he's a little concerned about confronting them without something more concrete to go on."

"That might take a while," Wanda Nell said.

"He's hoping to talk to one of the judges, but the particular judge he wants to talk to isn't available for a couple of days. So Elmer Lee's thinking we should back off until he's had a chance to talk to the judge."

"I see," Wanda Nell said. "Well, I have an idea. It might work, but it might cause a real mess."

"What is it?" Wanda Nell could tell by his tone in those three words that Jack was anxious.

Quickly she explained, and when she finished, he didn't say anything at first. "Well, honey, what do you think?" she finally asked.

"I think it's just crazy enough to work. Who knows? Let me ask Elmer Lee real quick."

Wanda Nell could hear the rumble of the men's voices, but not what they were saying. Jack was probably holding the phone so she couldn't. She was getting impatient, knowing she ought to get back to work, when Jack came back on the phone.

"He's a little nervous about it," Jack said. "And he wants us to think carefully about it, but he's not saying not to do it." He laughed. "Hang on a minute, he wants to talk to you."

"Wanda Nell." Elmer Lee's voice boomed in her ear.

"Yes," she answered, holding the phone away a little. "What is it, Elmer Lee?"

"I probably ought to have my head examined, but I'm thinking it won't hurt to stir things up a little. And being that it's not official, with me doing the stirring, it ought to be interesting to see what happens. I don't think you're in any danger, or I wouldn't be agreeing to this. I hope you realize that."

"I do," Wanda Nell said, "and I appreciate your concern. After all, what could either one of them do right there in the nursing home?"

"I reckon you're right. So when are you going to do it?"

"I have to call Mayrene first," Wanda Nell replied. "But I'm hoping maybe tomorrow morning. Look, I really have to get back to work. Tell Jack I'll talk to him later." She ended the call before Elmer Lee got any more chatty.

She speed-dialed the beauty shop, and when the receptionist answered, she asked for Mayrene. "Tell her it's Wanda Nell, and it's real important."

"Okay, honey. Just hang on there, and I'll get her."

A few moments later Mayrene's voice came on the line. "Hey, girl, what's up? Is something wrong?"

"No, everything's okay," Wanda Nell said. "Look, I'll explain it all to you later, but I need your help with something."

"Sure thing. What?"

"When's the next time Nadine is supposed to go out to the nursing home to do hair?"

"She usually goes Thursday or Friday. Hang on." Wanda Nell heard her yell a question at Nadine. After a moment Mayrene spoke into the phone again. "She's supposed to go tomorrow morning."

"Great. Do you think she'd let you go instead? Tell her I'll make up for any tips she'd lose. And don't ask me why right now, but I need to go with you."

"Okay, girl. Hang on a minute. Nadine, come over here."

Wanda Nell waited a short time. "It's okay by her, so we can do it. We need to be out there around eight, though. Is that okay?"

"Sure. And thanks. I promise I'll explain everything

tonight, or in the morning. It's real important; otherwise I wouldn't ask."

"I know that," Mayrene said. "I got to get back to Doris Cooper right now, or else that head of hers is going to start looking like a Brillo pad. I'll get all the details later."

Wanda Nell thanked her and ended the call. She then discovered that she needed to use the restroom after all, and when she was done, she hurried out. "Sorry, got a bit of an upset stomach," she said by way of apology to Patsy.

"It ain't exactly Grand Central Station here at the moment," Patsy said. "But now that you're back, I think I'll slip out back for a cigarette. Okay?"

"Sure, go ahead." With everything that was going on, Wanda Nell wished she could join Patsy. She had given up smoking nearly three years ago, but sometimes she still missed it.

Soon customers began to trickle in, and Wanda Nell had plenty to keep her busy. Mayrene dropped by after work to check in with her. Wanda Nell didn't have much time to tell her everything, but she was able to share enough of the details to satisfy her friend's curiosity for the time being.

"Okay, honey," Mayrene said. "I'd better get going, 'cause Dixon's stopping by later on, and I need to cook up a little something for us. You be ready to go about seven-thirty or so in the morning, okay?"

Wanda Nell said she would be ready, and Mayrene headed out the door after leaving money on the counter for her coffee and apple pie.

The rest of the evening passed quickly. Wanda Nell had no time to call Jack again, but she knew he'd be waiting up for her when she got home. As she pulled her car up beside the trailer, she reflected on just how wonderful it was to have Jack to come home to, along with Juliet. Her life sure was different now, and she thanked the Lord for that every day.

Jack was sitting on the couch watching television when she came in. He turned the volume down and got up to greet her with a kiss. "That sure is nice," Wanda Nell said. He smiled.

After a few moments Wanda Nell pulled away. "Has Juliet gone to bed already?"

Jack nodded. "She said she wanted to read a while."

"I'll just go and say good night," Wanda Nell said. "I'll be right back."

She walked down the hall toward her daughter's room. Light shone dimly through the half-open door, and Wanda Nell paused just inside the door. Juliet was fast asleep, her book at her side. Smiling, Wanda Nell tiptoed in, picked up the book, and placed it on the bedside table. She clicked the light off and tiptoed out again, pulling the door almost shut.

Back in the living room, she joined Jack on the couch. "Are you ready for bed, honey?" he asked. "I know you're pretty tired by now."

"I am," Wanda Nell admitted. "But it feels good, being able to sit here with you for a little while. Nice and relaxing, before we go to bed."

Jack pulled her close, and she rested her head against his shoulder. They sat quietly for a few minutes, and Wanda Nell was beginning to feel drowsy. Yawning, she sat up. "I guess I'd better get on to bed."

"I'll come with you. It's been a long day, and I'm pretty tired myself." Jack followed her down the hall to their bedroom.

When they were in bed, the lights off, and getting comfortable, Wanda Nell asked, "Are you sure you don't mind me going to the nursing home in the morning?"

"No, I know you and Mayrene will be careful," Jack said, after a big yawn. "And what could happen there? You might not find out much, but like Elmer Lee said, maybe stirring things up a little will produce some kind of results."

"I'm not afraid, at least not for me or for Mayrene. It's the stirring up part I'm thinking about. Or I guess I've been thinking about it more and more since I first came up with this idea."

"I've thought about that, too," Jack admitted. "It does make me a bit nervous, because we're not sure what we'll be stirring up. One other person has already died because of all this, and I don't want to see anybody else murdered." He sighed. "But I just keep going back to Jenna Rae. Thinking about her, and how terrible this whole thing is. I think we have to do it for her sake."

"You're right. I'm just praying that nobody else gets hurt, unless it's somebody who really deserves it. Like the person who killed her."

"That's what we have to focus on," Jack said. "And just watch out."

They talked for a few more minutes, but they were both worn out from the events of the past few days. Soon they were sound asleep, and when the alarm sounded the next morning, Wanda Nell came out of a sound sleep as Jack turned it off.

"What time is it?" she asked.

Jack picked up his glasses from the nightstand and looked at the clock. "Six-thirty," he said, yawning. "I think I'll get over to the school for a run this morning. What time are you and Mayrene leaving?"

"In about an hour."

"I probably won't be back by then," Jack said. "Y'all be careful, and call me right away if anything happens."

"I will," Wanda Nell promised.

Juliet was already in the kitchen when Wanda Nell walked in. "How about some breakfast, Mama?"

"What's on the menu?" Wanda Nell glanced at the stove.

"I'm cooking some bacon," Juliet said. "I thought I'd make a quiche for later. Belle gave me a recipe."

"Sounds good. I think I'll just have some toast and coffee this morning, honey. But you be sure and save me some of that quiche for later. I'm looking forward to tasting it."

"Thanks, Mama." Juliet went back to her bacon. "I'm glad you don't mind me cooking."

"Darling, if it's something you want to do, and you like doing it, then you go right ahead." Wanda Nell laid her head against Juliet's.

"Even if I wanted to go to cooking school instead of college?" Juliet asked.

Wanda Nell paused. She had always thought Juliet would be the one of her children who would actually go to college and get a degree, and she was disappointed to think that Juliet didn't want to. Suppressing a sigh, she said, "We can certainly talk about that, honey. You've still got some time to make up your mind about things."

"Okay," Juliet said. "I promise I'll think about it."

"Good." Wanda Nell popped a couple of slices of bread into the toaster and poured herself a cup of coffee while she waited. She buttered and ate her toast and had a second cup of coffee.

Wanda Nell was ready and walking out her door at seven-thirty. She met Mayrene outside. "I'd better take my own car," Wanda Nell said. "I'll have to be at the Kountry Kitchen at eleven-thirty."

"That should be enough time," Mayrene said. "Before we go, though, tell me just who it is you want to talk to. Last night you didn't exactly say, and I'm curious."

"Evangeline Connor and Jackson Dewberry. They're the two we think are connected. Dewberry could be Jenna Rae's father, or it might have been Miz Connor's husband."

Mayrene's eyebrows shot up. "Honey, if you're going to talk to Miz High-and-Mighty Connor, I hope you had a tetanus shot recently. That old biddy is something else."

"So you've done her hair?"

"I sure have. And she's as hard to please as an old maid on her wedding night." She laughed. "But if you keep telling her how young she looks, and how much you love her hair, she's a little easier to handle."

"Ernie said she was the meanest woman she ever knew," Wanda Nell said with a grimace. "What about Mr. Dewberry? Have you ever cut his hair or done anything for him?"

Mayrene shook her head. "Nope, never have. Some of the men have a barber come in. They don't hold with having a woman cut their hair." Glancing at her watch, she said, "We'd better get going, honey. They don't like you to be late. The old biddies start clucking if you're not there on time."

"I'll be right behind you," Wanda Nell said. True to her word, she followed Mayrene into town and out the highway to the nursing home. She parked beside Mayrene in the parking lot and helped her carry in her equipment.

A large, relatively new facility, the Lake Tullahoma Senior Living Center served as both a nursing home and an assisted-living facility. Wanda Nell eyed the place with curiosity. The grounds were immaculate, and there were a few people sitting out on the porch, smoking and enjoying the morning sun.

Mayrene nodded and smiled at them as they approached the front door. Inside, she went straight to the desk to sign herself and Wanda Nell in.

"Morning, Darlene," she said to the young black woman behind the counter. "This here's my assistant, Wanda Nell."

Darlene smiled at Wanda Nell.

"It's down this way," Mayrene said, leading Wanda Nell down one of the side corridors. "They have a little room set up like a beauty shop. All I have to do is bring my own scissors and so on. Everything else is here. There should be a sign-up sheet on the door, so we'll know who's coming and what they want."

Sure enough, there was a sheet taped to the door. Mayrene pulled it off and handed it to Wanda Nell before unlocking the door with the key Darlene had given her.

Wanda Nell scanned the list. Five women and two men had signed up for appointments. Her eyes widened when she saw that Evangeline Connor had signed up for eight-thirty. Her heart began to pound a little.

Would she be able to find out anything? She followed Mayrene into the room, thinking ahead to the challenge of dealing with the meanest woman Ernie Carpenter had ever known.

Twenty-eight

Mayrene's first appointment that morning, a small woman named Miss Roberta Simpson, proudly told them she was ninety-nine. She also informed them she was looking forward to turning a hundred in less than three months. She had walked into the room with the aid of only a cane. Wanda Nell hoped she would be in that good of shape when she was sixty, much less almost a hundred.

While Mayrene worked on Miss Simpson's thin hair, Miss Simpson chatted the whole time. She was lively, and when Wanda Nell asked her what her secret was for such a long life, Miss Simpson laughed and said, "Not minding my own business and eating right, dear. I've always been interested in everyone and everything, and I always eat sensibly. Stimulate the mind and feed your body right. That's all it takes."

By the time Miss Simpson was finished, Wanda Nell had almost forgotten about Evangeline Connor. When Mrs. Connor wheeled herself into the room, however, Wanda Nell felt her heart start to flutter. One look at the face of the thin, elderly woman in the wheelchair was enough to make her head start to ache. She had never seen anyone with such a sour expression. "Like all she's ever done was suck on lemons her entire life," Wanda Nell's mother might have said, and Wanda Nell would have agreed.

"Why, Evangeline," Miss Simpson said, her voice warm enough to melt butter. "Are you having your hair done today? How nice."

Mrs. Connor stared at Miss Simpson. "I thought I smelled something old when I came in here. Why don't you just go along, and let us get on with it?" She wheeled past Miss Simpson, barely missing the older woman's feet.

Miss Simpson merely smiled. "One of the joys of being as old as I am, ladies, is being able to tell someone like Evangeline here to go to hell and then sleep easily at night, knowing it's a forgone conclusion." She turned and left the room, leaving Wanda Nell and Mayrene trying very hard not to laugh their heads off.

Another look at Evangeline Connor, however, sobered them both pretty quickly. "Good morning, Miz Connor," Mayrene said. "Nadine couldn't come today, so I came in her place. This here's Wanda Nell. She's going to be helping me."

"I remember you," Mrs. Connor said in a grudging tone. "As I recall, you're competent at least." Her gaze raked Wanda Nell up and down. "And what are you going to be doing?"

"I'll be happy to shampoo your hair, if you'd like," Wanda Nell said. That was what she and Mayrene had agreed upon. Wanda Nell couldn't style hair, but she could do any shampooing that was necessary.

Mrs. Connor sniffed. "I suppose it will be all right." She thrust out a bag she had been holding in her lap. "Here's my shampoo. It's the only thing I use. My scalp is very delicate, and I can't tolerate rough hands. I hope you know what you're doing." Her tone indicated she might well be taking her life in her hands.

"I'll be very gentle," Wanda Nell promised, though the longer she was around the woman, the harder it was going to be to resist the urge to drown her and be done with it.

Suppressing such thoughts, Wanda Nell helped Mrs. Connor out of her wheelchair and into the chair in front of the sink. She turned on the water and adjusted the temperature before easing Mrs. Connor's head in the proper position for washing. She took every care to be gentle and, to her surprise, Mrs. Connor didn't complain once. She still looked like she was sucking on a lemon, but when Wanda Nell finished, she said, "That wasn't as bad as I thought it would be."

Wanda Nell responded with a strained smile. She and Mayrene worked together to get Mrs. Connor from the shampoo chair into the one where Mayrene would work on her hair.

Once Mrs. Connor was settled, Mayrene asked her what she wanted done. Mrs. Connor responded by saying, "I don't need my hair cut today, so don't think you'll be able to charge extra for that. I just want it rolled and styled. You can style it, and if I don't like it, you'll have to do it over."

"Sure thing, ma'am," Mayrene said. "I've got an idea of what will be perfect for you, and it'll make you look even younger." She winked at Wanda Nell over Mrs. Connor's head. Wanda Nell turned away for a moment.

When she turned back, Mayrene was busy putting rollers in Mrs. Connor's hair. Catching Wanda Nell's eye, Mayrene nodded. "So, honey, what did you think of Hattiesburg? Wasn't it the first time you'd been there?" She smiled at Mrs. Connor in the mirror. "Wanda Nell and her husband just got back from down there."

Mrs. Connor sniffed, but before she could say anything, Wanda Nell spoke. "Oh, it seemed like a real nice place. And we met some interesting people down there. In fact, one of them said he lived here in Tullahoma about fifty years ago."

"Really?" Mayrene said. "That was a long time ago. I was only about four or five." This time she winked at Mrs. Connor in the mirror. "And I bet you weren't much older than that, were you, honey?"

From the expression on Mrs. Connor's face, Wanda Nell figured the old woman couldn't make up her mind whether to be flattered by the years deducted from her age or offended by Mayrene's referring to her as "honey."

"Well, I wasn't around then," Wanda Nell said, her tone apologetic. "But this man we met said he wasn't here all that long, although he did know some people here. Now, what was his name?" She pretended to think for a moment. "It was Howell, and he had some kind of unusual first name. What was it?" She paused again. "Parnell. That was it. Parnell Howell."

Wanda Nell had been watching Mrs. Connor's face in the mirror as closely as she dared, and from what she could see, Mrs. Connor didn't react when she spoke Howell's name. She simply looked bored.

"I don't think I know any Howells," Mayrene said. "I guess his people weren't from around here."

"No, I don't think so," Wanda Nell replied. "I'm pretty sure he was originally from Hattiesburg."

"And what, pray tell, was so interesting about this man?" Mrs. Connor asked, her irritation obvious. "He sounds like a complete and utter nobody to me."

"He married a girl from here," Wanda Nell said, trying to figure out what Mrs. Connor's reaction meant. "She passed away some time ago, but I do know they had a daughter. I believe he said his wife's name was Margaret Lewis." Again, she watched Mrs. Connor carefully, but still the woman didn't appear to react.

"She sounds like a nobody, too. I don't know any family named Lewis in Tullahoma, and if I don't know them, they're not worth knowing."

Mayrene, her back to the mirror, rolled her eyes at Wanda Nell. "I don't know any Lewises either," Wanda Nell said, trying hard to keep her tone mild. "The really sad thing about it, according to Mr. Howell, was that his daughter, his only child, was murdered, right here in Tullahoma. Thirty-one years ago. Isn't that awful?"

Mrs. Connor's eyes narrowed, and she stared hard at Wanda Nell's reflection. "I remember that," she said. "They found some little tramp naked on the football field at the high school. They never did find out who did it, as I recall." She sniffed. "People like that, though, what are you going to do? If that girl had been raised by a decent family in the first place, it wouldn't have happened to her."

"So you think she deserved what happened to her?" Wanda Nell said, and this time she couldn't suppress the anger in her voice.

"Don't speak in that tone to me, missy," Mrs. Connor said. "I said nothing of the kind. You bleeding hearts are all the same." Her tone was nasty and mocking. "That girl was obviously doing something she shouldn't have been doing, sneaking around with Lord knows who. And somebody killed her. That kind of girl attracts bad men, and then they pay for it."

"I see," Wanda Nell said. Her head throbbed, she was so angry. She made herself take a few deep breaths, and as she began to calm down a bit, she started thinking. Was Mrs. Connor being deliberately provocative in order to distract her? Or was it just her natural meanness coming through?

Wanda Nell wasn't sure, but she decided to probe a little further. "I think it's just terrible that they never found out who killed her. It almost makes me think there was some kind of cover-up going on. Probably some rich man wanted to get rid of that poor girl, and he paid off somebody and walked away from the whole thing."

"I bet you're right," Mayrene said as she jabbed a bobby pin into one of the rollers on Mrs. Connor's head.

"Watch it," Mrs. Connor said, her face twisted in irritation. "That hurt."

"Sorry," Mayrene said with a sweet smile. "I'll be more careful."

Mrs. Connor glared at her in the mirror for a moment, but then she turned her attention back to Wanda Nell. "You might have something there. I hadn't thought about that. The sheriff we had back then was an incompetent fool who couldn't find his way out of his house unless someone showed him. And he'd do anything for money."

"I wonder, then, if there was some rich man in town who could have done it?" Wanda Nell said, staring at Mrs. Connor's reflection.

"I can think of a couple of men. It certainly wasn't my husband, if that's what you're thinking. He would never have been involved in that kind of thing." She frowned. "Now what was the girl's mother's name? Something Lewis, I think you said?"

"Margaret Lewis. Does that ring a bell?"

Mrs. Connor hesitated before she spoke. "No, it doesn't. Like I said, I don't know any Lewises here, and never did. Now can we change the subject to something less distasteful?"

Taking the cue, Mayrene started chatting about hairstyles. While they conversed, Wanda Nell sat and thought. She would swear that Mrs. Connor had lied when she said the name Margaret Lewis didn't ring a bell. Some kind of memory had surfaced, Wanda Nell was sure of it. The question was, what? What had Mrs. Connor remembered?

There wouldn't be any use in trying to talk to her any further about it, Wanda Nell decided. Mrs. Connor had put an end to the subject, and that was that. Mayrene had Mrs. Connor under the dryer a few minutes later, and Wanda

Nell was able to talk to her friend without fear of Mrs. Connor overhearing what they said. Just to be certain, they moved as far away from the dryer as they could.

"She knows something," Wanda Nell said. "Did you see her face when she asked about Margaret Lewis again?"

"I did. And you're right, she was sure lying at that point. But what do you think she knows? The rest of the time she seemed like she was telling the truth."

"It wasn't until I said that about it being a cover-up, with some rich man involved. That's when she really started to think about it. And you know what? I think she remembered that a girl named Margaret Lewis worked for some rich family in town."

"Do you think it could have been her family?" Mayrene asked.

"I don't know. I think if it had been, she might have had more of a reaction. I think she remembered that Margaret Lewis worked for someone else."

"Like the Dewberrys?"

Wanda Nell nodded. "That's what I'm thinking."

"So what are you going to do now?"

"I think maybe I'll go talk to Darlene at the reception desk, and see if I can find out where Mr. Dewberry's room is. Then I'll try to get in to see him, I guess."

"Sounds like a plan to me," Mayrene said. "Darlene's a nice girl. If you ask her real polite, and tell her he knew your daddy or something, I'm sure she'll tell you what you want to know."

"Good," Wanda Nell said. "I'll go check it out."

She headed back down the hall to the reception area. Darlene was on the phone when she approached the desk, but she smiled at Wanda Nell and nodded. When she finished her conversation, she said, "Can I help you?"

"I sure hope so," Wanda Nell said. "I got to thinking about whether I knew anybody who lived here, and then I remembered that somebody my daddy used to work for is here. He was always real nice to my daddy, and I thought I might stop by and say hello to him."

"That would be real sweet. A lot of these old people don't get much company, and I know most of them would welcome a visitor." She chuckled. "The problem is getting away from them. Some of them can talk your ears off. Who are you looking for?"

"Mr. Dewberry. Mr. Jackson Dewberry."

"Oh, him. Well, he has his good days and his bad days. Most of the time he knows who he is and all that, but sometimes he's totally out of it. My cousin Lauretta works in his wing, and she tells me all about it."

"I see," Wanda Nell said. "Well, do you think it would be okay for me to stop by and see him?"

"I guess so, but hang on a minute." Darlene consulted the visitors' book. "Actually, now might not be the best time." She made a face. "His daughter is here. She probably won't stay long, but while she's here, I sure wouldn't try to talk to him."

"That bad, huh?"

"Lauretta says his daughter is real mean to him. If my daddy was that rich, I sure wouldn't be talking to him the way she does."

"That's too bad. So you think I should wait till she leaves."

"I sure would. But sometimes after she's been here, he don't act too good. You'll just have to try your luck, honey."

"How long does she usually stay?"

Darlene shrugged. "An hour, not much more." She glanced at the visitors' book again. "She signed in about ten minutes ago, so I'd give it about an hour and then try. Or you might want to come back some other time."

"Where is his room?" Wanda Nell asked.

"His suite, you mean," Darlene said. "It's real nice, nicer

than my apartment, that's for sure. Anyway, you just go down that other hall until you get to the end. Take a left, and you'll end up in his wing. Just ask at the desk there."

"Thanks. I sure appreciate it."

Darlene smiled. "You're welcome." Her phone rang, and she answered. Lost in thought, Wanda Nell walked back to where Mayrene was.

Jackson Dewberry and his daughter, Marysue Avenel, didn't get along. Well, Ernie had told her that much. But it sounded even worse from what Darlene said. She really should go talk to him, and maybe after his daughter had been here would be a good time to do it. He might be too upset to guard his tongue, and that could work in her favor.

She decided that was what she would do. She walked back into the small beauty shop to find Mayrene's next appointment, an elderly man, already in the chair. Mayrene was giving him a quick trim while keeping an eye on Mrs. Connor under the dryer.

Mayrene was nothing if not expert, and Wanda Nell watched her with a certain amount of awe. Mayrene finished the haircut and had the elderly man out the door about two minutes before Mrs. Connor's dryer went off.

Wanda Nell helped Mrs. Connor back to the chair, and Mayrene began taking out the rollers. She chatted with Mrs. Connor, who barely responded, much to Wanda Nell's surprise. The old woman looked preoccupied.

Not having anything else to do while she waited until time to see Mr. Dewberry, Wanda Nell picked up an old magazine from the table by the door. She leafed through it, occasionally glancing up to note Mayrene's progress with Mrs. Connor's hair. Finally, Mayrene had finished, and she turned Mrs. Connor around so that she was facing the mirror.

"Now what do you think, ma'am?" Mayrene asked while Mrs. Connor studied her reflection.

Wanda Nell thought Mayrene had done a terrific job.

She had managed to take Mrs. Connor's thick white hair and tame it into a soft cut that framed her face very nicely. It was very flattering, and Wanda Nell tried to say so in a tactful manner.

Mrs. Connor still hadn't said anything, and Wanda Nell could see Mayrene starting to get ticked off with the old lady. "Very good," Mrs. Connor said. "Much better than what I hoped for. Help me to my chair."

Mrs. Connor was gone a few moments after that, and both Mayrene and Wanda Nell felt only relief. "Lord, that woman sure is a misery," Mayrene said.

"She is, but you managed to please her. You really made her look nice. Almost human, in fact."

"Did you find out how to find Mr. Dewberry?" Mayrene asked after they quit laughing.

Wanda Nell related what Darlene had told her. "I figure in about ten more minutes his daughter ought to be gone, and maybe I can talk to him."

"Okay," Mayrene said. "My next appointment ought to be here soon, and there's only one more. If either one of them needs a shampoo, I can do it if you're not here."

"Thanks, I really appreciate this." Mayrene waved her thanks away.

The next person came in, and Wanda Nell had time to give her a shampoo. Once she finished, she was ready to find Mr. Dewberry's room.

"I'll be back," she said to Mayrene.

Out in the hall, she headed toward the reception area, Darlene's directions in mind. Soon she came to another reception desk, and from what Wanda Nell could see, this section of the place was definitely where the rich old people lived. She stepped up to the desk and asked the young woman there for Mr. Dewberry's room. The woman didn't even ask her what her business was, simply gave her the number and told her how to find it.

Relieved that this part, at least, had gone easier than expected, Wanda Nell walked down the hall to Mr. Dewberry's room. The doors were much farther apart in this section, so the apartments—or suites, as Wanda Nell reminded herself to call them—were much larger here. Near the end of the hall, she stopped in front of Mr. Dewberry's door and knocked.

"Come in," a voice called out.

Wanda Nell opened the door and walked in. An elderly man, his face darkened by numerous spots, sat in a high-backed chair, his legs covered by a colorful afghan.

"Who are you?" he asked, his voice a bit shaky.

"My name is Wanda Nell, and I wanted to talk to you about something, Mr. Dewberry, if I may."

Mr. Dewberry looked at her for a moment. "I don't recall ever knowing a girl named Wanda Nell, but I sure would remember if she was as pretty as you." He smiled, and Wanda Nell tried not to shudder. His skin was stretched so thinly over his face, he looked like a death's head. He motioned to a sofa near him. "Come on in and sit down and talk to me. I don't often get pretty girls coming by to visit."

"Thank you." Wanda Nell took a seat on the sofa, being careful to sit out of his reach. He looked like a pincher or a leg squeezer, and she didn't want to give him an opportunity. From the disappointed look on his face, she had evidently made the right decision.

"What did you want to talk to me about, Miss Wanda Nell?" he asked. His hands moved restlessly in his lap, worrying the nubby yarn of his afghan. "I hope you're not coming to ask for money for something. My lawyers have all my money these days. What my son doesn't have, that is."

"I'm not here to ask for money. I wanted to talk to you about your daughter." She was gambling with this, but some instinct told her it was the right approach.

"Marysue?" Dewberry's face twisted in distaste. "She

was here just a few minutes ago. She didn't come complaining to you about something, did she? Always whining,
that girl. Never satisfied with anything." He scowled.

"No, it's not about Marysue. I want to talk to you about
your other daughter. The one who came looking for you
thirty-one years ago."

Wanda Nell watched Mr. Dewberry carefully. She was
hoping he wouldn't have a stroke right on the spot. To her
relief, he didn't appear to be having one.

The reaction she did see surprised her.

Tears began streaming down the old man's face.

Twenty-nine

Wanda Nell was taken aback. This was one reaction she had not expected. "Mr. Dewberry," she asked, "are you okay?"

Mr. Dewberry fumbled in his shirt pocket for a handkerchief. He freed it from the pocket and wiped his face with it. "Danged allergies. I swear they keep putting the wrong kind of flowers in this place on purpose, just because they know it makes my eyes tear up like that."

Wanda Nell stared at him. Was he telling the truth? Had it really been allergies that made his eyes stream like that? She couldn't be completely sure.

"That's too bad. Now, Mr. Dewberry, did you hear what I said? About your other daughter?"

"I heard you, Miss Wanda Nell," he replied with some asperity. "There's nothing wrong with my hearing, I'll have you know. I may not be able to walk too well anymore, but I can hear just fine." He frowned. "Now what's this about my other daughter?"

Wanda Nell noticed he didn't say outright that he didn't have another daughter. Taking that as a good sign, she went on. "She came here looking for you about thirty-one years ago. Her name was Jenna Rae Howell, and she was about nineteen or twenty at the time."

"Why do you think this girl would be looking for me? Didn't she know who her own father was? Some man named Howell, I reckon, not Dewberry." He watched her carefully.

"She was adopted," Wanda Nell said. He still wasn't denying that he was Jenna Rae's father. "Her mother was a woman named Margaret Lewis, and she was from here. She dropped out of high school and went to work for a rich family, and while she was working for them, she got pregnant."

"So you think I'm the man who got some maid pregnant?" Dewberry sounded neither offended nor amused, simply curious.

"I never said she was a maid. I just said she worked for a rich family."

Dewberry nodded. "So you did. So you did."

Wanda Nell was trying to think of what to say next when a knock sounded at the door. Before Mr. Dewberry could respond, the door opened, and Evangeline Connor wheeled herself in the room. "I need to talk to you, Jackson," she said. She broke off when she saw Wanda Nell sitting on the sofa.

"What are you doing here?" Mrs. Connor demanded. "Shouldn't you be shampooing someone's hair about now? I think you'd better get back to work."

Wanda Nell wanted to scream. Having that hateful old woman turn up had ruined everything. She doubted she would be able to get Jackson Dewberry to talk to her anymore after this, but she decided to fire another shot before she had to leave the room.

"I had some business with Mr. Dewberry," Wanda Nell said. "I wanted to talk to him about his daughter." She waited to see how Mrs. Connor responded to that.

The old woman stared at her, then at Dewberry. "What

the heck would you be interested in Marysue for? Nobody else is."

Before Dewberry could say anything, Wanda Nell spoke. "Not Marysue. His other daughter, Jenna Rae."

"I see." Mrs. Connor continued to stare at Wanda Nell for a moment. Dewberry had remained silent during this whole exchange, and Wanda Nell wondered about that. "Very interesting. Well, young woman, I think you'd better go peddle your tales somewhere else. I've known Jackson Dewberry for nearly seventy years, and I know all about his family."

Wanda Nell noted that Mrs. Connor had looked directly at Jackson Dewberry when she made that final statement. She also thought the choice of words was kind of odd. Surely Mrs. Connor ought to have said something about the fact that he had only one daughter. That is, if they were going to insist that Jenna Rae Howell wasn't Dewberry's daughter. Wanda Nell could feel the tension rising in the room, but it was between the two elderly people.

"In that case," she said, rising from the sofa, "I guess I'll be getting back to work like you said, Miz Connor. Maybe I was mistaken, but I guess I'll just have to dig a little deeper."

"I wouldn't bother, if I were you." Jackson Dewberry spoke at last, his voice harsh. He glared at Evangeline Connor. "You need to be looking for someone else, not me."

Wanda Nell merely nodded. She paused in the doorway for a moment to look back. The two others still stared at each other, obviously waiting for her to leave. Wanda Nell stepped into the hallway, pulling the door almost completely shut behind her.

After a swift glance down the hall to make sure no one was watching, she stuck her ear to the tiny opening at the door. She strained to hear the conversation going on inside Dewberry's suite.

". . . had to tell her you didn't know anything about it," Mrs. Connor was saying. "But she told me enough . . . few things together."

Mrs. Connor's voice faded in and out, and Wanda Nell could hear the rumble of Dewberry's voice. She couldn't really make out the words, however. She wondered whether she dared open the door just a little bit more. She pushed it, just barely, and she could hear a bit better.

". . . out of your mind, Vangie," Dewberry was saying. "Even if you were right, what does that get you?"

"Money," Mrs. Connor said, her voice ice cold. "That stupid shampoo woman can't prove anything. It's obvious she knows a lot, but she doesn't know everything. I can put a few things together, though, and I will, if you don't do as I say."

"How could you possibly need money? Atwell left you pretty damn well fixed for the rest of your life."

"That's none of your damn business," Mrs. Connor said. "Just that stupid son of mine. He's managed to screw things up, yet again, and I need cash. You've got more than you'll ever know what to do with, and I want some of it."

Dewberry said something, but Wanda Nell's attention was distracted, and she didn't catch it. She had just caught sight of someone at the end of the hall. With great care she pulled the door shut, wincing at the tiny click she heard, then strode down the hall, thinking furiously.

Evangeline Connor was trying to blackmail Jackson Dewberry. And that meant she knew something. Or else she thought she did. Wanda Nell could figure out at least part of it. Mrs. Connor had remembered that a girl named Margaret Lewis had worked for the Dewberry family. Also, she knew the family well, and she knew the kind of reputation old Dewberry had. It didn't take much to figure it out after that. Dewberry had gotten Margaret pregnant, then fixed up the scheme to have Howell marry her, adopt the baby, and move to Hattiesburg.

But what was the connection with Howell? And, other than the money, why would he be willing to do something like that for Dewberry?

By this time Wanda Nell was back at the room where Mayrene was working. Pausing at the door, she looked in. Mayrene was working on her last person, a plump woman with long, flowing hair.

"Are you sure, now?" Mayrene asked her. "It will be quite a shock to see yourself, and once I cut it off, it'll take time to grow back."

"I'm sure," the woman said in a firm voice. "It's getting too hard to take care of, and it's time. So cut away."

"Okay, honey." Mayrene caught sight of Wanda Nell. "Wanda Nell, this is Miz McDermott. Miz McDermott, this is my friend Wanda Nell. She came along to help me today, if I needed it."

Wanda Nell and Mrs. McDermott exchanged greetings while Mayrene began cutting the woman's hair. Wanda Nell winced as she watched Mayrene snip the long tresses and lay them aside.

Catching sight of Wanda Nell's expression in the mirror, Mrs. McDermott laughed. "I know, it looks shocking, don't it? But I'm going to donate the hair to one of those charities that make wigs for people who need them."

"That's a very nice thing to do." Wanda Nell couldn't help but think of the difference between this woman and Mrs. Connor.

"How did your visit go?" Mayrene asked.

"Okay," Wanda Nell said. "I'll tell you about it later." She smiled at Mrs. McDermott.

"It's okay, honey," Mrs. McDermott said. "I understand."

Nodding, Wanda Nell said, "Mayrene, if you don't need me anymore, I think I'll get going."

"Sure, girl, you go ahead. I'll shampoo Miz McDermott's hair when I'm done cutting it, and then I'm going to style it for her. I'll talk to you later."

When Wanda Nell reached the reception desk, she considered going back to Jackson Dewberry's room to see if Evangeline Connor had left him. But she decided that it was now Elmer Lee's turn to talk to them. She was convinced by what she had seen and heard that Jackson Dewberry was Jenna Rae Howell's father.

Who was her killer? That Wanda Nell didn't know. Had Jackson Dewberry killed her, after he thought he had safely gotten rid of her, in a manner of speaking? Or had his daughter done it, out of jealousy or anger?

Who else could it have been? Wanda Nell didn't think it was Evangeline Connor or someone in her family. If it had been, the woman wouldn't be trying to blackmail Jackson Dewberry. That was surely what she was doing.

Wanda Nell signed out at the reception desk and headed for her car. It was going on eleven, and she didn't have time to run home to see Jack before she went to the Kountry Kitchen. She started her car and turned the air conditioner up to cool the car. It was blazing hot already, and she could imagine how miserable it would be this afternoon.

As the car cooled, Wanda Nell pulled her cell phone out of her purse and speed-dialed Jack. He answered quickly. "Hey, love, how's it going? Are you okay?"

"I'm fine," Wanda Nell assured him. She started to give him a rundown of what she had heard, from both Mrs. Connor and Mr. Dewberry, while trying to keep an eye on the time. It would take her only six or seven minutes to get to the Kountry Kitchen from here, so she had a little time to talk.

When Wanda Nell finished her summary, Jack whistled. "You've got to be right. Jackson Dewberry has to be Jenna Rae's father. That's the only thing that makes sense at this point. Especially if Miz Connor is trying to blackmail him. She sounds pretty nasty."

"She is. Every bit as mean as Ernie said she was."

"I think we'd better call Elmer Lee," Jack said. "Sounds to me like we have more than enough to get him to act now. It's still nothing really concrete, but maybe if he goes to talk to both of them, he can get something out of them. The threat of an investigation might get some results."

"I think that's probably what it's going to take. Maybe if Elmer Lee pushes hard enough, one of them will crack."

"Something's got to give," Jack said. "We can't get this close and not be able to identify the killer and prove he or she did it."

"I know, honey. We'll give it everything we've got." Jack replied, but Wanda Nell didn't hear what he said. Her attention shifted to a car that had driven into the parking lot a little too fast. While Wanda Nell watched, the car, an old, beat-up Jeep, lurched into a parking space, barely missing a much more expensive car on the right. Wanda Nell breathed a sigh of relief. The last thing she needed at the moment was to be a witness to an accident.

"What did you say, honey?" Wanda Nell asked. The driver of the Jeep was a woman of average height, dressed in a denim skirt and a white blouse. Her hair, a mousy brown, flopped around her face as she hurried toward the front door of the nursing home. Wanda Nell had caught a brief glimpse of the woman's face, and she looked really angry. Somebody was going to catch hell, she had no doubt of that.

Wanda Nell realized there was something odd about the way the woman walked, like she had a sore foot and was favoring it. Despite that, she was fast. She disappeared inside the nursing home.

A memory of something Miss Lyda had said surfaced in Wanda Nell's mind.

"Jack," Wanda Nell said, interrupting her husband,

"what does Marysue Avenel look like? And do you know what kind of car she drives?"

"She drives an old rattletrap Jeep. I've seen her driving that thing, and it ought to be put out of its misery. Marysue is a bit shorter than you, brown hair. Most of the time she's wearing a denim skirt, or something like that. Why are you asking?"

"Because she just drove back here, and she's in a real hurry. I've got a bad feeling about this. You'd better call Elmer Lee and tell him to get over here as fast as he can."

"What are you going to do?" Jack asked, obviously alarmed. "I'll call Elmer Lee, but what are you going to do? You're not going back in there, are you?"

"I am." Wanda Nell turned the key in the ignition with her free hand. "Look, honey, don't worry about me. I'll be fine. You just call Elmer Lee, okay?"

"I will, but what are you going to do? Tell me."

"Prevent another murder, I hope."

Thirty

As she got out of her car and slammed the door shut, Wanda Nell groaned over what she had just said to Jack. She had meant what she said, but it sounded like something out of a really bad movie.

She ran for the front door, slowing down only to make sure she didn't bowl over anyone inside near the door. The way was clear, so she hurried down the hall to where Mayrene was. If she was right about what might happen, she wanted someone with her.

Mayrene was alone, tidying up, when Wanda Nell skidded to a stop in the doorway. "Grab something, and come with me," she said.

Mayrene didn't even blink. She grabbed a can of hair spray and a pair of scissors, and followed Wanda Nell as fast as she could down the hall.

Wanda Nell flew past the desk in the wing where Jackson Dewberry and Evangeline Connor lived, and Mayrene was only a few paces behind her. Making a beeline for Jackson Dewberry's door, Wanda Nell skidded to a stop when she reached it. Mayrene came panting up behind her.

"What's going on?" Mayrene hissed.

Wanda Nell shook her head. She tried the doorknob, praying that Marysue hadn't locked it behind her.

She hadn't. The door opened with a tiny click, and Wanda Nell opened it just wide enough to be able to hear what was going on in the room.

A low, furious voice was all she heard at first. Figuring the speaker had to be Marysue, Wanda Nell pushed the door open a fraction more. She still couldn't see anything, but the voice was more distinct now.

". . . make one more noise like that," Marysue said, "and I swear to God I'll blow a hole in you before you can open your mouth again."

Oh, Lord, Wanda Nell thought, *she has a gun*. She turned to share that news with Mayrene. Mayrene's eyes grew big, but she didn't back away. She handed Wanda Nell the hair spray, and she kept a firm grasp on her scissors.

"Marysue, don't talk to Vangie like that." Jackson Dewberry's tone lacked conviction, however, and his daughter laughed, a harsh, grating sound.

"I ought to blow a hole in you, too, Daddy," she said. "Daddy. The word makes me sick even to say it. When were you ever like a father to me? You couldn't stand the sight of me. Why didn't you just have me drowned at birth, when you saw I was deformed?"

"Don't be ridiculous. Stop acting like a hysterical child, Marysue, and put that down." Dewberry's words sounded like he was giving orders, but the tone said otherwise. He was begging. Marysue just laughed again.

Wanda Nell pushed the door open a little farther, praying that it wouldn't make a sound and that Marysue had her back to it.

She paused a moment. Marysue went on talking, so Wanda Nell figured she hadn't seen or heard anyone at the door. Marysue went on spewing hateful words and recriminations at her father and Mrs. Connor. Wanda Nell kept inching the door open, and Mayrene was close behind her.

Now Wanda Nell could see Marysue, along with her father and Mrs. Connor. Marysue had her back to the door, and both Jackson Dewberry and Evangeline Connor were facing it. Neither one of them gave any sign, however, that they saw two women sneaking up behind Marysue.

"Stop it, Marysue!" Mrs. Connor's voice broke into the diatribe. "Just shut up. Your father and I know what you did, and why you did it. You're too old to be blaming your mommy and daddy for everything wrong in your life. So what if your daddy didn't love you? Mine didn't love me, either, but you never hear me whining about it."

The sheer acid in Evangeline Connor's voice took Wanda Nell's breath away. The old woman was probably doing her best to keep Marysue's attention engaged until Wanda Nell and Mayrene could jump her and get the gun away from her, but Wanda Nell was afraid Mrs. Connor was pushing Marysue too far.

A stream of profanities issued from Marysue's mouth, and Wanda Nell and Mayrene got close enough to tackle her. Wanda Nell had the can of hair spray up and ready, just in case.

Before either she or Mayrene could make another move, however, Marysue snapped. Wanda Nell hadn't seen the gun yet, but she heard it go off, and she jerked back a step. A hole appeared in Evangeline Connor's chest, and blood began to blossom from the wound. Mrs. Connor's eyes went dark, and she died right in front of them.

Mayrene didn't let the gunshot stop her. While Wanda Nell stood staring at the dead woman, Mayrene tackled Marysue. The smaller woman went down under the force of Mayrene's attack. The gun flew out of her hands as Mayrene landed on top of her and knocked the breath out of her.

Wanda Nell stood there, still staring at Evangeline Connor. After a moment her gaze shifted to Jackson Dewberry. She dropped the can of hair spray on the floor and ran out into the hall to yell for help.

The next few minutes were sheer pandemonium. A security guard, followed quickly by a nurse and two aides, crowded into the room. They stared for a moment at the two women on the floor, and then at the dead woman in the wheelchair.

"Mr. Dewberry," Wanda Nell said. "I think he's having a heart attack."

At those words, the nurse snapped into action. Wanda Nell moved out of the way, grabbing at the security guard. She tried her best to explain what had just happened, and the guard listened long enough to determine who had fired the gun. Mayrene got off Marysue, who was still pretty winded, and the guard took her into custody.

"I'm going to put her into a room with no windows and only one door until the police get here," the guard said. "They're already on the way. In the meantime, don't you two go nowhere."

"What about the gun?" Wanda Nell asked, and the guard grimaced.

"I'm going to leave it for the police," he said after a moment's thought. "It's under that table, and I don't think nobody'll step on it."

With that, he escorted Marysue from the room. Marysue moved slowly, her arms hanging listlessly by her side. Wanda Nell caught one glimpse of her face, and she had to turn away from the absolute despair in the woman's eyes. Mayrene went after them, just in case the guard needed help subduing Marysue again. Wanda Nell moved into a corner, keeping anxious eyes on the gun, but the nurse and the aides didn't get too near it as they worked on Jackson Dewberry.

Someone else had come into the room in the meantime,

carrying some sort of equipment. When they began to use it on Jackson Dewberry, Wanda Nell realized it must be a defibrillator. They had Dewberry stretched out on the floor, and they were working hard to bring him around.

Not long after that, the paramedics arrived, followed by the police. The room was so crowded now, Wanda Nell could hardly breathe. In the confusion, she managed to slip into the corridor. Anxious residents were milling about at the other end, and a couple of policeman barred them from coming any closer.

Trying to stay calm, Wanda Nell stared down the hall. Jack arrived, only to be stopped by the cops. As Wanda Nell started toward him, Elmer Lee turned up. Wanda Nell waited, and sure enough, Elmer Lee came down the hall, Jack at his heels.

Jack outpaced Elmer Lee, and Wanda Nell flew into his arms. "Are you okay, love? What happened?"

Wanda Nell couldn't talk. Instead, she started crying. She couldn't hold off the horror of what she had seen any longer, and it took Jack several minutes to calm her. He held on tight and kept stroking her hair, murmuring over and over, "It's okay, love, I'm here."

Elmer Lee had disappeared into Jackson Dewberry's room, and by the time he came out again, Wanda Nell was calm.

"I'm sorry, Wanda Nell," Elmer Lee said. "You saw it happen, didn't you?"

Wanda Nell nodded.

"I'm sorry about that. And I sure hate to do it, but I'm going to have to ask you to talk about it with the police. Can you do that?"

"I can," Wanda Nell said, her voice shaky. "Somebody's got to call Melvin, though, and tell him I'll be late for work." For some reason, that struck her as funny, and she started laughing.

When she couldn't stop, Jack pulled her into his arms again. Putting her head against his shoulder, he did his best to comfort her.

Elmer Lee retreated, leaving the two of them together.

Two weeks later, when Wanda Nell had a Saturday off, she and Jack drove down to Hattiesburg to visit Miss Lyda Fehrenbach. They had spoken with Rufus King, and he had agreed to meet them at Miss Lyda's house to have lunch. They wanted to tell Miss Lyda about everything, and they figured Rufus King should be there as well, though he already knew what they would have to say.

The drive down was pleasant. It was hot but clear. Wanda Nell hated driving in the rain. She stared out at the passing scenery.

"Okay, love?" Jack asked. They had both had trouble sleeping recently, and they often felt tired during the day as a result. "Why don't you nap a little?"

"No, I'm okay. I'm just thinking."

Jack didn't have to ask her what she was thinking about.

"At least some good has come of all this," she said. "Thank goodness, Rocky has rescued Sandra June from that awful husband of hers."

"And Rocky doesn't have to worry about being arrested for murder anymore," Jack added. "But the fact that he had to wait so long to be exonerated still makes me angry."

"I know, honey. That's the worst part of it, how much time it took."

They both fell silent again, and when they did talk, they made an effort to speak of something else. "Thank the Lord Mayrene wasn't hurt when she tackled Marysue." Wanda Nell shuddered at the memory. "If she'd gotten shot, I don't know what I'd do."

"Well, she wasn't." Jack reached out a comforting hand, and Wanda Nell smiled. "She's pretty tough."

"She is." Wanda Nell drew a deep breath. "I wish we could get other things to work out as well as that."

"You mean Teddy, don't you?"

Wanda Nell nodded. "At least he's willing to talk to us about it, so I guess that's some progress."

"It's a positive sign." Jack squeezed her hand. "He'll come around before long, honey. He's got a good heart. I think he's just a little confused, with his daddy telling him one thing and us telling him something else."

"I sure hope you're right." Wanda Nell sighed and leaned her head back.

A little after eleven-thirty, Jack pulled up in front of Miss Lyda's house in Hattiesburg. Wanda Nell had actually dozed off, and Jack wakened her gently. "We're here, love. Miss Lyda's on the porch waiting for us."

Wanda Nell yawned and stretched. "I'm awake."

Jack came around and opened her door, and together they proceeded up the walk to where Miss Lyda waited for them.

"Oh, I can't tell you how good it is to see you," Miss Lyda said, with a huge, happy smile. "I know it's on sad business, but I can't help feeling glad that you're here."

Wanda Nell and Jack took turns hugging Miss Lyda and kissing her cheek. "We're so glad to see you, too," Wanda Nell assured her.

"Now come on in the house," Miss Lyda said. "Rufus ought to be here any minute, and I declare it's too hot to be out on this porch for more than a few minutes. So y'all just come on into the kitchen, and we'll have something cool to drink."

They were seated at the kitchen table, sipping ice-cold lemonade, when the doorbell rang. "I'll go," Jack said, rising from his chair.

Miss Lyda beamed up at him. "Thank you, Jack."

Jack was soon back with Rufus King. The policeman greeted Miss Lyda warmly, then spoke to Wanda Nell. "I hear y'all had a bit of a rough time."

"Yes, but things are getting better. It's just going to take time."

"Rufus, you sit down, and let me get you some lemonade," Miss Lyda said, popping out of her chair. King knew better than to protest, so he did what he was told. Miss Lyda handed him a glass of lemonade, and he raised it in a toast. "To Jack and Wanda Nell. Thanks to them, Jenna Rae Howell can rest in peace now."

"Amen to that," Miss Lyda said. "Now I know some terrible things happened, but I've said a prayer of thanks to the Lord every night on behalf of that dear girl."

"Thank you both," Jack said. "That means a lot to us."

"It sure does," Wanda Nell added. She appreciated their words, and the thoughts behind them, but she knew it would be a long time before she could rest completely easy. Would Evangeline Connor be dead now if she hadn't gone to the nursing home and stirred things up?

When she had confessed those thoughts to Ernie Carpenter, Ernie had regarded her with sympathy. "I can understand how you feel, Wanda Nell, and I'd like to be able to tell you that things would have happened differently if you hadn't gone to the nursing home that day. But you're not stupid, and I'm not going to lie to you. But believe me when I tell you this, Evangeline Connor was a nasty, venal, heartless woman. She put herself in that situation by trying to blackmail Jackson Dewberry. If she had left well enough alone, she'd still be alive and terrorizing the poor folks at the nursing home. But she wanted money, and she was determined to get it. She got something else instead, and it may not be very Christian of me, but I don't feel one bit sorry for her. Especially since she's the one who called Marysue back to the nursing home. She always wanted people dancing to her tune, and look where it finally got her. It's poetic justice, if you ask me."

Wanda Nell had tried to take heart from Ernie's words, and she understood how Ernie felt. She knew that Mrs. Connor had made her own choices, but still couldn't help feeling guilty over the role she had played.

"So what did Mr. Dewberry do after they revived him?" Miss Lyda asked. "I would have figured a heart attack would have been the end of him, right then and there."

"He's got a strong heart, which is pretty ironic," Jack said. "He came out of it a good bit weaker, but he's hanging in there." He shook his head. "After all that happened, I'm still having a hard time believing he survived."

"He did admit that he was Jenna Rae's father," Wanda Nell said. "Elmer Lee Johnson, the sheriff, told us about it. He was there when Mr. Dewberry talked to the police."

"Did you ever find out what Howell was doing in Tullahoma in the first place?" Rufus King asked. "That's one thing I haven't been able to find out."

"Dewberry explained that," Jack said. "Turns out Howell served in Korea with Dewberry's youngest brother, Raymond. Howell had done a few favors for the brother, and when Howell got out of the army, he came to Tullahoma looking for Raymond. Raymond Dewberry helped him get a job at the high school, and he worked there for almost two years."

"And then when Jackson Dewberry needed someone to take Margaret Lewis and the baby off his hands, he paid Howell to do it," Rufus King said.

"Exactly. Dewberry promised Howell three hundred dollars a month, and over the years, he increased the amount, until it was a thousand dollars a month."

"Surely he wasn't spending that much money on liquor every month." Miss Lyda was appalled.

"No," Rufus King said. "We've dug further into his finances. He was pretty heavily in debt. Turns out he had a gambling habit, too. On the Internet, if you can believe that." He shook his head.

"If that don't beat all. What about Dewberry's daughter? Marysue, isn't that her name?" Miss Lyda asked.

"That's right," Jack replied. "She's in jail right now. They're holding her without bail until she can be indicted. She still hasn't admitted anything, but her father says she killed Jenna Rae."

"And we know she killed Howell," Rufus King said. "We've traced the phone calls he made that night, and one of them was to her number. She had moved back into her father's house, and I guess that was the only number he knew to call. As soon as she knew what he wanted, she drove down here and killed him."

"And to think I saw her going into that house." Miss Lyda shivered. "It makes my blood run cold."

"It was your description of her that made me realize she really was the killer," Wanda Nell said. "You remember what you told us, about the odd way of walking she had?"

Miss Lyda nodded.

"I saw her running, and she ran funny," Wanda Nell said. "Like she had some problem with one of her feet. And it turned out that she has a club foot."

"No one at school knew about it," Jack said. "I certainly had never seen her running, and she didn't seem to have any problems with walking."

"But when she ran, she couldn't run evenly, and that's what we both saw," Wanda Nell said. "Elmer Lee said there's something wrong with the muscles in the leg that has the club foot."

"And her parents never did anything about it?" Miss Lyda asked, plainly incredulous.

"Who knows?" Jack said. "It was pretty obvious that they didn't pay much attention to her."

"If you could have heard the hate coming out of her . . . It was horrible." Wanda Nell looked away for a moment.

Miss Lyda reached over and patted her hand. "It's okay, dear. Don't dwell on it." She sighed. "But that sure seems to be a theme here, doesn't it? Unhappy daughters."

"Yes," Jack said. "There was Marysue, growing up in Tullahoma with rich parents and a nice house. But she didn't feel loved or wanted, and she felt deformed. Then there was Jenna Rae, beautiful, poor, but loved at least by her mother. When Jenna Rae went to Tullahoma, the first member of the family she met was Marysue."

"How old was Marysue?" Miss Lyda asked.

"She had just turned sixteen," Wanda Nell said.

"Oh, my." Miss Lyda sighed. "To think of a girl that age, killing someone. But I guess when she looked at Jenna Rae, she saw a girl who was everything she was not."

"According to her father, that was exactly it," Jack said. "Once he knew Marysue was safely behind bars, he couldn't talk fast enough. Marysue had come to him, thirty-one years ago, and she told him what she had done. In order to keep her out of jail, he paid for a cover-up."

"Who left Jenna Rae on that football field?" Miss Lyda asked.

"It was Marysue," Wanda Nell said.

"According to the statement I read," Rufus King added, "she lured the victim to the football field late that night on some pretext, and she killed her right there. With a baseball bat. She stripped off all her clothes, took her purse, and drove the victim's car back to the motel where she was staying."

"How did she get home?" Miss Lyda asked. "She surely couldn't have walked very far."

"She walked about half a mile down the road to a service station," King said. "She called her mother, and her mother came and got her. According to Mr. Dewberry, the girl told her mother she had gone out with a boy, and he had put her out of his car because she wouldn't have sex with him."

"Oh, dear, that poor girl," Miss Lyda said. "Both of them. Poor girls. It just breaks my heart to think of them, and all they wanted was the same thing."

They talked for a while longer, and then Rufus King said he had to be going.

"Are you sure you can't have lunch with us?" Jack asked. "We'd love to have you come with us."

"Thanks," King said with a smile. "I'd love to, but if my wife found out, she'd have my hide. She's real serious about me eating healthy and losing weight. And if I go with y'all, I sure won't be able to restrain myself."

They bade him goodbye, and King said, "Y'all have a safe trip back. I'll see myself out."

"We will, and thanks for everything," Jack said. The two men shook hands, and King departed.

"Now, Miss Lyda, where would you like to have lunch?" Wanda Nell asked.

"I know a wonderful little place that makes the best fresh rolls. I know you'll love them. But before we go, I wanted to ask you something else."

"What was that?" Wanda Nell asked.

"Did you find her grave?" Miss Lyda asked, her eyes suspiciously damp.

"We did," Jack said. "And Dewberry is arranging to have a headstone placed on it. He's going to acknowledge that she was his daughter."

"I'm glad," Miss Lyda said. "I'm so very, very glad."

Recipes from the Kountry Kitchen

Tuck Tucker's
Spaghetti and Meat Sauce

1 medium onion, finely chopped

2 cloves garlic, minced

2 tablespoons olive oil

¼ pound lean ground beef

5 small mushrooms

½ cup ketchup

¼ cup chili sauce

1 teaspoon each oregano and tarragon (dried)

½ pound spaghetti

Grated Parmesan and chopped parsley for garnish

Sauté onion and garlic in olive oil over medium heat. Add ground beef and stir until beef is brown. Add mushrooms, ketchup, chili sauce, and herbs; stir and simmer slowly for about 7 minutes.

Meanwhile, cook spaghetti. When spaghetti is done, drain, but retain liquid.

Add drained pasta to meat sauce. If sauce is too thick, add a little of the pasta water. Ladle mixture onto plates and sprinkle with grated Parmesan and chopped parsley.

Serves 2–4.

T.J. Culpepper's
Greek Salad

4 large tomatoes, chopped

2 dozen medium or large mushrooms, quartered or chopped

1 large onion, copped

1 cucumber, peeled and chopped

1 red bell pepper, chopped (substitute yellow or green, if desired)

1 green bell pepper, chopped (see above)

1 cup feta cheese

2 dozen or so black olives

2 tablespoons lemon juice

2 tablespoons white wine vinegar

1 teaspoon oregano leaves (dried)

1 teaspoon salt

½ teaspoon cracked black pepper

½ cup olive oil

In a large mixing bowl, combine the vegetables, cheese, and olives.

Mix the rest of the ingredients in a smaller bowl. Pour over salad and toss to coat.

For best results, the salad should be served within a few minutes of completing preparation.

Serves 4.

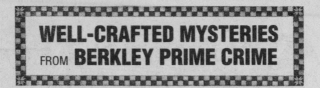

The Quiche
AND THE Dead